PRAISE FOR

STRANGE TRUTH

(Previously titled *We Know It Was You*)

"A fast-paced, sassy, and sultry whodunit."
—School Library Journal

"The definition of a page-turner. Thrash's unique ability to balance humor, mystery, and teen angst blew me away. Hilarious, twisty, and full of unforgettable characters—this is damn good stuff."
—John Corey Whaley,
Printz Award–winning author of *Where Things Come Back* and National Book Award Finalist *Noggin*

"*[Strange Truth]* has all the elements of a great read: mystery, humor, romance, and drama. . . . Thrash's writing is so mesmerizingly good I found myself rereading sentences for the sheer pleasure and surprise of them."
—Cecily von Ziegesar,
New York Times bestselling author
of the Gossip Girl series

"A complicated and twisty tale that blends noir mystery, gothic romance, and dark humor."
—VOYA

ALSO BY MAGGIE THRASH
Strange Lies

A _STRANGE_ NOVEL
Previously titled _We Know It Was You_

MAGGIE THRASH

Simon Pulse
New York   London   Toronto   Sydney   New Delhi

SIMON PULSE
An imprint of Simon & Schuster Children's Publishing Division
1230 Avenue of the Americas, New York, New York 10020
First Simon Pulse paperback edition August 2017
Text copyright © 2016 by Maggie Thrash
Previously titled *We Know It Was You*
Cover title illustration copyright © 2017 by John Harwood
All other cover illustrations copyright © 2017 by Thinkstock
Also available in a Simon Pulse hardcover edition titled *We Know It Was You*.
All rights reserved, including the right of reproduction in whole or in part in any form.
SIMON PULSE and colophon are registered trademarks of Simon & Schuster, Inc.
For information about special discounts for bulk purchases, please contact Simon & Schuster
Special Sales at 1-866-506-1949 or business@simonandschuster.com.
The Simon & Schuster Speakers Bureau can bring authors to your live event. For more
information or to book an event, contact the Simon & Schuster Speakers Bureau
at 1-866-248-3049 or visit our website at www.simonspeakers.com.
Cover designed by Jessica Handelman
Interior designed by Mike Rosamilia
The text of this book was set in Adobe Garamond Pro.
Manufactured in the United States of America
2 4 6 8 10 9 7 5 3 1
The Library of Congress has cataloged the hardcover edition as follows:
Names: Thrash, Maggie, author.
Title: We know it was you : a Strange truth novel / by Maggie Thrash.
Description: Simon Pulse Hardcover edition. | New York : Simon Pulse, 2016. |
Summary: When the Winship Academy mascot jumps off a bridge during a
halftime show, she leaves behind a lot of questions, and two students who
witnessed the scene firsthand are determined to find out what really happened.
Identifiers: LCCN 2015041347 (print) | LCCN 2016018998 (eBook) |
ISBN 9781481462006 (hardcover : alk. paper) |
Subjects: | CYAC: Mystery and detective stories. | Suicide—Fiction. |
High schools—Fiction. | Schools—Fiction.
Classification: LCC PZ7.1.T53 We 2016 (print) | LCC PZ7.1.T53 (eBook) |
DDC [Fic]—dc23
ISBN 9781481462013 (*Strange Truth* pbk)
ISBN 9781534411289 (*Strange Truth* eBook)

For Mr. Wayne Parker, a genius

It was very God-like, the thing she was doing.

And that meant it couldn't be bad, right? If God was good, then anything done in imitation of God was also good. That's what she reminded herself as she stared into the mascot's bulging plastic eyes.

"You know what you have to do," she said. "Trust your body; follow your mind."

There was no reply. The mascot stood motionless under the locker room's dingy fluorescent lights.

"Can you hear me?" She snapped her fingers and raised her voice. "Nod if you can hear me."

The huge plastic wildcat head slumped forward on its shoulders, apparently nodding.

"All right, then . . . ," she said, uncertain how to wrap things up. "Bye." She gave the mascot a small wave and started walking toward the door. Then she turned back.

"You know . . . I wish this weren't the end. Do you believe me when I say that?"

But instead of waiting for an answer, she turned her eyes away and left.

Friday
The football field, 8:55 p.m.

Gerard Cole was in love with the Montague twins, and not for the same dumb reason as everyone else. Obviously they were hot, their two mind-blowing bodies mirroring the perfection of each other. But they were also the nicest girls at Winship Academy. They were nice to everyone, even Gerard.

Angie Montague waved to him from the sidelines, where all the cheerleaders were stretching and drinking pink Gatorade. Gerard waved back, aware that a huge dumb grin was probably taking over his whole face. Being a water boy may have lacked prestige, but it more than made up for it in proximity to cheerleaders. In one month Gerard had talked to more girls than he had in his entire life. But the only ones he cared about were the twins.

They were both on the squad, but Angie was the real cheerleader. Brittany was the mascot. She spent every game stuffed inside an immense wildcat suit. It seemed like a crime to hide such a beautiful person inside an ugly, smelly costume, but Brittany never complained. She actually *liked* being the mascot. She always said it made her feel like "a big, cuddly stuffed animal." The twins looked so much alike that this was the only time Gerard could ever tell them apart: Brittany was the one with the enormous, toothy cat head. He didn't like thinking of them as individuals, though. He was always relieved at the end of the games when Brittany emerged from the mascot suit, unrecognizable from her sister once again.

Gerard looked around, expecting to find Brittany bouncing around, doing her usual routine. Instead, he saw her on the bench by herself. She was just sitting there, the bulbous wildcat head drooping a little on her shoulders. Gerard squinted, noticing the bulging nose and comically huge eyes, which suddenly didn't seem so comical. They seemed . . . Gerard didn't know what. A little weird. He looked around. No one else had noticed Brittany's uncharacteristic lack of energy. He shrugged to himself and turned his eyes back to Angie—lovely Angie, with her bright smile and white-and-blue pom-poms.

The pep band, 9:05 p.m.

The problem wasn't a lack of mysteries. Mysteries were everywhere, and Benny Flax knew this to be true. The problem was a lack of people who cared.

Most of the clubs at Winship Academy were stupid and based on either the consolidation of social power (School

4

Spirit Club, the Young Republicans) or the padding of college applications with bogus interests (Nature Club, History of Barbeque Club). Benny had to fulfill the after-school activity requirement somehow, so he'd started his own club, a mystery-solving club that he called, unimaginatively, Mystery Club. He'd always been interested in puzzles and games and documentaries about unsolved crimes. What *wasn't* interesting about a mystery? Every day, someone, somewhere, was getting away with something. How did they do it? What really happened? Questions like these consumed him.

When he'd founded the club, he'd expected to be inundated with inquiries about all the unexplained stuff that happened all the time. *Who's been sending dick pics to my private e-mail? Who stole my lunch card and charged thirty cinnamon rolls? Who wrote* SKANKY YANKEE *on the new girl's locker?* There was always something weird going on at Winship, but people just accepted the unknowns in their lives; they shrugged and moved on. It wasn't like in the movies where the detective sits back and desperate people throng him with their problems. Benny had quickly realized that if he wanted to solve life's mysteries, he'd have to find them himself, and no one would actually thank him for it.

We sound really awful, Benny thought, trying to sync his flute melody with the severely off-tempo snare drum. Their conductor, Mr. Choi, hadn't even bothered to show up to the game, which meant the marching band sounded even worse than usual. The frazzled assistant was shouting, "Halftime! Don't leave your instruments on the ground, please! They'll get stolen. Right, Scooby?"

Benny looked up, embarrassed. Were even teachers calling him Scooby now? He hated that nickname. It was infantilizing and undermined the legitimacy of Mystery Club. He gritted his teeth. "Right . . . ," he managed.

Last year Shelly Jenner's French horn had been stolen from the band room. Benny had jumped on the case immediately, not that Shelly had asked him to. In fact, she'd seemed kind of embarrassed by Benny's interest and said she'd rather just buy a new horn than make a big deal of it. But Benny persisted and ultimately caught the thief—a moronic eighth grader who thought he could melt the horn down to gold. Benny hoped, after this, that people would finally start to take Mystery Club seriously. But the only change was that now everyone called him Scooby-Doo.

Benny shouldn't have been surprised. He'd always been, if not quite ostracized, vaguely dismissed by his classmates. He was one of few Jews in a school where 90 percent of the student body were members of FCA, the Fellowship of Christian Athletes. Most Jews in Atlanta sent their kids to the Jewish Academy or to Pace, which had more diversity and a better reputation for tolerance. But Winship had offered the best scholarship, so Winship was his cross to bear. And while he didn't particularly covet a place among their popular ranks, being called Scooby-Doo was annoying. People already treated him like a kid because he didn't have a car; he didn't need a nickname from a little kids' cartoon on top of that. Besides, Fred and Velma were the ones who actually solved mysteries on that show. Scooby was just a foolish nuisance who compulsively snacked and freaked out at the slightest provocation.

The Mystery Club's loserish reputation wasn't helped by the fact that the only person to join the club since the disappearing-horn incident was Virginia Leeds—the strangest and most annoying girl in school. Honestly, Benny would have preferred being in a club by himself, but for whatever reason, Virginia seemed determined to solve a mystery. *Maybe you should start with the Mysterious Case of Your Annoying Personality,* Benny sometimes thought, though he'd never have said it out loud. The key to dismissing someone, Benny knew from years of getting the same treatment, was to act like you couldn't be bothered to take the time to actually insult them.

A loud cheer went up from the stadium as the cheerleaders got into formation. They always did the same halftime dance to that eighties song about trying not to ejaculate. Benny began cleaning the head joint of his flute. Then, in the course of several seconds, he sensed the mood of the stadium shifting. The clapping became scattered, and the cheers turned to murmurs.

"What's going on?" someone asked. Benny looked up from his flute. The song continued to blare from the speakers, but the cheerleaders had stopped dancing. They were turning around in circles, looking lost and disorganized. Then he realized why: The mascot was out of control.

"What's happening out there?" someone was shouting. Other people were laughing. "The mascot's on drugs!" The cheerleaders yelled, "Get back in line, Brittany!" But the great wildcat continued to lurch across the field, leading with its heavy plastic head in a zigzagging path. The football coaches stood on the sidelines, debating whether to intervene or stay put.

Benny stood on the bleachers, observing the scene. At first glance the mascot seemed to be running wildly, with no direction. Benny squinted at the field, focusing on the wildcat's feet, the way she placed one in front of the other. *She's trying to get somewhere,* Benny thought, scanning the football field. *There,* he realized. *She's heading for the woods.*

He dropped his flute on the ground and set off running.

The bleachers, 9:05 p.m.

Virginia Leeds sat in the bleachers, trying to look bored, but not too bored. If she looked too bored, people would look at her and think, *If she hates football so much, she should just leave.* What she wanted them to think was, *Virginia Leeds has a mysterious look on her face. She must be watching this football game for reasons unfathomable to us.*

That was Virginia's goal for the year: to become unfathomable. But it was hard because she was already fifteen, which felt like too late. She hadn't been careful with her identity—for years she'd just done what she wanted and said what she wanted, not realizing that her identity was forming in the process. And now it felt like this was her last chance to change it before it became totally permanent.

Virginia wasn't stupid; she could see how it had happened. She'd always loved gossip and other people's business. And the more she dug up about people, the more she wanted to dig, and the more it became this web of information that took over her life. She'd even had a website called Winship Confidential, where she collected rumors and social news items and provided in-depth analysis. But at some point all that gossipmongering had become *who she was*. Even worse, what had taken Virginia four years to realize was that having a popular blog didn't necessarily make you a popular person.

It wasn't just that people hated her for slamming them on the Internet, it was that people thought she was lame for even caring. Maybe secretly they devoured her website— the Google analytics didn't lie—but outwardly they acted like they were sick of it. And Virginia truly was sick of it. She was sick of everybody's stupid business, and sick of herself for being obsessed with it. She needed a change; she needed *mystique*. So she'd shut down the site and joined Mystery Club. It was literally a club of mystery—what could be more perfect? But so far the club involved less mystique and more sitting around boredly.

Benny always said the number one secret to solving a mystery was to Be There. "Wherever you go," he said, "something might happen. Don't just be a detective—be a witness. Be watching."

The main disconnect between him and Virginia was that Benny wanted to solve mysteries, while Virginia just wanted to be part of one. But it was Benny's club and Benny's rules. So Virginia sat on the bleachers, trying her best to Be There. Not that it mattered. No one was going to notice her, and nothing mysterious was going to happen. Nothing ever happened at this school.

Then, out of nowhere, something did.

She was watching dopey Gerard Cole ogling the cheerleaders when suddenly there was chaos on the field. The cheerleaders were wandering aimlessly. And the mascot was running off, stomping and lurching gracelessly. Then someone else was running too. His neatly combed black hair and dorky maroon turtleneck were unmistakable. It was Benny.

The woods, 9:12 p.m.

When something strange happens, particularly in a crowd, the average person will immediately lose the ability to focus their senses. Things that should be obvious become obscured by the disorder of excitement. *It all happened so fast,* people always say. But it doesn't have to be this way, Benny knew. Not if your brain can be faster.

"Following the leader, the leader, the leader!"

There was pandemonium in the forest. Benny had followed the mascot, the cheerleaders had followed Benny, and the football players had followed the cheerleaders. Someone had begun to sing "Following the Leader," and soon everyone was singing it. *"We're following the leader wherever he may go!"* Benny tromped through the underbrush, eager to get away from the noise. As he moved farther into the woods, the chorus echoed behind him, no longer jolly-sounding, but eerie and distorted. *"We're following the leeeeeeader . . ."*

The mascot was here, Benny was sure of it, but he'd lost her. He spun in circles, looking, listening. But the throng was catching up with him again, engulfing the quiet with their annoying singing.

Then he saw it: a great, lumbering shadow moving in the darkness toward . . .

The bridge.

This section of the river was called the White Bend for a reason. It surged past the school in a great gush, its cold white water frothing over the jutting rocks and cutting a deep, dangerous forty-foot ravine. A one-hundred-year-old footbridge stood tenuously across it, connecting the campus to a black patch of forest on the other side. The bridge wasn't very safe. The rails were low, and the drop was deadly. It wasn't a question of drowning—it was breaking your neck and your skull on the massive, slick rocks. Benny remembered some kids getting drunk and falling to their deaths a few years ago. But since they weren't Winship students, the response had been minimal. Winship was a snobbish old place, not likely to sink a bunch of money into ruining a historic bridge just because some no-name townies couldn't handle themselves. But this was no townie, it was Brittany Montague—the prize of the school—and Benny stared as she began crossing the bridge, pausing at the center to lean perilously over the rail.

What is she doing? he thought. *She's going to fall.*

But she didn't fall. She jumped.

Benny watched, frozen, as the mascot flipped head over heels and plummeted toward the rushing water. In seconds she was gone.

The bridge, 9:20 p.m.

"We're following the leader wherever he may go!" The throng had swarmed the bridge, singing and yelling. Benny located one of the coaches, the one with the bushy white mustache, and tried to explain what had happened. "It was Brittany! I saw her jump," he shouted, fighting to be heard above the raucous din.

"What, son? What? You need to get back to the field. Everyone get back to the field!"

Benny didn't know exactly how it happened, but within minutes everyone seemed to have heard. Brittany Montague had jumped off the bridge in her mascot costume. The mood changed instantly. The singing morphed into wails and sobs. Benny found himself crammed against the bridge railing, the crowd swelling dangerously. *It's going to collapse,* he thought. He looked down at the gushing river below and felt momentarily dizzy.

"Benny. Benny!" A hand grabbed his arm. It was Virginia.

"Virginia. Oh my God. I saw—"

"I saw it too!" she shouted. "I can't believe it!"

Next to them, Angie Montague was leaning over the rail, sobbing. "I dropped my pom-poms!" she cried, reaching toward the watery abyss. "I DROPPED MY POM-POMS!"

Virginia burst out laughing. Luckily the scene was so chaotic that only Benny noticed. "Stop laughing," Benny hissed at her. "She's obviously traumatized."

"Well so am I!" Virginia yelled. "I just witnessed a suicide!"

"I did too," Benny snapped back, "but I'm managing to not be an imbecile about it."

"Sorry, sorry," Virginia said. "It was a nervous reaction."

"There she is!" a girl shrieked behind them, pointing downriver. Benny squinted and saw the mascot floating facedown in the dark water, gliding like a ghost. It sank, then the water heaved it up again. Then it disappeared around the bend.

"Christ, let's get off this bridge!" Virginia shouted.

They were pinned in on either side by sobbing people. He could hear the coaches yelling at everyone to calm down. Benny craned his neck, trying to see a way out, but the bridge was impossibly crowded.

"Look," Virginia said, pointing her finger toward the dark forest.

"God, somebody's elbow is digging into my spine."

"Benny, *look*." She grabbed his jaw and forcibly turned his face.

"I don't see anything. Let go of—" Then he saw it. A tiny, tiny speck of red light. At first it looked like a burning cigarette. Then he realized what it was: a camera.

Somebody is recording this.

Virginia began elbowing people left and right. She pushed over two sobbing girls, accidentally stepping on one. Benny followed as she wormed her way off the bridge, shoving stupefied football players, brushing past the frantic coaches who continued to scream at everyone to get back to the field. Virginia's pushiness had always annoyed him, but in this case it was proving useful. There was no way Benny could have elbowed his way off this bridge on his own.

As soon as they reached the shadowy trees, Benny broke into a sprint.

"Whoever it is," Benny shouted back to Virginia, "just tackle them. Can you do that?"

"Yes," Virginia answered, though truthfully, she didn't know. She'd never tackled anyone before.

But it turned out she didn't have to. Because when they

arrived at the site of the tiny red light, no one was there. It was just a small camera on the ground, recording everything.

The Boarders, 10:30 p.m.

Virginia rooted around in the common-room refrigerator, looking for something exotic and interesting to offer Benny. Surely there was a mango in there, or some seaweed or something. But all she could find were reduced-fat cheese slices and some old turkey rolls.

"Mom, I'm fine. I'm at the Boarders with Virginia. . . . Yes, her."

Virginia flinched at the way he said "her." Clearly Mrs. Flax wasn't her biggest fan.

"I don't know, maybe eleven thirty? We have . . . homework. Mom, stop; we're just friends."

Virginia slammed the refrigerator door shut.

"Mom, please? I'll unload the dishwasher. I'll take Grandma to synagogue. . . . Okay. Love you too. Bye." He snapped the phone shut. "Sorry about that. My mom's picking me up at eleven thirty. Is that enough time?"

Virginia checked the computer, glad for an excuse not to look at Benny. Her cheeks felt hot, and she knew she was probably blushing. It wasn't a sweet or coquettish look on her; it made her look angry. "I don't know," she said. "Depends on how much footage there is on the camera."

There was a small echo to her voice. All the rooms in the Boarders echoed, because they were always empty. The

Boarders was a neglected old building at the edge of campus where the resident students lived. Winship Academy used to be a boarding school back in the sixties and seventies. But the residence program was being gradually phased out, and now there were only about two dozen boarders in the entire school. Every year the trustees threatened to cut the program entirely. It created a weird distance between the regular students and the boarders, like it wasn't worth getting too attached to them, because at any moment they could disappear.

Benny wasn't sure exactly what Virginia's deal was. He knew she usually went to Florida during school holidays, but he never got the feeling that she was actually *from* Florida, only that Florida was where she went. Maybe her family had a beach house or something. He'd never asked. It seemed rude to pry into the boarders' home situations. There was probably something dysfunctional about them, or else why would they be here?

He and Virginia sat side by side on a pair of wheeled desk chairs, waiting for the common room's ancient computer to buzz to life.

There was a soft, low whistle above their heads. They both looked up.

"That's it," Virginia said, pointing to the ceiling. "Do you hear it?"

There was a ghost living in the attic—at least that's what all the boarders thought. Virginia had been trying to get Benny to investigate it for weeks, but he was always reluctant. Investigating a ghost was way too much like a *Scooby-Doo!* episode, and he didn't want to encourage any more comparisons. And anyway there was no ghost, just scuttling squirrels and the whistle of wind and the magnolia tree casting twisted shadows. And the boarders below padding around like ghosts themselves, probably wishing there *were* a ghost so that they could have some company.

"Hm," Benny grunted, uninterested.

Virginia connected the camera to the computer and stared at the little icon that indicated the video was loading. She gave Benny a quick glance. He looked so dorky and serious in his voluminous turtleneck, but actually he was kind of a rebel. Back in the woods, he'd just grabbed the camera and breezed past the throng of police officers who had descended upon the scene. She'd seen enough *SVU* to know that this was tampering with evidence, but Benny didn't seem to care. She knew he didn't like the police— something to do with his childhood dog? She didn't know the whole story. Old Virginia could have wheedled it out of him in no time, but new Virginia wasn't obsessed with people's weird dog traumas.

"It has a bar code," Benny said, pointing to the bottom of the camera. "I think it's from the library."

Virginia opened a viewer on the computer and pressed play. A bright, white-and-gray room filled the screen. At the edge of the frame they could make out the brown fur of Brittany's mascot costume beside the camera.

"It's the locker room," Virginia said, surprised. She'd expected the footage to begin at the bridge.

There was giggling, and a pair of white-and-blue pom-poms sailed across the screen. Then a girl appeared in a pink bra and shorts with the word PRINCESS across the butt. The camera angle raised slowly, surreptitiously, showing her face. Blond hair, radiant skin, faintly flushing cheeks. It was Angie Montague.

"Brittany, get off your ass," Angie was saying, swiping her pom-poms toward the camera. Another cheerleader bounced into the frame for a second, carrying a pink Gatorade. She was completely naked.

"Oh my God," Benny said, quickly covering his eyes. "They don't know there's a camera."

Virginia stared at the screen. "Omigod. Corny Davenport's boobs are gigantic. She must wear like ten bras to keep those puppies down." It was the exact kind of tidbit that would have exploded in the old days on Winship Confidential.

"What else is happening?" Benny asked, still covering his eyes.

"Um . . ." Virginia squinted at the screen. "They're just, you know, bouncing around. They're changing into their uniforms."

"Are they still naked?"

"Yep."

Benny could hear giggling and locker doors opening and slamming. He knew he should open his eyes. He didn't want Virginia to think he was a pervert, but he couldn't trust her not to miss something important.

About a dozen cheerleaders were bouncing into and out of the frame in various stages of undress. The lens slowly zoomed in and out, showcasing whichever girl happened to be the most naked. One girl had a large powder puff of glitter and began patting it up and down the long, smooth limbs of the other girls, until their skin shimmered and clouds of glitter formed in the air around their bodies. The dingy locker room was suddenly transformed into an ethereal place where the beauty of the girls was so magical it caused the atmosphere to literally sparkle.

Benny realized his mouth was hanging open slightly. He snapped it shut. It felt very wrong to be watching incredibly beautiful naked girls when someone was dead and he was supposed to be figuring out why. He wished he didn't have to watch this in front of Virginia. It was so awkward he felt almost ill.

"Is Brittany obsessed with boobs or something?" Virginia said loudly. "Why would she need to record them? She can see them in the locker room every day."

"Maybe the tape was for someone else," Benny answered, not looking at her. "The football players. Or some voyeur website."

"Putting her own cheerleading squad on the Internet?" Virginia said. "That's pretty messed up."

Benny shrugged. People *were* pretty messed up; it didn't surprise him.

"Here we go," Virginia announced. The video moved jerkily out of the locker room and onto the brightly lit football field. An enormous shout rose up from the bleachers as cheerleaders skipped past the camera, waving their pom-poms and doing cartwheels. Occasionally the image was blocked out by the large furry arm of Brittany's mascot costume.

"I wonder if the camera was sewn into the costume," Virginia said. "She may not have known it was there."

"No, she knew," Benny said. "She's using the zoom button. She's getting specific shots. It's probably why she got a real camera instead of just using her phone."

For a long time the camera was very still, pointing inertly at the football field. In the background, the pep band played an abysmal rendition of "We Will Rock You." The two teams scuttled back and forth, first in one direction, then in the opposite direction. Was there a stupider game than football?

"Look at that dope Gerard," Virginia said. "Could he be any more obvious? He's been gaping at Angie the entire game."

The timer blared from the speakers. The camera moved as the cheerleaders started getting into formation for the halftime show.

"Okay, watch carefully," Benny said. "Watch for anything strange."

But it was hard to see anything at all. The camera was jerking around, almost spinning. "Brittany, get it together!" one of the girls was shouting. "Brittany. Brittany!"

Then the camera lurched forward. Brittany was running from the field.

"And she's off," Virginia said. The blackness of the forest bounced wildly in the frame as Brittany careened toward it. For a while there was just darkness and the sound of the mascot costume swishing as she ran. Then the camera was on the ground, and it was still.

"She dropped it," Benny said.

"On purpose?" Virginia asked.

Benny didn't answer; he didn't know. The camera was pointing toward the bridge, which appeared brightly illuminated by the moon. The whole scene had seemed much darker in real life.

"It's a wide exposure," Virginia said, answering his thoughts. "That's why it looks so much brighter. But it also distorts the image quality. See how grainy it is?"

Benny nodded. Seconds passed as the video played footage of the empty bridge.

"I bet this is all a dumb prank," Virginia said. "Watch, I bet we'll see Brittany sneaking out of the costume and then tossing it over the rail. 'Mascot Commits Suicide.' It's kind of funny."

"Not really," Benny said, still staring at the screen.

"Well, yeah, obviously not. But it's the sort of thing those dumb football guys would think is funny."

"Shhh, listen," Benny said. In the background they could hear a faint melody: *We're following the leeeeeeader.* "It's about to happen."

Sure enough, a great lumbering lion came crashing out of the woods. Benny shivered. An hour ago he'd watched a girl jump off this one-hundred-foot bridge, and now he was about to watch it again. The spookiest part was how disconnected he felt from it, from the gravity and finality of death. It was like Brittany wasn't a real person; she was just a question: Why?

"Look, that's you," Virginia said, pointing to a figure at the edge of the screen.

Benny squinted at it. "That's not me."

"What?"

"That's not where I was standing. I wasn't that close to the bridge."

"Well maybe it's me. . . . No, I wasn't standing there either. Um, who is that?"

Benny put his ear to the computer speaker. The raucous chorus of "Following the Leader" still sounded pretty remote. "It's definitely not me," he said. "The football players and cheerleaders were right behind me. Listen to how far away they sound right now. This guy's out there on his own."

A muffled sound came from the speaker.

"Turn it up," Benny said. "I think one of them just said something."

Virginia rewound the video and cranked up the sound.

Benny leaned his ear to the speaker. "Sounds like 'fun.' He's yelling 'fun.' Did you hear it?"

Virginia nodded. "But how did we not hear him when we were standing right there an hour ago?"

"Those stupid idiots were singing right behind us. He could have been shouting a foot away and we wouldn't have heard it."

Benny switched off the sound.

"Fun, fun," Virginia was repeating. "Maybe we misheard it. Maybe they're saying *money*? Maybe Brittany had a bunch of cash in her mascot suit, and they were trying to steal it."

Benny shook his head. "No, look at the way he's just standing there. He's not trying to catch her; he's just . . ."

"What? *What?*"

Benny felt a shiver as he stared at the grainy shadow blocking the exit to the bridge. *He's closing in on her,* he thought. *He's trying to trap her.*

Benny's house, midnight

Every day when Benny came home, his house felt like a theater set that had been carefully staged for his much-anticipated entrance. A glass of milk and a plate of Oreos sitting on the kitchen counter next to his *Scientific American* or whatever had come in the mail that day. His clothes freshly laundered and stacked neatly at the edge of his bed. An autumnal-scented candle burning on the living room table. Every surface spic-and-span and shining. It was a conspiracy between Benny's mother and grandmother to make every detail perfect and pleasant, as if that could make up for the one huge and very imperfect aspect of the Flax household, which was currently slumped in the living room easy chair with the canned laughter of *The Golden Girls* blaring in his face.

"Don't make him watch that," Benny said, setting his book bag down. His mom followed him inside.

"Your grandmother's watching it. And he doesn't know the difference."

Yes he does, Benny thought, but he didn't feel like having the same argument for the ten-thousandth time. He went over to the TV and changed the channel to PBS. It was a show about South American slugs, which wasn't much better than *The Golden Girls* in terms of mental stimulation, but at least it was science.

"What did he say today?" Benny asked.

"Light cold no fine," Mrs. Flax answered, as if "light-cold-no-fine" were one single word instead of four.

Benny sat at the kitchen counter and pulled a *National Geographic* calendar from his backpack. He felt fidgety and overexcited. He wanted to go on a long walk outside to calm his nerves and review the events of the night over and over in his mind. But he had a job to do.

In the square for October 3 he wrote *light, cold, no, fine*. Then he highlighted the word "cold" in yellow and "fine" in green. Yellow meant a new word; green meant a word his dad had said twice within the space of five days. There were more than fourteen highlighter colors in Benny's system, and 480 words so far, most of them with only one or two syllables—words like "cup" and "door" from a man who had once said things like "orbital mechanics" and "hyperbolic trajectory" on a regular basis.

Mr. Flax had been an aerospace engineer for twenty years. But sixteen months ago there'd been an accident on the test flight for the AeroStream V4 *Spinetail*, designed to be the fastest, most advanced plane ever commercially flown. It was the *Titanic* of planes, and just like the ship, it had sprung a leak. Mr. Flax was running diagnostics in the back of the plane when it depressurized. The tertiary back-ups failed to bring the aircraft down to breathable airspace, and the pilots stopped responding. As the plane seeped oxygen, Mr. Flax's brain cells died by the millions. It was a full twenty minutes before the autoland system recovered. By then the pilots were already dead.

Mr. Flax lived but was left with extreme brain damage from hypoxia. Benny had seen the CAT scans showing purple splotches indicating areas of his father's cerebrum that were irreversibly damaged. But it was too depressing to think that the brain could be broken, like a ligament or a collarbone. It wasn't just a muscle; it was *the mind*! Surely it was more than tissue and cells. Surely his old dad—his *real* dad—was in there somewhere, lost in that lavender-colored fog.

To prove this, Benny had embarked on a project of obsessively documenting every word his father said, convinced that his father was trying to say something. The ironic thing was that before the crash, Benny and his dad could have talked all the time, but they hardly ever spoke to each other. Mr. Flax had been a workaholic and wasn't home much. Few conversations from before the accident stuck out in Benny's mind. There was really only one: When he was thirteen, Benny had discovered that the *Spinetail* was costing AeroStream eighty-eight million dollars to build, which seemed like an ungodly amount at the time. He remembered asking his dad if it was wrong to spend that much money on a faster plane when people in the world were starving and homeless. His father had answered, "Progress should never wait. If we waited for everyone in the world to be clothed and fed before we advanced ourselves, we'd have no civilization."

Now, on the sofa, that same man stared blankly at the TV, drinking from a child's sippy cup decorated with bright cartoons of planes. Mr. Flax could still feed himself, but his left arm was paralyzed, and his right arm had periodic spasms and twitches that made normal glassware impossible. Nana had bought the sippy cup, cheerfully pointing out, "Look, it has planes on it!" Benny had almost cried.

"Now what's this foolishness about someone dying?" Mrs. Flax asked, dumping leftover spaghetti into a Tupperware.

"A cheerleader jumped off the bridge," Benny said. "I'm trying to figure out why. It's for my club."

Mrs. Flax sighed loudly. "Well I'm sure no one asked you to. I don't see why you have to create problems for yourself and make life difficult." She glanced at Benny's color-coded calendar. Obviously she wasn't talking about Mystery Club.

Benny stood abruptly. He scooped up his calendar and highlighters and dumped them in his book bag. He took his plate of cookies and started toward his room.

"Good night."

"Do your homework," Mrs. Flax called after him.

Benny closed his door and sat at his desk. He pulled out his chemistry book and stared at it for a second. Then he pushed it aside. He reached under his desk and grabbed his freshman yearbook, flipping to his class and scanning the *M*s.

Montague.

Angie's and Brittany's pictures were side by side. Identical faces, identical smiles. People thought of the two of them as basically interchangeable, which they'd never seemed to mind. In fact they exploited it all the time—dressing alike, wearing their hair the same, making little effort to carve out separate identities. But now one was a corpse, and one was still alive.

What made Brittany different?

Saturday
The football field, 8:30 a.m.

It was sunny but windy, a wind that accentuated the emptiness of the football field. It swooshed across the crisp green grass, with not a single body to offer resistance. Benny checked his watch. Virginia was late.

"Sorry, sorry," she panted as she ran up to him. "They were late serving breakfast."

"Oh," Benny said. It was depressing, imagining the boarders having Saturday breakfast in the cafeteria. Empty tables, lukewarm eggs, toast from the bread heels left over from the sandwich bar. Always late because the weekend staff didn't give a shit.

"So what are we looking for?" Virginia asked, still catching her breath.

"You don't look *for* anything," Benny said. "You just look."

Virginia stood still, trying to look like she was looking. A huge white cloud passed overhead. It was so quiet, it took her a moment to notice the sound of distant chatter. It was coming from the woods.

"It's the cops," Benny said, nodding toward the voices. "There are about ten of them at the bridge. Probably destroying the crime scene." He gave an impatient sigh. "Not that they know it's a crime scene. Idiots. They still think it's a basic suicide."

Virginia looked at him. She knew Benny was weird about police, but it seemed kind of unreasonable to call them idiots. The only reason *he* knew it wasn't a "basic suicide" was because *she* had spotted the camera in the woods.

"So . . . are we waiting for them to leave?" she asked him.

"No. It's a mistake to be obsessed with the bridge," Benny said. "The field is where it started. It's where she started running."

He kept staring at the field. Virginia glanced at him a few times.

"She was sitting on the sidelines," he said, "looking that way." He pointed across the field. It was an unusual football field because there was only one side of bleachers. On the other side was a small bit of woods, half concealing a three-level parking garage. They were the only school with a garage in addition to a lot, a recent one up in an ongoing facilities race between Winship and its rivals.

"Maybe she saw someone on the roof of the garage. Someone she wanted to get away from. And then when they saw her running into the forest, they ran down to corner her at the bridge."

"Stop, stop," Benny said, holding up a hand. "It's way too early to start forming a narrative. You'll confuse your brain and start seeing things that aren't there."

"What, like hallucinating?" Virginia asked.

Benny rolled his eyes. "I'm gonna look under the bleachers."

He ducked under the metal stands. The air instantly felt about five degrees cooler. Dirty paper cups and napkins littered the ground. Benny took out his phone and snapped a few pictures. A torn, crumpled French quiz. Someone's half-eaten hot dog, lying in its own ketchup like it was a blood splatter. A few cigarette butts, but not too many. Winship had an incredibly strict no-smoking policy, and for most people it wasn't worth getting kicked out of school just to seem cool. A used condom caught his eye, half shoved in its torn wrapper. Benny frowned at it. People were so gross and callous. If Benny were going to have sex, he hoped he'd treat his ejaculate with a little more reverence. Not in a perverted way—it's not like he'd frame it or something—but didn't people realize their fluids were the wellspring of life? You don't just pump them out and leave them on the ground.

"Benny!"

Benny jumped, and his head slammed against the metal stands. "Ow, fuuu . . . ," he said, stumbling forward. Benny never cursed, at least not completely. He always stopped himself before the whole word came out.

"BENNY!" Virginia shouted again.

"What, what?" Benny said, crouching to get out from under the bleachers.

"I'm hallucinating, just like you said." Virginia's voice was weirdly calm.

"Um, what?" Benny said, rubbing his head.

Then he saw it. A blond boy had appeared out of nowhere in the middle of the field. At first it didn't look like he was going anywhere. He was staggering in small circles. He looked lost, or drunk. He wore red pants that stood out starkly against the green grass. He continued spinning aimlessly in circles, then he bolted suddenly.

"Is that . . . is that Gottfried?" Benny asked. But before Virginia could answer, Benny took off running.

The woods, 9:12 a.m.

It was like a strange replay of the night before—Benny following someone into the forest, and Virginia following him. But this time it was daylight, and the forest was empty, and instead of chasing a mascot, they were chasing a German exchange student.

How is Benny so fast? Virginia wondered as she strained to keep up with him. He wasn't on any sports teams. She knew he took some weird karate class that was about trying to punch people with your mind or something. Maybe he had some supernatural mind-body connection that allowed his body to siphon power from his brain in times of physical need. Or maybe he secretly worked out. He could be ripped under those voluminous turtlenecks, and no one would ever know.

She reached the edge of the woods, leaping over a line of yellow police tape. She almost smacked right into Benny.

"Where is he?" she panted.

Benny didn't say anything, just pointed.

Gottfried stood hunched at the edge of the bridge, his hands on his knees. He was vomiting his guts out. The brackish spew splattered across the ground and the edge of the bridge. Virginia recognized the congealed chunks of cafeteria oatmeal, which had already resembled vomit in the first place.

"Oh my God," she said, covering her eyes. "Gross."

"Uh, you okay?" Benny shouted to him. Gottfried stumbled and coughed quietly. Then he wretched again. Leaves formed unflattering shadows on his face.

"I don't think he heard you," Virginia said.

"Hey, what's goin' on here?" A cop was climbing up the steep riverbank toward them. But he was balancing a clipboard and a tray of coffees and almost immediately started to slide back down the mud. One of the coffees tipped over and sloshed on his shirt. "God daymit," he hissed.

"Gottfried, come on," Virginia called out. Gottfried was staring vacantly, wiping his mouth. He looked baffled and ill. Virginia strode toward the bridge and gently took his arm.

"You kids git outta here!" the cop shouted. "You blind? That's po-lice tape!"

"He's from Germany!" Virginia shouted, dragging Gottfried away from the bridge. "Police tape is red there! He was confused!"

Benny was already far ahead of them. Virginia led Gottfried through the trees back toward the field. It felt like leading a cloddish horse. He kept stumbling and slowing her down.

"Geez, Gottfried, what the hell were you doing over there?" Virginia demanded as soon as she'd dragged him into the end zone.

"Give him a second to breathe," Benny hissed at her.

They could hear the policeman still shouting, but he was far-off now. Apparently he'd decided it wasn't worth the effort to scale the muddy bank and go after them. Soon even the shouts stopped. *Lazy fools,* Benny thought. If some random kids trampled over *his* crime scene, he wouldn't just let them run away.

Gottfried was squinting up at the sky. He shook his head a little and blinked. Some of the color was returning to his face. Benny studied him. Gottfried was kind of a spacey, weird guy. No one really knew what his deal was. He'd appeared in the ninth grade as part of a one-semester exchange program. But then when everyone came back from Christmas, Gottfried was back too, with a room in the Boarders. And then he was back the next semester, and the next semester. He'd been at Winship for almost two and a half years now. Evidently he was very attached to the place, but Benny couldn't imagine why. He wasn't particularly popular. People thought he was funny and goofy, but more in a laughing-*at*-you way. He was known for saying strange things—like once Benny had heard him tell a teacher he needed an extension because he thought he'd done his homework, but actually it had been a vivid dream. People assumed his English was bad, attributing his weirdness to foreignness, even conflating the two. But Gottfried's English was fine, Benny knew. He was just a weird person.

"Are you really drunk or something?" Virginia asked tactlessly.

"Hm . . . eh . . . ," Gottfried mumbled.

Benny's phone buzzed. "Ugh," he said, checking it. "I have to go. My grandma's picking me up for temple. Um . . ." He looked from Virginia to Gottfried, and back to Virginia. Was it wise to leave her alone with him? It wasn't her safety that concerned him—Gottfried was harmless, and Virginia could take care of herself anyway. It was the fear that she'd screw up his investigation somehow. Tell Gottfried the wrong thing, ask him the wrong question.

"So . . . I guess . . . ," he said stupidly.

"I'll take him back to the Boarders," Virginia said.

"Sure, just don't, you know . . . ," Benny said, eyeing Gottfried. He didn't seem to be paying attention, but Benny couldn't risk being explicit.

"Don't what?" Virginia asked obtusely.

Benny fidgeted with his phone. "I dunno. Whatever. I'll call you later. Bye." Then he turned abruptly and sprinted from the field.

The Boarders, 10:15 a.m.

"Would you feel better if you took a shower?" Virginia asked, eyeing a tiny fleck of vomit on Gottfried's shirt.

Gottfried shook his head, which didn't surprise her. People avoided showering in the Boarders on the weekends, because for some reason the hot water tended to run out. It was a running joke that the boarders always smelled on Mondays—an affectionate joke, for the most part, but one that nevertheless emphasized their general apartness.

"Well . . . do you want some tea or something?" Virginia offered. She started opening and closing cabinet doors, looking for the herbal tea Mrs. Morehouse kept stocked in the common-room kitchen. Mrs. Morehouse was the Boarders' house mom. She was supposed to live with them and supervise their every move. However, in her ancientness, she seemed to grow disinterested in her duties, making up for long stretches of absence with fierce disciplinary tirades whenever she randomly appeared. The tea she liked was always fruity flavors paired with an abstract quality, like "passion fruit persuasion" or "peppermint spice tranquility." Zaire Bollo, the British girl—or part British, who really knew—read the ingredients list out loud once and declared that it contained no actual tea, just artificial flavors. Zaire was always complaining about the food in America, which Virginia thought was snobbish. Gottfried was from Europe too, but he never complained.

"No sank you," Gottfried said. His accent was faint, but you could always hear it when he made the "th" sound, which came out like a hiss, instead of soft and velvety like it was supposed to.

Virginia flopped onto the sofa next to him. It felt weird to be hanging out together. She wasn't sure if she should leave. People always assumed that since there were so few of them, the boarders were all best friends and had orgies every night—cooped up with all those empty rooms. But actually they tended to feel kind of awkward around one another. The building was just too spacious and too quiet. There was a "Boarders Bash" in the common room once a semester, but it was always dysfunctional—everyone showed up at different times and missed the others, or else they just refused to relax and ended up pretending to go to the bathroom and never coming back.

Gottfried stared at the wall while Virginia chewed her thumbnail. *I'll call you later.* Had Benny actually said that? He'd never called her before, but he'd said it like it was no big deal, like they talked on the phone all the time. *Just don't, you know. . . .* And what had he meant by that? Don't lose Gottfried? Don't make out with him? Virginia glanced at him. Maybe Benny saw something she didn't.

Maybe Gottfried was in love with her. Or maybe he was Brittany's murderer, and what Benny was saying was *Don't get killed*. That would be so like him, to send her off with a murderer while he went to synagogue with his grandma. Benny never let her know what was going on.

"How did you know police tape in Germany is red?" Gottfried asked suddenly.

Virginia looked at him. "Huh?"

"What you told da police officer. Have you been to *Deutschland*?"

"Oh! Um, no, I just said that. Is it really red?"

"*Ja . . . ,*" he murmured. "*Polizeiabsperrung . . .*"

People were always commenting on Gottfried's eyes. They were so blue they were fake-looking. No imperfections or flecks or brown or gray—just a seamless ring of pure pale aquamarine. Virginia made herself look away. She didn't want to be like everyone else, going gaga for Gottfried's eyeballs. She liked to think of herself as a person who was unimpressed by superficial things.

"What were you doing out there?" she asked, redirecting the conversation. "Were you channeling the mascot or something?"

"Hm?" Gottfried's eyebrow cocked curiously, in a way that Virginia couldn't quite read.

"You did the same weird dance as Brittany," Virginia pressed, "and then you ran to the bridge just like she did."

Gottfried shrugged, and then yawned hugely.

He's on drugs, Virginia decided. A long, silent moment passed.

"I sink I will take a small siesta now," Gottfried announced. "I am so tired . . . tired all da time." He stood up and looked right into Virginia's eyes again. "You helped me today. It was very kind. Sank you." Then he bent down in a swift, smooth motion and kissed her cheek. Before she felt it, she smelled the faint rotten odor of his vomitus breath on her face. It made her stomach turn. But then she felt his lips, and her stomach turned again, in a different way.

"You're welcome . . . ," she said lamely.

Gottfried stood up and left the room. Then she heard him say, "Oh," as if he'd bumped into someone in the hall. Virginia stiffened. Was someone there? Was someone listening in on them? Virginia scanned their conversation in her mind. Had she said anything weird or incriminating? She got up quickly and poked her head into the hall. Gottfried was gone. A door shut upstairs. And then it was quiet—that familiar sound of no one being there.

Congregation Mikveh Israel, 10:30 a.m.

Benny paced back and forth in front of the row of rabbi portraits. He turned his face away from them; some of the portraits were the creepy kind where the eyes follow you, and Benny didn't feel like dealing with their reprimanding gaze.

"Well, what was his facial expression when you

mentioned Brittany's name?" he was saying in a half whisper.

"It's hard to describe," Virginia said over the phone. "It was like . . . when a dog hears a sound it recognizes? Like its food being opened?"

"Huh . . . ," Benny said, not quite sure what to make of that. "Not, like, guilty or anything?"

"No, he didn't look guilty. Mostly he looked incredibly spaced out. I think he was on drugs."

Benny could hear the children's choir singing, which meant they were about to start the Torah service.

"I have to go," Benny said. "Keep an eye on Gottfried. If he leaves the Boarders, follow him."

"Okay," Virginia said. "Anything else I should do?"

"Get ahead on your homework. It could be a big week, so school can't be in the way."

"Okay. I have a paper due Thursday, but I'll do it now."

It was always surprising how obedient Virginia could be. She never argued with him or tried to be in charge. It was strange for someone so pushy and assertive.

"Should we go to that vigil tomorrow?" she asked.

"What vigil?"

"Oh, there's a thing at the fountain, to light candles and stuff. Everyone's going."

Everyone's going. Benny usually never heard about these sorts of things until they were already over and "everyone's going" had become "everyone was there."

"Yeah, definitely," he said. "We should definitely be there."

The Boarders, 2:30 p.m.

She had lost him almost immediately. Surveilling someone was pretty much impossible if you didn't have a car. Virginia reread her pathetically brief report, trying to come up with ways to pad it and make it look more impressive.

> Subject was in his room for an hour and a half, sleeping probably. At 1:22 someone showed up and started throwing rocks at his window to wake him up. It was the delivery guy from Domino's. Everyone at the Boarders calls him Corn Flakes because he has cornrows and really bad dandruff. He tries to hang with us all the time, but pretty much only Gottfried will talk to him. They drive to the gas station sometimes to buy cigarettes. That's probably where they went, but I couldn't figure out how to follow them.

There was a ton more she could say about Corn Flakes—how he was obsessed with Lindsay Bean and always got her free toppings, how he tried to take her to prom and Lindsay was so embarrassed she pretty much died, and how he supposedly went to Georgia State but was more likely just a townie loser. But was all that intel or just gossip? It was hard to know the difference.

Post siesta, subject looked refreshed and revived. He didn't seem sick anymore. He'd changed his pants.

Virginia frowned, erased the part about changing his pants, then wrote it back in again. She didn't know what was important to report. Maybe in some weird universe Gottfried's pants could unlock the Mystery of the Suicidal Mascot.

Gottfried and Corn Flakes had this elaborate high five they gave each other, which struck me as interesting because I didn't think they hung out all that much. But maybe it's just one of those high fives that all dudes preternaturally know. I will investigate this and report back.

She folded up the paper and went to the common-room computer to google "guy high fives." The results were pretty useless, like guys high-fiving their dogs or accidentally smacking each other in the faces. She came up with a great plan to ascertain whether the high five was a standard dude one or unique to Gottfried and Corn Flakes:

She'd wait for Gottfried to come back in the hope that they would do the high five again, but this time she'd be waiting with the camera. She'd film the high five, study it, and practice it until she could do it perfectly. Then she'd go up to Gottfried and do it, and if he was incredibly shocked, she'd know the handshake was personal between him and Corn Flakes.

And then what? she thought, suddenly discouraged. *What would that even prove? That Gottfried and Corn Flakes were buds? So what? Total myopic fixation.*

"Myopic fixation" was what Benny called Virginia's principal weakness as an investigator. She'd looked up "myopic" in the dictionary; it meant being shortsighted. And "fixated" meant being obsessed. Together they meant a tendency to get sidetracked by small details.

Zoom out, she thought, and found herself envisioning the Earth from outer space. *Christ, not that far,* she told herself. She closed her eyes. What did football, boobs, and a German exchange student have in common?

She sighed, opening her eyes. She just wasn't good at seeing the big picture. All she saw was a big blank.

Virginia closed the Google tab and folded her pathetically inadequate field report on Gottfried. Then she left the common room and went back to her hall. A pair of white-and-blue pom-poms was lying in a fluffy pile next to one of the doors. *Her* door. Virginia looked around. The pom-poms hadn't been there before. Someone must have dropped them there while she was in the common room.

There was a Post-it note stuck to the door, written with messy handwriting in blue ballpoint pen:

You LEFT THESE IN MY CAR. HOPE YOUR OK

Chrissie White was the only cheerleader in the Boarders; someone must have mixed up Virginia's room with hers. Virginia picked up the pom-poms and crossed the hall to knock on Chrissie's door. Virginia and Chrissie hadn't talked in ages, though they used to be best friends. Chrissie was a total social climber, which Virginia could have respected if she weren't so bad at it. She got way too drunk at parties, gave blow jobs to the wrong guys, and then bragged about it to the wrong girls. And the fact that she'd started snubbing Virginia was proof that she had zero sense of social strategy. Not that Virginia cared anymore. She had her own reputation rehab to deal with, which was challenging enough without getting sucked into Chrissie's downward spiral.

The door cracked open. "What?" Chrissie's voice was small, and she looked like she'd been crying. She was still wearing her nightgown even though the afternoon was half over.

"Someone left these at my door," Virginia said, handing her the pom-poms.

Chrissie wiped her nose on the sleeve of her nightgown. "These aren't mine. They're Corny's."

"Oh. How can you tell?"

"They have glitter on the handles. Corny puts glitter on everything." Chrissie sighed sadly, as if everything—even glitter—was ugly and meaningless now that Brittany was gone.

"Oh . . . ," Virginia said. "Well, someone left them at my door. Will you take them?"

"Sure," Chrissie sighed again. Then she closed the door, presumably to resume weeping in her nightie.

Virginia stood in the hall for a second. Who was clueless enough to think Corny Davenport lived in the Boarders? None of the really popular girls were resident students; they were all Atlanta-born-and-bred types whose parents had also gone to Winship back in the day. Winship had a reputation for being one of the more cliquish schools, which its students wore like a badge of honor. Everyone knew where everyone belonged. And in no universe did Corny Davenport's pom-poms belong at the Boarders.

Virginia turned and crossed the hall and opened the door of her room. The air felt different inside, muggy and sticky. Was her window open? She looked; it was closed. But the air was thick and smelled like the magnolia tree outside. She gave the window a closer look. There were smudges from fingertips at the bottom of the glass. She pressed her own hand on the window next to them. She held it there a second, then drew it away.

"What the hell . . ."

Side by side, the smudges weren't the same.

Someone else had been in her room.

Sunday
The fountain, 8:10 p.m.

The dusk light glowed with a hundred twinkling flames. It would have been romantic if not for the cloud of death hanging over everyone's heads. Corny Davenport reached for her boyfriend's hand, but he seemed reluctant to touch her. He fiddled with his candle, pretending to be distracted by a drip of wax. He was obviously embarrassed. Corny wished he would relax and submit to being comforted by her. They were sixteen; no one expected them to be strong.

"Hold my hand," Corny whispered to him. Winn looked over his shoulder first, checking if anyone was looking. Corny felt a twinge of irritation, but it only lasted a second. *Poor Winn*, she thought. He didn't know how to deal with death. None of them did. They especially didn't know how to deal with suicide. Everyone had some crazy explanation for why Brittany jumped, mostly involving the supernatural: The mascot costume was cursed because the football team lost to Lowell four years in a row; the bridge was cursed because those kids who'd died a few years ago had been Satanists.

Why is it easier to believe in curses than to believe that a cheerleader could have depression? Corny thought. Being a cheerleader could be very depressing! You were responsible for the happiness of the entire school! Which was a hard job when the football team was having a terrible season, and it was raining a lot, and Lillian Davis's grandfather died so they couldn't have parties at his plantation anymore, and it was just generally not being the greatest year. Everyone leaned on the cheerleaders to keep their spirits up, and clearly Brittany had collapsed from the pressure.

The whole thing gave Corny a sad, motherly feeling, like she wanted to scoop up the entire school into a big hug. She was always hugging people—it's why everyone called her Corny. Her real name was Courtney Anne, but Corny fit her personality; she was a completely sentimental dork. And she'd never felt so purely in her element as she did at that moment. Everyone was vulnerable; everyone needed a hug. She'd given at least a hundred hugs today and felt like she could give a hundred more. Especially to Winn, who really needed one, even if he wouldn't admit it.

"It isn't fair!" one of the cheerleaders was moaning. "Heaven is full of angels! Why did they need to take Brittany, too?" Then she began crying bitterly. Corny spotted her like a hawk, swooping upon the needy soul to envelop her in a deep, warm hug.

Winn wiped his hand on his pants. His palm had been sweating for a while, and he'd been wishing Corny would let go of it. But as soon as she was gone, he almost immediately wished she would come back. It made him twitchy and jealous, the way she smothered other people with attention. It was embarrassing, and it undermined him as her boyfriend. All Winn's teammates on the football team had an exact idea of her body, because she was always affectionately plastering herself on them, pressing her huge, pillowy boobs against their broad chests. Sometimes she even hugged them when they were sitting down, which was pretty much just smashing her boobs in their faces. Winn was always scanning the crotches of his friends to see if they got hard-ons when she jumped on them. It was a gross, paranoid habit, but Winn told himself he was doing it to protect her. Corny was kind of clueless. Actually she was a lot like Brittany in that way. And it was easy to take advantage of girls like that. Girls who didn't understand the power of their bodies.

8:30 p.m.

Benny squeezed his way into the crowd. It was unclear who had organized the vigil, but now almost the entire high school was gathered together holding candles and crying. Bouquets of flowers had been tossed in a disorganized pile around the gurgling fountain, which looked less like a scene of mourning than a pile of pleasantly scented garbage.

Everyone was waving pictures of Brittany on their phones, adding to the weird glow. No one had bothered to print out pictures, no one except Benny anyway. He quickly folded his up and hid it in his pocket, not wanting to stand out. He and Virginia weren't there to grieve; they were there to observe.

"Do you see Angie?" Benny asked. "Or Gottfried?"

Virginia scanned the crowd. "No . . . But Angie may be in the middle of that bunch of cheerleaders." They were all wearing their uniforms, as if they hadn't changed since the game Friday night. Maybe they hadn't. Virginia pushed through the crowd toward the cheerleaders, careful not to catch her hair on fire from all the carelessly bobbing candles. The cheerleaders' weeping sounds were soft, unlike their hysteria on the bridge. They were probably exhausted from crying for two days straight.

"Ashes to ashes, dust to dust. You gotta be a Wildcat to cheer with us," a pair of cheerleaders chanted in a weepy whisper. Virginia looked at them.

"Could y'all not do that?" she said loudly. "It's kind of creepy."

The girls glared at her, and then turned their backs and kept chanting.

"Don't talk to anyone," Benny told her. "Just be in the space."

He'd never seen this many people packed around the fountain. Apparently it was Brittany's favorite place to eat lunch. There were already rumors of deliberations to rename the area Brittany Park, which Benny suspected had more to do with obfuscating a certain decrepit old bench under the magnolia tree. The bench had been erected in the sixties as a scanty peace offering to the first black students to desegregate Winship. It had not been a smooth transition, and now the bench was a daily reminder of a very embarrassing period in the school's history. While the trustees couldn't actually remove the bench without drawing further attention to it, renaming the entire area Brittany Park would at least overshadow it. Better to remember Brittany Montague—sweet, shining Brittany—than some fraught, bitter time that just made everyone uncomfortable.

"Stop blowing out your candle," someone behind Benny was saying.

"I'm not blowing it out. It was the breeze."

"You just did! You blew it out!"

Benny turned around. It was Winn and Corny, the junior class couple. They'd been together since the sixth grade. Everyone envied them, but Benny thought it was weird. Kissing someone you kissed when they were eleven was kind of abnormal. And besides, Benny knew Winn was a creep even if no one else saw it.

Corny was lighting his candle. Winn immediately blew it out again.

"Is this a trick candle or something?" Winn said,

sounding really annoyed. "How did I get a trick candle?"

"You're blowing it out," Corny insisted. "I just saw you. Benny, didn't you see it?"

"Um, I guess," Benny said. "Have y'all seen Angie? Is she here?"

"I don't think so. . . . Winn, seriously, stop blowing out your candle."

"She's over there," Benny heard. He turned around and saw Zaire Bollo. He was surprised he hadn't noticed her— Zaire tended to make herself known. She was imperious and a little stuck-up, in a way that was sort of similar to Virginia, but somehow Zaire pulled it off better. A matter of stage presence, Benny guessed. Composure. And the fact that she looked like a model, with the kind of face you'd find etched into the wall of a pharaoh's tomb.

She was pointing to the bench under the magnolia tree. As his eyes adjusted to the darkness, Benny could suddenly make out a person lying in a ball, tangled blond hair catching a small bit of light. He could tell she was crying.

"Why isn't anyone helping her?" Benny asked.

"I dunno." Zaire shrugged. "I guess we're the only ones who see her."

Benny stood there for a second, staring at the dark lump shrouded in shadows. Just as he decided to go over to her, Angie righted herself abruptly and started walking toward the parking garage, a key ring hanging limply from her fingers. *She shouldn't be driving*, Benny thought. Benny started to walk after her, but then stopped. He barely knew Angie. It would be invasive, not to mention self-important, for him to sweep in like some pushy hero.

At that moment, apparently realizing that the center of their hurricane of sorrow had drifted away, a swarm of cheerleaders appeared at Angie's side. In the darkness they all looked dimly alike, as if they were a dozen twins trying to take the place of the one Angie had lost.

8:55 p.m.

"I KNOW IT WAS YOU!"

The scream—hysterical, anguished—jolted the soft hush of the vigil. Everyone looked around.

"Oh my God?"

"What the . . ."

"What's going on? Who is that?"

"I KNOW IT WAS YOU! I KNOW IT WAS YOU! I KNOW IT WAS YOU!" The scream repeated over and over.

Virginia spun around. *Where the hell is Benny?* she thought. *Is he hearing this?* She didn't know what to do. Her MO was just to follow Benny and do what he said. But she couldn't find him. It was hard to see anything in the crowd, because everyone was pushing and trying to find out what was going on.

Then she saw it. It was Gerard Cole, the water boy. He was screaming and pointing at someone in front of the fountain.

But then some freshmen moved in front of Virginia, and she couldn't see him anymore. She pushed a gap between them and shoved herself through.

"I KNOW IT WAS YOU!" Gerard continued to scream. But his voice was getting hoarse and weak. He was pointing at two immense upperclassmen, Trevor Cheek and another one whose name Virginia didn't know. The boys were looking sort of baffled but also pissed. Suddenly Gerard launched himself at Trevor, beating his fists against Trevor's broad chest.

"Get the FUCK off me!" Trevor shouted, giving Gerard a swat that sent him flying to the ground. Trevor's face had turned completely purple, engorged with rage. "I will FUCKING kill you."

Gerard immediately picked himself up and flung himself at Trevor again. The crowd formed a tight circle around them, everyone yelling, candles being dropped or snuffed out by all the jostling. Trevor blocked Gerard with an effortless wave of his arm, and Gerard was back on the ground. His head was bleeding now.

"Eeeeh . . . ," Gerard moaned, trying to sit up. He pointed up at Trevor. Tears streamed down his face. "I know it was you."

"You are a FUCKING psycho," Trevor sneered at him. Virginia had never heard a more menacing voice in real life. "If you touch me again, you DIE." Then he turned and stomped away, knocking down several people in his path.

"Nobody move!" boomed an adult voice from across the fountain. It was Principal Baron. "Nobody move" was what he always shouted when he was on the warpath.

Virginia quickly shoved her way to the center of the circle and knelt next to Gerard. "Gerard, come on. Quickly, come on."

"No one believes me!" Gerard wept to himself.

"I believe you!" Virginia whispered. She had no idea what Gerard was talking about, but it seemed like what he wanted to hear. All around them, people were staring, and the principal was elbowing his way toward them. She had to get him out of there and find Benny.

"You do?" Gerard asked, and his eyes contained such sad, innocent hope that he looked like a child.

"Yes," Virginia said. "Now come on." Gerard got up, and Virginia ducked between two groups of upset cheerleaders. She looked over her shoulder to make sure Gerard was following. The small circle of space where he and Trevor had fought was gone; bodies had immediately pressed in and filled it. Like they'd never even been there.

The Boarders, 9:00 p.m.

"I'm invisible to them. They don't even see me." He sounded alert, but dulled.

"Well, they're cheerleaders, Gerard, what do you expect?" Virginia was trying to be patient, but she hadn't brought him here for a pep talk, she'd brought him here to find out why he'd moronically attacked Trevor Cheek.

Gerard slumped on the common-room sofa with a vacant look in his eyes. Virginia was sitting next to him, but as far away as she could get without insulting him. She didn't want someone to walk in and think they were *together*. It's not that Gerard was even that bad. He was a dope though, very low-hanging fruit, and people would think she had low self-esteem if it seemed like she liked him.

"Not the cheerleaders," Gerard moaned softly. "They're *nice*. It's the football players."

"Oh," Virginia said.

"They say things in front of me. They don't even notice I'm there."

"Things like . . . what?" Virginia asked.

"I heard them . . . I heard them talking about Brittany. They're disgusting."

"Omigod, what were they saying?" Virginia asked, and was immediately embarrassed by the overeagerness in her voice. She wasn't a gossip queen anymore, she reminded herself; she was an investigator. She needed to be cool. But if Gerard was put off by her obvious salivating, he didn't show it. He was probably so starved for attention he would have told anyone.

"They talked about her and the mascot suit. They wanted to hear her growl like a wildcat while they . . . banged her."

"In the *suit*?!" Virginia yelled. She burst out laughing.

"Don't laugh! It's not funny! I think they banged her before the game. R-r-raped her." His voice stuttered over the word. "Raped her in the wildcat suit."

Virginia stopped laughing.

"And that's why she killed herself!" Gerard sobbed. "Because she was ruined! She was the best mascot in the world! The mascot of beauty and innocence and joy!"

Virginia's lip curled. She really didn't want to believe this. It was the most disgusting and perverted thing she'd ever heard. It wasn't mysterious; it was gross and sad.

"Okay, just . . . calm down," she said to Gerard. "Come here." She went over to the computer and sat down. Gerard continued to weep on the sofa.

"Come *here*," Virginia repeated, slapping the chair next to her. "I want you to look at this."

Gerard sniffed and looked at the ceiling. "What's that sound?" he said, his face wet with tears.

Virginia listened and heard a familiar whistle, breathy and low and emanating from inside the walls. "It's just the ghost," she said. "Don't pay attention to it. Now come here."

"Y'all have a ghost?" Gerard asked, wiping his nose on his sleeve. Virginia didn't answer. She pulled out a silver flash drive and plugged it into the computer. Then she clicked open the video from Friday night, pointedly fast-forwarding past the locker room footage so she didn't have to endure Gerard weepily ogling the cheerleaders in their underwear. It had been awkward enough watching that with Benny.

"Okay, watch this," she said, pointing to the screen. It was the bridge, all muddled gray hues with a touch of blue. "See that guy? He's making her jump. He's intimidating her."

Gerard wiped his eyes. "Hang on, whaaa . . ."

"And look at his shape. He doesn't have football gear on. His shoulders are narrow. It's definitely not Trevor."

"Well . . . he could have run ahead of her! He could have ditched the gear in the woods!"

Virginia shook her head. "I was there. The cheerleaders were behind me, and the football players were behind them. There wasn't time for anyone to cross the bridge before Brittany got there. Whoever it was, they were already there. Waiting."

"Can you zoom? Enhance it?" Gerard said, his voice eager and little high-pitched. "Can you tell who it is?"

"That's just TV," Virginia said. Those scenes always annoyed her, the ones where cops zoomed in on a piece of grainy footage and suddenly a million pixels magically appeared, providing a crisp, clear image. "In real life what you see is what you get."

Gerard didn't say anything. He seemed confused, staring at the grainy image and blinking dumbly.

"I mean, I guess it doesn't really change much. Brittany's still . . . gone. But, I mean . . ." Virginia didn't know what she meant. "I mean we still don't have the answers."

Gerard inhaled slowly, then started crying again.

"Christ, Gerard," Virginia sighed. Why had she even showed him the video? Because she felt sorry for him, she guessed, but now he was just annoying her again.

She closed the file and yanked out the flash drive.

"I'm going to bed. Can you get yourself home? You can sleep here on the sofa if you want, I guess, but if Mrs. Morehouse checks in, you'll be dead meat."

Gerard sniffed and wiped his eyes. "I'll go." He began shuffling to the door. Then he turned back and looked right at Virginia.

"Do you think Brittany's a virgin in heaven?" he said. His voice cracked.

"Uh . . ."

"Or when we die, do we bring all the bad shit that happened to us?"

Virginia gaped at him for a second. Was she actually supposed to answer that?

"The first one," she managed. But actually, that one seemed depressing too. What was the point of all this shit happening if when you died it just got erased, like it hadn't meant anything at all?

The fountain, 9:30 p.m.

Benny dialed the number again, but she didn't pick up. *She must not be in her room. Where is she?* It was weird and inconvenient that Virginia didn't have a cell phone, but he didn't want to embarrass her by bringing it up. Which was ironic, because Virginia never hesitated to embarrass anyone, pointing out all the little ways they were lacking in her opinion.

Benny bent down to pick up another burned-out candle rolling on the ground. Why was he picking up everyone's litter? It's not like anyone would thank him for it. There was no one around; after the loud kerfuffle by the fountain, everyone had quickly dispersed and gone home, dropping their candles like they were trash, even though most were only barely used.

Benny sat down on the ledge of the fountain, depressed. It was quiet. They'd turned the water off, so now instead of a gushing, sparkling spray, it was just a pointless cement pool of stagnant water.

A baby cried. *A baby?* Benny turned around. He'd been sure he was alone. Then something low and slinky caught his eye. It wasn't a baby; it was a cat.

"Wildcat," Benny said. "What're you doing out here, little guy?"

The cat meowed again and hopped up beside him. He was a brown, fluffy part-Manx, slightly mangy looking, with big expressive yellow eyes. He was the school cat and had the run of the campus, but usually avoided the students.

Benny hesitantly ran the tips of his fingers over Wildcat's

long fur, matted in places and in need of a good brushing. Wildcat wasn't generally very friendly. He was one of those moody cats who test people—rubbing up against you, then attacking out of nowhere, just to see if you'll still like them.

"Did you see what happened, Wildcat?"

Wildcat nuzzled Benny's arm. Benny reminded himself that this was the same cat who had literally scratched Connor Tate's eye out and sent him to the hospital. The Tates wanted to have Wildcat put down after that, but everyone agreed it was Connor's fault. He was an asshole and an idiot and was trying to put a sock on Wildcat's head.

Benny called Virginia's room again. No answer. He left a message. "Hi. It's me. . . . Umm . . . could you bring the camera to school tomorrow? We should take it to the AV lab, find out if Brittany checked out equipment like that a lot. Maybe videotaping the locker room was, like, a habit of hers. . . . Okay, anyway . . . bye." He snapped his phone shut. Next to him, Wildcat stretched, gave Benny a random, offended-seeming hiss, and then hopped to the ground. "Bye," he said to Wildcat.

Benny put his head in his hands and moaned quietly. He was furious with himself for missing the action with the fight or whatever it was. He'd been at the edge of the crowd, watching Angie Montague shuffle toward the parking garage. He must have been staring for a full minute, just spacing out. Then he'd heard shouting and immediately turned around.

Virginia was gone, and the crowd had compressed, forming a wall of bodies that blocked Benny from whatever was going on at the center. Benny had circled the crowd desperately, like a dog circling a tree. But there was no way in—they were packed too tight. Maybe Virginia could have shoved her way to the center, but Benny couldn't. He was stuck there, missing everything. Which proved the entire point of the philosophy of Being There. You could *never* get inside from the outside. Your only hope was to Be There.

The Boarders, 2:11 a.m.

Virginia realized she was awake. She wasn't sure how long her eyes had been open, or why she'd woken up. She was lying on her side, staring blankly into the darkness. In the corner her coat hung from a metal hook, creating a bulky shadow. She kept staring at it, like her eyes were magnetized. The room had a faint bluish tint from the streetlamp filtering in through the thin curtains. As Virginia's vision slowly adjusted to the dimness, the coat's outline started morphing, taking on eerie details. A pale sheen of gold on top. Shadows almost seeming to form a face. And it was moving slightly.

It's October, Virginia thought suddenly. *My coat's in storage.*

Instantly she was wide awake. Her arm shot out to reach for the desk lamp. But she knocked it over, and there was a loud thump and a clatter as the power cord dragged everything on her desk down with it.

"GET OUT!" she screamed. She fell out of her bed in a tangle of sheets, landing hard on her hip. She picked herself up in the darkness, then tripped on the sheets and fell down again. She scrambled to her feet and lunged for the light switch. Bright yellow light flooded the room. Virginia blinked, looking around frantically. Her heart was pounding and her breath was ragged. Her lamp was on the floor, her sheets in a messy knot.

There was no one there.

Virginia poked her head out into the hall. It was dark and silent.

Chrissie White's door opened and light spilled into the hall. "What's going on?" she said groggily, squinting at Virginia across the hall.

"Nothing," Virginia said, rubbing her eyes. "I don't know. I was dreaming. Did you hear someone in the hall just now?"

"Be quiet!" someone shouted from inside their room.

"I just heard you screaming," Chrissie said. "Go back to sleep." She closed her door, and her light disappeared.

Virginia stood there for a second, feeling foggy and confused. It wasn't the first time someone had woken up screaming in the Boarders. Yancey Kemper had nightmares all the time, and no one paid attention. The boarders tended to have little sympathy for one another. They were all stuck in the same shitty situation; no one had it particularly worse than anyone else.

Virginia went back into her room and looked at the corner. There was no coat. There was no person, either. It was just her normal room. She gathered her sheets and threw them back on the bed. Then she flicked off the light and went to sleep.

Monday
The girls' locker room, 11:00 a.m.
I love you and you're my best friend. You have the biggest heart!

I love you and you're my best friend. Your smile makes my day!

I love you and you're my best friend. Never ever change!

Corny began carefully taping the notes to the locker doors, using tape she'd sprinkled with pink and silver glitter. She'd stayed up until two a.m. writing a special note for every girl on the varsity and junior varsity cheer squads, each with a unique message to lift their spirits and help get everyone through this sad and awful week.

I love you and you're my best friend. You have the most beautiful hair!

She taped up the last one with a flourish, and then plopped down on a bench. She closed her eyes and made herself breathe in and out. It was important to take a moment for yourself every now and then. It was called self-care. Corny had read that in a magazine.

"Okay!" she said after five seconds. She opened her eyes. *This locker room is disgusting,* she thought. Stuff was strewn everywhere—clothes, bras, pairs of tennis shoes. No one had bothered to clean up after the game on Friday. Everyone had just gone home and cried. And now it was like a moment frozen in time, the moment before Brittany's light had gone out and left the world a darker place.

Corny noticed a puddle on the floor near the pom-pom closet. It looked like urine. *Gross.* Had someone been so sad they'd peed themselves? Grief pee? Maybe that was a thing. Corny got up and went closer to it, to see if it really was pee. It was disgusting, but she couldn't help being curious. Then she realized it was coming from under the pom-pom closet door.

Oh my God, she thought. *There's someone in there.*

There was a burgundy backpack leaning against the door. It had initials embroidered on it: GWC. *Gerard Cole.* She knew Gerard came in and out of the locker room sometimes to refill their pink Gatorade. No one really minded—Gerard was practically one of the girls. But did he, like, hang out in there when they were all gone? Just by himself? That was kind of weird.

"Um . . . Gerard?" Corny knocked gently on the closet door. "Gerard, what are you doing in there?"

She heard him groan softly.

"Don't be embarrassed," Corny said. "I think we all deserve to cry in the pom-pom closet today. Let me in and we can cry together." She jiggled the door handle, but it was locked.

"Did you pick a fight with Trevor again?" she asked through the door.

She waited, but he didn't seem to be moving.

"I'm going to get the spare keys from the lounge. And a mop. Don't go anywhere. I'll be back in five minutes, and I'll give you a nice foot massage."

She gave Gerard's backpack a little push with her foot so the urine puddle wouldn't touch it. Then she dashed from the locker room, buzzing with all the love inside her.

The AV lab, 12:30 p.m.

Skylar Jones sat in the dark, blinking back tears. He was in the equipment closet, watching *The Lion King* on Mr. Rashid's laptop. The circle of life—it was so beautiful! Skylar swiped a match against his pant leg, preparing to light up for the third time since breakfast. On a day like this you really couldn't be too high, Skylar figured. Everyone was freaking out about Brittany Montague. Apparently she'd jumped off the bridge in her mascot suit and was dead. About a hundred people had seen her do it, right in the middle of the football game. Skylar shuddered, not wanting to think about it. He turned up the volume on Mr. Rashid's computer. *Hakuna matata*, right?

Ding ding! It was the little bell at the front desk. Skylar considered ignoring it. The school was barely functioning today. Half the student body hadn't even shown up, and the other half was crowded into "grief circles" in the guidance hall. *Ding ding!* The bell rang again. Skylar sighed and paused the movie. He poked his head out of the closet to see who was there.

Great. It was that Scooby-Doo guy and god-awful Virginia Leeds. Just being in the same room with Virginia was a buzzkill. She'd worked at the AV desk for a few weeks at the beginning of the semester, and she'd driven Skylar crazy. The AV lab had always been Skylar's place to chill out, but Virginia's vibe was anything but chill. She was always in your face, and she was incredibly nosy. He'd even caught her going through his backpack once. When he asked her what the hell she thought she was doing, she said, "I'm just trying to get to know you!"

And now here she was, leaning across the desk and holding a small digital camera. "Skylar, can you give us the checkout history on this camera? It has a library barcode. Just tell us how often it gets checked out."

"Um . . . no?" Skylar said. "We don't fork over that information."

"We're just trying to return it," Virginia said. "We found it on the ground. . . . Are you crying?"

Skylar wiped his eyes. "Shut up."

"It's okay to be one with your emotions," Virginia said, smirking.

The Scooby guy looked impatient. "Yes, yes, everyone's upset. So can you give us the checkout history?"

"You just found it on the ground?" Skylar asked. "Why do you care who checked it out?"

"Why do *you* care that *we* care?" Virginia said.

"I *don't*," Skylar said, scowling, wishing he'd never left the equipment closet.

"If you could just check," the Scooby guy persisted.

Skylar sighed loudly and scanned the barcode on the camera. He squinted at the computer screen. "Um . . . nobody checked this out. Well, not a student anyway."

"Yes they did," Virginia said. "It was definitely a student."

"Well if you know so much, why are you asking me?" Skylar sighed.

"Here, let me look," Virginia demanded, leaning over the desk to see the computer screen for herself. Her elbow bumped a cup full of pens.

Skylar swatted her away. "Quit. You're knocking things over. Let me a do full scan."

"Patrick Choi," Virginia said, reading the scan result. "Mr. Choi? The pep band conductor? Mr. Choi?"

"Mr. Choi?" Scooby repeated. "Mr. *Choi*?"

Now Skylar *really* needed a joint. "Let's say 'Mr. Choi' five hundred more times."

Virginia grabbed the camera and started walking off with it, followed by her nerdy friend. "Thanks, Skylar."

"Hey, you have to give that back," Skylar shouted after them. They ignored him. He sighed and returned to the equipment closet, resolved not to come out again until he was high enough to tune out this entire day.

The girls' bathroom, 2:45 p.m.

Virginia stood at the mirror, spritzing herself with perfume. *I can't believe I used to think Skylar was cool,* she thought. She'd applied to work at the AV lab in September because Skylar Jones had seemed like the most mysterious boy in school. He was a senior, he wore sandals, he had a bumper sticker on his car that said THE TAO OF CHILL, and Virginia had started the school year determined to be his girlfriend. She had spent every free period in the AV lab, probing Skylar's mind for the mysterious, philosophical thoughts that she was certain must be in there somewhere. But after a few weeks Virginia learned the important lesson that some people who seem mysterious are actually just incredibly stoned.

Virginia eyed the camera in her backpack. *Mr. Choi?* she thought for the hundredth time. It was so weird and random. Maybe he'd been paying Brittany to do his lecherous peeping for him. Except that didn't make sense, because the Montagues were already rich.

"That smells really nice," came a girl's voice from inside one of the stalls.

"Thank you," Virginia said, taking a final spritz of the perfume.

"It smells like . . . I dunno. Like a rose."

Virginia frowned, annoyed. She didn't want to smell like a rose. She wanted to smell like *yearning* or *eternity*.

"Can I use some?" The stall door swung open, and a tall blond girl stepped out, dramatically wobbling on a pair of high heels. One glance at her face and it was obvious that the girl was way on drugs. But for once Virginia reserved her snotty judgments, because this wasn't just some druggy low-life skulking in the girls' room. This was Angie Montague.

Virginia's mouth hung open stupidly for a moment. *What is she doing here?* Half the school was missing today, and Angie was the last person anyone expected to show up. And who could blame her for wanting to drug out—only why was she doing it *at school*?

"Uh, sure," Virginia managed to say finally, holding out the perfume bottle.

"Thanksss," said Angie. She reached out and swiped the perfume, then immediately dropped it. The glass bottle shattered on the filthy bathroom tiles, and within seconds the air was thick with the pungent smell of perfume. Angie looked at her hand with confusion, as if she expected the perfume bottle to rematerialize. Then she burst into tears.

"I'm so sorry!" she cried out, crumpling to her knees. The perfume's smell wafted up from the floor.

"Whoa, it's okay," Virginia said, coughing a little from

the smell and wondering if she should go get a guidance counselor.

"I'll pay you back!" Angie said, sobbing into her knees. "How . . . how much was it?"

"Um, forty dollars . . . but don't worry about it, really."

"Forty dollars?" Angie gasped. "Where am I going to get forty dollars? MY PURSE WAS STOLEN!" Then she collapsed in tears, burying her face in her hands.

Virginia felt her lip curl in irritation. She'd been prepared to excuse Angie's histrionics, but this was just insulting. She didn't need to make up some story about her purse being stolen. She was Angie Montague; she could probably reach up her ass and pull out forty dollars.

"I said don't worry about it," Virginia said icily. "You can write me a check."

"Do you have anything to eat?" Angie demanded. "I'm fucking starving." And she actually looked kind of starving. Her cheeks were hollow and colorless, and she seemed weak.

Virginia rummaged in her bag and found a crumbly old granola bar. "Here," she said, handing it to Angie. Angie took it, but then just stared at it.

"So . . . are you gonna eat it or what?" Virginia asked her.

Angie glared at her, and her eyes were suddenly clear and ferocious. "Oh my GOD, get OUT of here! I want CORNY! I want a HUG! Not you and your disgusting trailer-trash perfume!"

Virginia stumbled backward, startled by Angie's outburst.

"Sorry," she muttered. The heavy perfume was making her dizzy. She turned and ran out the door, and immediately crashed into the soft, hefty chest of Corny Davenport.

"Sorry," Virginia found herself saying again. "I think I touched your boob."

"Is she in there?" Corny breathed urgently.

"Yeah . . . she was asking for you."

Without another word Corny whirled past her. Virginia watched her dash on her tiptoes toward the bathroom, the door whooshing open in front of her. Virginia peered in for a second—and immediately wished she hadn't. It was possibly the saddest thing she'd ever seen: Angie Montague weeping on the filthy bathroom floor in a puddle of perfume.

The music hall, 2:50 p.m.

Benny leaned his ear against the heavy wooden door. Silence. He knocked lightly. No answer.

In a way he was relieved. He hadn't planned what to say if Mr. Choi had actually answered. The two things detective work required were intuition and authority: the ability to see through your suspect and the ability to make him crack in front of you by trickery or intimidation. But Benny didn't know if he could do that with a teacher. Benny was the kind of guy who said "yes, sir" compulsively, even to Rick the janitor who was twenty-four years old and always laughed at him. He had been raised to be respectful.

He looked for the appointments roster on the door. It took him a moment to find it, because the door was covered with posters of famous jazz musicians. Mr. Choi was obsessed with jazz. He was in the house band at the Sapphire Lounge, and was always trying to persuade his students to come see him play. But the Sapphire Lounge was in the bad part of town, and Benny knew there was zero chance that his mom would ever let him near it. "Monday through Thursday, I'm always there!" Mr. Choi was constantly reminding the class. Nobody ever went. It used to make Benny feel guilty, and also kind of embarrassed. It seemed a little desperate, not to mention inappropriate, for Mr. Choi to be inviting his students to a place like the Sapphire Lounge.

Benny found the roster half concealed behind a black-and-white print of Charles Mingus. The roster was blank, except for the hour between three-thirty and four: Marty Robeson. Private lesson. 3 and 3:30.

Benny Flax, he wrote beneath it. Question.

The football field, 3:20 p.m.

Benny felt a little weird watching the cheerleaders halfheartedly doing stretches on the field. He knew he probably looked like some clueless pervert hoping to prey on one of the grief-stricken girls after practice. It didn't help that Gerard Cole, the sappy water boy, was there too, staring at the cheerleaders and periodically weeping.

I wish Virginia would get here already, Benny thought. She'd left a note on his locker reading, in bright pink marker, *Meet me at cheer practice this aft— important clue to discuss.* It was just taped to the front of his locker for anyone to see. Virginia had yet to absorb the finer points of investigating a crime, for instance that you don't advertise to the world when you have an "important clue."

Only about half the cheerleading squad was in attendance. The principal had declared all extracurricular activities optional until after Brittany's funeral, which kept getting pushed back. It was supposed to be Wednesday, then Thursday—now people were saying next week. The problem was that the body had been drifting downriver so fast that no one could catch it. It might have been funny if it weren't so grotesque.

Yesterday the immense, waterlogged wildcat head had finally washed ashore, but the body it had encased was proving more elusive. There had been sightings as far south as Troup County. People were calling the police hotline claiming to have seen the body floating right past their backyards. A video had popped up on the Internet of a white, corpselike form floating past the Cherokee Trail Bridge. It already had more than one hundred thousand views. Benny had watched the video himself at least thirty times. It was about ten seconds of footage, taken on a jerky camera phone: a grayish expanse of skin—the naked back of Brittany's corpse—bobbing into view before disappearing around the river bend. Just remembering it made Benny shudder.

The local news had been dominated all weekend by outraged community members demanding to know how the police force could possibly be so incompetent. The river was basically a one-way street. All they had to do was stake out a position downriver and wait for the body to float past. But so far no one had been able to catch it. *Maybe Virginia was right,* Benny thought. *Maybe this really is some horrible, morbid prank.*

"Can you believe they're keeping the mascot costume?" Benny turned and saw Virginia clomping down the bleachers toward him.

"They're keeping it?" Benny repeated incredulously as Virginia plopped down next to him.

"Apparently the wildcat head was like three thousand dollars, and there isn't any money to get a new one. I just saw Coach Graffe scrubbing it down in the locker room. Some poor girl's going to have to wear it at the game next week. After Brittany, like, *decomposed* in it for two days."

At this Gerard Cole suddenly snapped out of his stupor. He glared at Virginia and shouted, "Don't talk about Brittany like that!"

Virginia scoffed. "What? I barely said anything."

"Brittany will never decompose in our hearts!" Gerard shouted, thumping his chest with his curled fist.

Virginia snorted, trying not to laugh, but obviously not trying very hard.

"Leave him alone," Benny said. He wished Virginia would just ignore Gerard and explain what they were doing here.

"You should give that video to the police," Gerard said, standing up and pointing at them. "You think this is a game, you and your silly club!"

"What is he talking about?" Benny whispered.

"Oh, the bridge footage," Virginia said. "I showed him."

"You WHAT?" Benny hissed.

"You're both jerks," Gerard went on. "You don't care about Brittany at all."

"Shut up, Gerard," Virginia snapped at him. "Leave us alone. Go cry on Corny's boobs."

"You're jerks!" Gerard repeated, and with that he turned and stumbled over to the far end of the bleachers.

"Wow, that guy needs to get a grip," Virginia said. She glanced at Benny, expecting him to agree. But he was just gawking at her. She realized Benny probably didn't think it was cool to make fun of dweebs, because he was one.

"Oh my God, Benny, you're not even close to that bad," Virginia assured him quickly. "He's *pathetic*."

But Benny just looked confused. Finally he said, "What on earth possessed you to show the video to him? *Gerard*, Virginia! Gerard!"

"Oh, that? I don't know. He had some revolting theory

about Brittany being raped in her mascot suit by Trevor Cheek. I felt sorry for him."

"Well for all we know, that was him on the bridge, and now he knows somebody saw."

"Oh . . . I didn't think of that."

You never think, Benny thought. It was Virginia's main liability. He'd known something like this would happen eventually. He should never have let her join Mystery Club in the first place, but Benny believed in justice and inclusivity, and that everyone deserved the chance to improve themselves through the act of mystery solving.

"I'm sorry," Virginia was saying. "I'm really sorry."

Benny looked at her. She looked sorry. She looked more than sorry—she looked scared, like she was afraid Benny was about to kick her out of the club or something.

"It's okay," Benny said, trying to swallow his irritation. "I mean, it probably wasn't Gerard on the bridge anyway, or else he wouldn't be telling us to give it to the police. He'd be glad we were keeping it to ourselves. It's just . . . the principle. Don't ever show anything to anyone without asking me first."

"I won't," Virginia swore, actually making the cross-my-heart sign like a kindergartener. Benny looked at her and felt tense. He wasn't sure Virginia actually got what he was saying. Maybe she could be obedient, but it would be better if she could just understand.

"Do you know that expression 'knowledge is power'?" he asked.

Virginia nodded.

"Well it's not true," Benny said. "Not intrinsically, anyway. Knowledge is only powerful when you have it and other people *don't*. And that's why we don't share information—not with the police, not with anyone. Not even harmless-seeming people like Gerard. Every person you share information with, you reduce your own power. I reduce my power by sharing information with *you*. But I choose to do it, because I choose to trust you."

Virginia looked at him, nodding earnestly. "I appreciate that. And I totally trust you, too."

Benny winced a little and felt his cheeks getting hot. "I mean, it's not a big deal. It's just a matter of . . . machinery. The more moving parts in a machine, the weaker the machine is. So . . ." Benny trailed off. *Oh my God, what am I rambling about?* "So what are we doing here?" he asked.

"Oh!" Virginia exclaimed, suddenly excited. "I have a *hunch*!"

Benny rolled his eyes. Virginia was way too into the mystery-solving lingo like "hunch" and "gumshoe." "What kind of hunch?" he pressed, humoring her.

"You'll see. Watch." She pointed at the cheerleaders, who had begun running in a small circle in the football field. Benny raised his hand to shield his eyes against the afternoon sun.

"Brittany would want us to keep cheering," Coach Graffe was saying to the girls somberly. "We still have a tri-county championship to win!"

"There," Virginia said. "Look at their feet."

Benny looked. They just seemed like normal feet to him. "Um, okay . . ."

"They run on their *toes*. Every single cheerleader does it. I noticed it when I ran into Corny Davenport in the hall today."

Benny nodded slowly. Virginia went on. "It's totally unconscious. Like, ingrained in their feet. They could be running for their lives, and I bet they'd still do it just like that—on their toes."

Benny closed his eyes, the memory of Friday night flashing in his mind. The bright stadium lights, the music blaring from the speakers. The great lion charging across the field, carried by a pair of stomping, flat feet.

The music hall, 3:45 p.m.

"I think Angie's having a nervous breakdown," Virginia declared. She and Benny were sitting on the floor outside Mr. Choi's office. The halls were empty and quiet. "She seemed, like, disconnected from reality."

"I can't believe she even came to school," Benny said. He checked his watch. It was three forty-five, and nobody had entered or exited Mr. Choi's office. He was starting to feel like they were wasting their time.

"Apparently she's been wandering around school all day, randomly napping. Like, sleeping in bushes and stuff. That's what I heard."

"Someone should drive her home," Benny said. Why did no one ever take responsibility in these situations?

"And she said my perfume was trailer trash, but it's not," Virginia continued. "It's French."

Benny looked at his watch again.

"Do *you* like my perfume?" she said, shoving her wrist in Benny's face.

"Hey, are you guys waiting for Mr. Choi?"

Benny and Virginia looked up. It was Marty Robeson, dragging his giant stand-up bass.

"Yeah, do you know where he is?" Benny asked.

"No. He's not here. I've been dragging this bass around for half an hour trying to find him."

"Couldn't you just put the bass down?" Virginia asked. Next to her, Benny rolled his eyes again. Why did Virginia have to harp on everyone all the time?

"*No,*" Marty said. "It might get stolen. Right, Scooby?"

Benny nodded weakly. The Case of the Disappearing Horn felt childish and ludicrous to him now. He wished people would stop reminding him of it.

The parking lot, 4:00 p.m.

Virginia dropped some change into the Coke machine and pulled out a Dr Pepper. "They're replacing this with a juice machine next semester," she said. "Which is stupid, because juice has just as much sugar as soda. It's like the biggest impostor of healthy beverages."

Benny was standing behind a tree, peeking his head out to scan the parking lot for Mr. Choi's blue Honda.

"Did you know that?" Virginia asked, crossing toward him. "About juice having just as much sugar as soda? It's like, you may as well drink a soda. Are you even listening to me?"

"Hm? Yeah, I'm listening. . . ."

"Well what did I just say, then?"

Benny pointed suddenly. "Look, there it is!"

"There's what?"

"Mr. Choi's car. Way over there."

Virginia looked where Benny was pointing and saw Mr. Choi's dented blue Honda parked at the end of the lot. Benny got out his phone and started dialing a number.

"Who are you calling?" Virginia asked.

"My mom. I have to tell her I'll be late for dinner."

"Why, are we going somewhere?"

"We should stay here until Mr. Choi shows up."

"A stakeout!" Virginia cried excitedly.

Benny sauntered off to argue with his mother on the phone. "Mom, it's for *Mystery Club*. . . . I can't; I'm the *president*. . . . I have barely any homework. . . . Mom, *please*?"

Virginia dug a pair of sunglasses out of her bag,

prepared to wait a while. She'd grown used to overhearing this weird ritual between Benny and his mother. It wasn't very suspenseful—Mrs. Flax always let Benny do what he wanted in the end. But she always made him fight for it first. *Maybe that's the difference between Benny and everyone else,* Virginia thought. *He's been trained to have convictions.*

She looked up from her Dr Pepper and noticed a girl walking toward the parking lot. She immediately recognized the lithe frame and billowing blond hair: It was Angie Montague. Quickly Virginia ducked behind the tree and motioned frantically for Benny to hang up the phone.

"Hm? Mom, I have to go. I love you. Bye." He snapped the phone shut. "Virginia, what?"

"It's Angie!" she hissed, pointing across the parking lot. "I don't think she saw me." They watched Angie striding between the cars, heading toward her silver Lexus. Her gait was graceful and quick.

"She doesn't seem very drugged out to me," Benny said. "I thought you said she was, like, a wreck."

"Well maybe the drugs wore off . . . ," Virginia answered. Angie seemed very crisp and put together for someone who had been on drugs and sobbing in the girls' room an hour ago.

"Is that how drugs work?" Benny asked. "One minute you're a wreck; the next you're fine?"

"She changed her shoes," Virginia observed. "When I

saw her, she had on these ludicrous high heels. Wait, look." She pointed to the Lexus. "There's someone waiting for her in the passenger seat."

Benny squinted. A thick white cloud reflected on the windshield, making it hard to see. "I can't tell."

"Here, look." Virginia took off her sunglasses and placed them awkwardly on Benny's face. Her fingers brushed against his temple as he straightened them on his nose. Benny already wore glasses, and adding the sunglasses on top made him look like the Terminator.

"They have polarizing lenses," she explained.

Benny peered at the Lexus.

"You look cool in sunglasses," Virginia said.

"Everyone looks cool in sunglasses."

Virginia shrugged. "I guess so. . . ."

"Wait a second. That's . . . Whoa."

"What, what? Let me see!" Virginia snatched the sun-glasses off Benny's face and put them on. She looked back to the Lexus. Overhead, the cloud passed. Now Virginia could clearly see a blond girl, barely conscious, slumped in the passenger seat. At that moment Angie reached the car and jumped in the driver's side. She gave a quick glance to the knocked-out girl beside her, and then turned on the ignition.

"It's . . . it's both of them," Benny was saying.

Virginia felt a surge of excitement as the sight of both twins in the car confirmed her vague suspicion.

Someone else was in the mascot suit that night, Virginia thought. *That was no cheerleader.*

4:10 p.m.

There was a crack as the soda can slammed against the tree and exploded. In her excitement, Virginia had just hurled it, and now she was gripping Benny's shoulders and shaking them hard.

"Ow, stop! Please calm down."

"Oh my God," Virginia said feverishly. "This is really exciting. This is really mysterious. You know what word I just made up? *Twin*ister. 'Twin' plus 'sinister.'"

Benny gritted his teeth, wishing Virginia would stop rambling and help him think. Across the empty parking lot, Angie had gotten out of the car and was dragging Brittany into the backseat. Corny Davenport appeared, scurrying to the trunk and pulling out a Wildcats blanket. She unfolded it and threw it on top of Brittany, who was curled in a lump.

"Are they trying to hide her under a blanket?" Virginia asked, her voice way too loud.

"Shhh!" Benny hissed.

"Maybe Gerard was right, and there *is* a mascot rapist, and they've been hiding her from him this whole time!"

Benny had about two seconds to decide what to do. The brain can do a lot in two seconds, he knew. When people have a near-death experience and report their lives "flashing before their eyes," what's actually happening is that the mind is reviewing the entire sum of their experiences, seeking some tidbit that might help them survive this life-or-death scenario. And it all happens in the space of a microsecond.

Benny had always scorned the idea of the action-adventure detective, the guy who scales buildings and wears elaborate disguises and puts himself in reckless and dangerous situations in order to solve a case. Real mysteries weren't about being a daredevil; they were about being patient and observant. For instance, at the start of the school year a bunch of the really popular guys kept getting their tires slashed. Everyone assumed the culprit was some trashy townie who was jealous of their cars. "The Slasher," people called him, almost fondly, like they felt sorry for him. But to say the tires were "slashed" was inaccurate, Benny found upon examination. "Stabbed" was a better word. The tires hadn't been cut; they had been *punctured*.

Benny went online and studied common types of knives. He knew all the boys at Winship had bowie knives for deer hunting. But bowie knives had long, rounded edges designed for slicing, not stabbing. The perpetrator could have used a throwing knife or a butterfly knife, but only hicks and rednecks had those kinds of knives, and Benny was convinced the Slasher was a Winship student. Lots of kids had nice cars, but the only ones getting slashed were from a particular circle of guys, and never girls. The

Slasher had *targets*; it wasn't just some random townie.

It was possible the Slasher had acquired a pointed knife specifically for tire-stabbing purposes, but to Benny that seemed unlikely. Tire slashing was an unoriginal crime, an immature offense usually motivated by spite. Whoever did it wasn't the most creative person in the world and probably used a pointed knife because that's just what he happened to have access to.

Then Benny remembered that rusty old gun Winn Davis kept in his car. It was a Confederate musket with a short bayonet on the end, "a real Richmond rifle," Winn bragged to everyone. The teachers let him bring it to school because the shooting action was long broken. But the bayonet was still sharp, its blade ending in a nice stabby point. After one hundred and fifty years you could probably still kill someone with it, and you could definitely puncture someone's tire. They were all Winn's friends, the guys who kept getting messed with. And the more Benny watched Winn, the more he sensed something weird about him—a hidden rage maybe. *Something.*

In any case, as soon as Benny realized the Slasher was Winn, he dropped it. It was enough to have privately solved the mystery; he didn't need to cause a sensation by accusing Winn Davis of slashing his own friends' tires with no apparent motive. The point of the story was that you didn't need daring heroics to solve a mystery, just the ability to look closely.

But now the Lexus was pulling out of the parking

spot, and Benny had the agitated feeling that he should stop looking for once and *do* something. But do what? He couldn't follow them because he didn't have a car. And it wasn't like he could just run up to them—that idea seemed insane. Beyond the fact that they had a girl who was supposed to be dead in their car, they were cheerleaders and he was nobody. The social order was so rigidly in place that even in this bizarre scenario Benny couldn't bring himself to defy it.

"What should we do?" Virginia asked. The question felt like it was a spotlight on his ineptitude. It was time to act—even Virginia knew it—and she was looking to him for instructions. But Benny didn't have a clear idea.

The Lexus pulled out and turned directly toward them. Benny tried to hide behind the tree, but then stopped, knowing it was too late and that hiding was pathetic. Then, in a swift, unexpected motion, Virginia leaped from the curb. She planted herself in the middle of the parking lot, legs apart, blocking the exit to the street.

The car stopped, waiting.

Virginia didn't move.

4:15 p.m.

The glare from the windshield made it hard to see the girls inside. For a moment the car just stood there, the engine idling. Then Virginia could see Angie raising her hands from the steering wheel like, *Hello?*

The passenger-side window lowered with a whirr.

"Excuse us?" came Corny Davenport's small voice. She was glaring at them. Virginia had never seen Corny glare at anyone. Her fat pink lips were pressed into a hard line. It made her look like an indignant four-year-old. But the look only lasted a moment before it was gone, as though Corny lacked the essential meanness to sustain it. "Um, can we help you?" she asked with a small smile.

"Where are y'all going?" Virginia asked loudly.

Corny opened her mouth to answer, but Angie cut her off. "Don't tell her. She'll tell everyone."

Virginia crossed her arms, looking very offended. "No I won't!"

"Yes you will. You'll tell everyone and put it on your gossip site."

"I will *not*," Virginia practically shouted. "I'm not that person anymore. People change."

"Well obviously you didn't, or you wouldn't be butting into our business."

Virginia fumed. "Oh my God! You are *so* rude!"

"*You're* rude," Angie spat back. "You're standing in our way."

"Virginia, we really have to go," Corny said in an excessively gentle tone. "It's an emergency, honey. Let's have donuts tomorrow, okay? We'll talk, woman to woman."

"Get out of our way!" Angie shouted.

Meanwhile Benny was studying the car. There was a faint smell of urine mixed with exhaust from the idling engine. A GPS was poised on the dashboard. And Corny kept glancing back at Brittany heaped in the backseat, as if checking to make sure she was still there. Benny narrowed his eyes at the lump of a person wrapped in the Wildcats blanket. It looked like a corpse. Blond hair stuck out in greasy-looking clumps. A pale, lifeless wrist poking out, hung with a sterling silver charm bracelet, the kind all the girls wore. It had always amazed Benny how everyone at Winship seemed to know what to wear, like it was their birthright, these Patagonia fleeces and charm bracelets and backpacks with the little polo players on them.

Is she dead? Benny's stomach twisted. Surely she wasn't dead. Surely Angie and Corny weren't dragging a corpse around in the middle of the afternoon. The idea made Benny feel repulsed, but also faintly impressed. People thought girls were the squeamish ones, but he was the one who was on the verge of throwing up all of a sudden, while Corny and Angie and Virginia bickered in the parking lot.

The blanket moved, and there was a quiet moan. "Ooohhm . . ."

At the sound, Corny's eyes snapped to Benny. She held her arm up to the car window, feebly trying to block his view. Benny just looked at her. What were they *doing*? It was hard to imagine Corny and Angie carrying out some sinister twin-hiding plot, yet there they were with Brittany's unconscious body in the backseat. And Corny didn't even seem that upset about Benny seeing everything. She just seemed a little flustered.

Virginia was still refusing to move, and now she was looking at Benny like she expected him to back her up. He just gave a tiny shrug. He wished he could disappear. Or that he could make Virginia disappear. It was one thing to jump in front of the car with no plan, but now she expected him to save her and finesse the whole thing?

"I know who's in there," Virginia declared, her arms crossed. Then, in a faintly threatening tone: "Maybe someone should call the police."

"We already did," Angie said. "Now will you move?"

Virginia looked at Benny again to see if he would step in. Benny did nothing. "Well . . . fine!" she said, stepping back.

"We'll get donuts at Glaze tomorrow, okay, Virginia?" Corny called, flashing a fake-looking smile. As soon as Virginia was out of the way, Angie slammed the gas. The tires screeched as the car tore away.

Once they were gone, it was quiet. The leaves swished in the breeze, but other than that it was silent. For a while neither of them said anything. Virginia breathed heavily, clearly still mad.

"You can't let people get to you like that," Benny said finally, not looking at her but at the empty street.

"Like what?" Virginia asked, kicking a clump of dirt.

"You totally let Angie control the conversation."

Virginia scoffed. "Well at least there *was* a conversation. If it had been up to you, we would have stood here like blobs and nothing would have happened."

"Sometimes it's better to do nothing than to do the wrong thing," Benny said.

"Well that doesn't sound very American."

Benny looked at her. "What does that mean?"

Virginia was sort of pacing. Her face was red. "Just that it's better to try and fail than to never try at all. I mean it's the American way. It's why we have the bankruptcy system."

What is she talking about? Benny thought. "Okaaay," he said, "but what I'm saying is, you know how people say, 'Don't just sit there; do something'? Well I saw a YouTube video of a Zen master who said, 'Don't just do something; sit there.'"

He waited for her amazement. It didn't come.

"A YouTube video of a Zen master," she repeated.

"Whatever, it doesn't matter. It's fine. While you were busy sniping with Angie, I was examining the scene. That was definitely Brittany in the backseat. And they were taking her to the hospital."

Virginia stopped pacing. "Wait, how do you know that?"

"I saw it on the GPS."

"Wow . . . you really know what you're doing, don't you?"

Benny looked at her face—was she making fun of him?

It didn't seem like it, but he couldn't be sure, so he just sort of grunted.

"Anyway, hopefully you can find out even more tomorrow," he said. "You can practice controlling the conversation. With Corny it shouldn't be that hard."

Virginia looked at him like she had no idea what he was talking about. Then she said, "Oh, that? I doubt we'll actually go to Glaze. Corny constantly invites people places, and then it never happens. She's a flake."

"Oh . . ."

They were always embarrassing, these moments when Benny realized how little he understood about the people he'd been surrounded by for five years. Not only was it embarrassing, it was a problem. Investigation only got you so far if the minds of your suspects were a mystery to you.

"So should we follow them?" Virginia asked.

"Do you know anyone with a car?" Benny asked half-heartedly. He liked to think a real detective didn't need anything but a brain to solve a mystery, but it wasn't true. The fact was, you needed a brain and a car.

"Your mom," Virginia said with a shrug. Then she giggled. "That sounded like a 'yo mama' joke."

Benny grimaced. "How can I get her to drive us to the hospital without asking a billion questions?"

"Tell her we're visiting a cancer patient," Virginia suggested. "Tell her it's for Compassion Club."

Benny looked at his cell phone, apparently considering

it. Then he sighed. "There's no point. Angie said they called the police? It's over. It's beyond us now. God, I hate being fifteen."

Virginia looked at him. She'd never seen him get mad before. Benny hated things? It was a revelation.

"So . . . who was in the mascot suit?" she asked, hoping the question would distract Benny from his tantrum. She didn't like seeing him all perturbed. It was unsettling, like seeing your dad cry. "I mean, there was a body, right? People saw it. It was on the Internet."

Usually Benny enjoyed these moments, the moments where it turned out everything you thought you knew was wrong. But this time felt different. Instead of being energized by the twist of events, Benny felt baffled and lost. Maybe it was just embarrassment from how badly Virginia screwed up the altercation with Angie, but everything felt like it had gotten suddenly out of control.

He took a breath. "Okay. Let's just pause. We'll go home, and we'll see what happens tomorrow."

"Are you sure?" Virginia asked, sounding disappointed. "Shouldn't we Be There? At the hospital or wherever?"

"We can't Be There after you accosted them like that," Benny snapped. Then he changed his tone, trying to be patient. "We'd be conspicuous and they'd run us out. Do you see what I mean about doing nothing being better than doing the wrong thing? We talked to them, sure, and we found out some stuff, but in doing so, we were cut off from other opportunities. Your initiative is an asset, but it's also a liability."

Virginia felt annoyed, but she couldn't articulate exactly why. Why was her initiative a liability, but Benny's total timidness wasn't? Probably because he'd call it *conscientiousness*. Benny was so full of shit sometimes. But they were his club and his rules, which he'd never let her forget.

The media lab, 6:00 p.m.

STILL FLOATING, SAYS LOCAL RESIDENT.

Zaire Bollo hit the refresh button, but the headline was the same. For three days Brittany's body had eluded the police, bobbing to the surface of the Chattahoochee River and then disappearing again into its murky depths. Pictures of the corpse showed it morphing into a bloated and purplish sack as it floated on downriver. It was becoming a joke. People needed resolution, they needed to say good-bye—but instead all they could do was watch helplessly as the inept police continued to let the body slip through their nets. Maybe they'd never get the body out. Maybe it would just disappear into the Gulf of Mexico, poured from the river into the sea. The thought haunted her, and she couldn't stop thinking about it. She felt obsessed.

She hit the refresh button again for the billionth time. Then she checked her e-mail. There was a message from Chrissie.

Hi Zaire this is so awkward but it's like, people are dying and life is so short, I just want to make sure I follow my heart. No regrets, you know? So anyway would you be mad if I liked Gottfried? I know you two were pretty intense but it's been six months so I don't know. I'm too nervous to ask you this in person. xoxoxo, Chrissie

Zaire read it twice, then deleted it without responding. Chrissie had been hinting for months that she liked Gottfried. It gave Zaire a kind of cruel enjoyment to pretend not to catch her drift. She knew she was being ungracious. But the idea of Chrissie and Gottfried getting together made her want to throw up.

She clicked back over to the news site and hit refresh again. *STILL FLOATING.* Across the lab some sophomores were talking loudly:

"And Trevor was like, get the fuck off me! And Gerard was like, I know it was you! Or something like that, I don't even know. And then Gerard *punched* him."

"He punched *Trevor?* Christ, did he have a death wish?"

Everyone was talking about Trevor and Gerard's big fight at the vigil. Apparently Gerard had started it, which was insane. You don't touch football players. They were animals who had no control over their aggression. It wasn't their fault—the coaches trained them to be violent and thuggish, and yet everyone was surprised when they beat kids up or were insensitive to women. They'd been hard-wired to be barbarians, and they couldn't just turn it on and off. Your best defense was to stay out of their way. It was one of the first things she'd learned at Winship. She'd never been to a school with a football team before. Her schools in England and Nigeria had rugby—which was arguably *more* violent—but somehow football was scarier. Something about the bulky equipment the players hid inside, making them impossible to distinguish from one another as they rammed and slammed and heaped in piles.

She clicked refresh again, barely seeing the screen. She'd been in the lab for three hours, refreshing and rereading. Which is why it took her a moment to realize that the headline had changed:

BODY FOUND.

Benny's house, 6:00 p.m.

Benny folded his hands in the *furitama* position and shook them up and down. The name of the exercise literally meant "shaking the soul."

It is my wish that the world should know everlasting peace.

Benny thought the words, but his mind was elsewhere. He kept seeing Brittany heaped in the backseat. If she was alive, who was the body in the river? Whose purplish, bloated sack of skin had been floating past houses and under bridges for three straight days? He got a chill every time he thought of the video, and once the image of the corpse was in his head, it stuck there until he forced himself to think of something else.

"Rodrigo, can I get you a drink?" Mrs. Flax called from the kitchen.

"I'll get it," Benny said, quickly dropping his pose. He went into the kitchen and poured a bourbon on the rocks. That was Rodrigo's drink, and the smell didn't feel new anymore. Before the accident Mr. Flax had been a scotch man; scotch had a cold, smoky smell, like a campfire extinguished by rain. Bourbon was different—rich and warm like leather or toast. It had taken Benny a while to get used to it. A little-known fact is that the nose is the strongest memory architect of all the senses. The connections made by olfactory receptors stay with the mind forever. In this way Benny's life was defined and divided by two aromas: before the accident, scotch; after the accident, bourbon.

For more than a year Rodrigo had been coming to the house five times a week for Mr. Flax's occupational therapy. His job was to help Mr. Flax relearn physical tasks like holding a cup and dressing himself, as well as complex mental functions like how to read.

"It . . . felt . . . like . . . rain. . . ." Mr. Flax read slowly from a special large-print book. At this stage he could see words and recite them, but was unable to articulate the meaning of sentences. What did "It felt like rain" *mean*? To Benny it seemed very deep and existential. What *did* "It felt like rain" mean? Why did anyone attempt to communicate at all? It was futile; no person was capable of understanding another person through words. Everyone was alone in their minds. An impassable gulf existed between what people said and what they thought. Brain damage just made the case more obvious.

"*Gracias, amigo,*" Rodrigo said as Benny handed him the bourbon.

"*Ein davar, chaver,*" Benny said back.

Rodrigo swirled the glass so the ice clinked. He held it up and smiled at Mr. Flax. "You know this one, don't you?"

"D-drink," Mr. Flax said, his mouth twitching. His expression was always in flux. One second his eyes would seem as sharp as ever, almost impatient, as if the idea of having to demonstrate that a drink is called a drink was too stupid to bear. But then the next second his eyes would glaze over, and Benny wouldn't really recognize him anymore.

"Not going to write that one down?" Mrs. Flax said from the kitchen.

"Rodrigo prompted him. It doesn't count." Benny had explained that to her about a million times.

"Mm-hm." It was a classic Mrs. Flax utterance, meant to convey precisely how foolish someone was being. She used it with his father whenever he made some addled, unintelligible demand. When she used it on Benny, it made him want to scream, *I don't have brain damage! Don't* mm-hm *at me!*

"I'll be in the other room," she announced in a clipped

voice. Mrs. Flax was always formal and awkward with Rodrigo. It was like she saw him as a stranger who'd just shown up one day, and whom they were all too polite to ask to leave. Which Benny found ironic, because at this point Rodrigo felt more familiar to him than his actual dad, who had been remote before but was now *beyond* remote—he was on another planet.

Sometimes Benny had dumb fantasies where Rodrigo and his mom fell in love against all odds and got married. His father's role in this was always dim and ambiguous. In some versions he miraculously recovered but still lived with them, like an uncle or a much older brother. In other versions he just sort of disappeared. Benny always felt embarrassed emerging from these fantasies; they were childish and disloyal. Rodrigo was a nurse, not a substitute dad, and Mrs. Flax was too old for him anyway.

Benny looked at his watch. It was six thirty. He turned on the news and resumed his stance on the yoga mat.

It is my wish that the world should know everlasting peace.

He repeated the mantra, trying to clear his mind. Aikido was meant to be practiced with tranquility of spirit, not with visions of unidentified waterlogged bodies floating before your eyes.

Benny always did his aikido exercises in the living room during the news. He felt it was beneficial for his father to observe this ritual, in whatever foggy capacity he was able to. The translation of aikido meant "the way of unifying with life energy." It was a Japanese martial art unlike karate or tegumi, where the winner of a fight was determined by which opponent could force the other into submission. In aikido, the goal was not to use force, but to evade and redirect your attacker's strike in such a way that no one, including your attacker, was harmed. The idea was that everyone was deserving of empathy and compassion, even those who sought to destroy you. The aikido fighter blended himself seamlessly into the motions of his opponent, like a magnet, anticipating each movement and deftly redirecting it using the attacker's own momentum. It didn't require physical strength or brute aggression: only focus and awareness and the desire to understand, rather than hate, the person who wanted you dead.

"Hey, Rodrigo, did Mom tell you I'm getting my black belt?" Benny asked, doing a wide side stretch.

"Very cool," Rodrigo said, sipping his bourbon. "Mr. Flax, can you point to something in the room that's the color black?"

Mr. Flax sort of twitched and stared mutely ahead.

"Yeah, black sucks," Rodrigo said. "It's not even a real color. How about pointing to something red?"

Mr. Flax pointed at the TV. On the news a bright red body bag was being heaved onto a stretcher.

"Nice," Rodrigo said. "Now point to something—"

"Oh my God," Benny interrupted. He stared at the TV. Police officers were standing aimlessly on the riverbank holding what looked like an enormous soggy piece of fur.

Who is in that body bag?

Tuesday

The assembly hall, 8:30 a.m.

Everyone was talking excitedly. There was an undercurrent of explosive giddiness in the room. People were actually shaking. Every so often someone would shout, "You can't kill a Wildcat!" and the entire assembly hall would break into a cheer. The room sparkled with glittering plastic tiaras. Corny Davenport was passing them out, and everyone was wearing one, even the teachers.

"Where do you get three hundred tiaras at a moment's notice?" Virginia asked loudly. She was supposed to be sitting with her homeroom, but no one was paying attention in the disorder, so she'd grabbed a seat in the front next to Benny.

Benny shrugged, turning his tiara over in his hands, as if inspecting it. "You should put it on," Virginia told him. "You'll look suspicious if you don't."

Benny frowned, and then put the tiara on his head. Virginia snorted. If there was anyone who looked really ridiculous in a tiara, it was Benny Flax. He looked younger, like a deeply dissatisfied thirteen-year-old whose mother had forced him to have a princess-themed bar mitzvah. Suddenly his serious expression didn't look so serious—it looked pouty and sulky and babyish.

Virginia adjusted her own tiara, cocking it a bit to the side at what she hoped was a jaunty, careless-looking angle. You should never let your accessories dominate your look—it made you seem insecure. There was a way to look good in a tiara, but irony was key. Virginia didn't want it centered on the crown of her head like an actual princess, or perched goofily like a cake topper the way some people were wearing them.

A loud cheer went up, louder and more raucous than any of the previous cheers. Virginia looked up at the stage and saw a pair of blondes, Corny and Angie, with their arms around a third blonde they were lovingly escorting to the podium: Brittany Montague. She looked weak, but happy. She waved at the crowd like a pageant contestant. Benny and Virginia clapped mechanically.

Brittany gave Corny and Angie a hug, and then they stepped back, seeming reluctant to let Brittany out of arm's reach. Brittany gazed out serenely as the house lights dimmed and everyone went quiet.

"As most of you know at this point, I'm alive." She giggled, and the crowd giggled back at her. "But what you don't know is how much I love you." A huge cacophonous cheer erupted. It lasted more than a minute.

"And love is what got me through the last three days. Well, love and strawberry-kiwi Gatorade!" Everyone laughed again, though it wasn't a joke. The Gatorade was the reason she was standing there and not in the hospital hooked up to an IV. The local news headline was THANK GOD FOR GATORADE, SAYS ABDUCTED CHEERLEADER. Corny Davenport had found her locked in the pom-pom closet yesterday, where she'd been trapped since Friday night. She'd been drugged before the game and ditched there. There were no signs of abuse (the paper had reported this), and though Brittany's purse had been stolen, it had contained no cash, and no charges had been made to the many credit cards. The attacker appeared to have wanted only one thing: the mascot suit.

Onstage, Brittany pulled out a bottle of pink Gatorade and took a long, dramatic sip. The audience cheered wildly. She wiped her mouth and giggled.

"What do you bet this whole thing is a scam by Gatorade," Virginia whispered.

Benny didn't reply or even register that he'd heard her. He just stared ahead with his arms crossed. Several newspaper articles were clenched in his fist, the ink blackening his clammy palms. Things were moving ahead of him now, and fast. Brittany was alive. For a precious few moments, that information had been his and his alone. Well, his and Angie's and Corny's and Virginia's, anyway. But as the twins' Lexus had zoomed away yesterday, his control over the case had zoomed away with it. And now he was reduced to reading the paper for information like a clueless yokel.

According to the *Atlanta Journal-Constitution*, the last thing Brittany remembered before her abduction was standing in the shower with her clothes on. But she seemed confused—in the online edition of the story she reported that the shower occurred *after* Corny had rescued her. According to the *Marietta Daily Journal*, there may have been no shower at all; the reporter suggested Brittany had invented the shower to cover up her embarrassment at having repeatedly urinated on herself while trapped in the pom-pom closet. Normally Benny would have pounced on such discrepancies, analyzing every possibility, but at the moment he was too distracted by an overwhelming sense of failure.

"I'm going to go home and rest for a while," Brittany was saying, reading from a piece of paper in front of her. "But I just wanted to say how much everyone's love and support means to me. Thank you for all the flowers and brownies and cookies and cards. And I appreciate everyone cooperating with the police as we figure out what happened on Friday night. I hope none of you ever have to find out what it feels like to be locked in a closet for sixty hours with no food or bathroom. But I do hope you get to find out what it feels like to be as loved as I feel right now, because it feels amazing!"

The reaction from the crowd was deafening. "WILD-CAAAATS!" someone shouted, and then everyone was shouting it. That was the weirdest part of all this—the sudden Wildcat zeal that had seized everyone, as if Brittany not being dead were the result of school spirit.

"And you all look beautiful in your tiaras!" Brittany shouted, smiling stupendously. Then she took Angie's and Corny's arms, and they walked her off the stage as the audience gave her a standing ovation.

Mr. Choi, Virginia couldn't help noticing, had been pointedly left out of Brittany's speech. No one wanted to spoil the school-wide emotional high of Brittany being alive by dealing with the creepy, baffling fact that, in her place, Mr. Choi was dead. They'd finally caught the body, and it wasn't a young blond cheerleader. It was a middle-aged Asian man with a tattoo of a saxophone on his left butt cheek. Which meant it hadn't been Brittany filming the locker room footage; it had been Mr. Choi himself, *inside the suit.* The idea made Virginia so hyper she could barely sit still. All those girls with their boobs out, giggling and jiggling around, no idea that a middle-aged man with a saxophone butt tattoo was hiding in plain sight, watching them. Probably with an erection! It was gross and thrilling and weird all at the same time, and Virginia had never felt more thrilled in her life. Benny, on the other hand, looked wilted and defeated. Virginia rolled her eyes at him. He was just mad he hadn't figured it all out himself.

The principal took the podium, beaming with smug pride, like they all had him personally to thank for their favorite cheerleader being alive after all. "We'll see you at the spirit show on Friday, Brittany," he called after her. Then, to the crowd, "Sign-ups are on the bulletin board in the main hall. Let's make this the best spirit show ever, whaddaya say, Wildcats?"

The crowd roared wildly in assent. Then the bell rang, and people began filing out of the assembly hall. Everyone was grinning and talking and waving their tiaras in the air.

"So what now?" Virginia asked Benny. He was slumped in his seat. Virginia copied his body language, slumping down too. "At least there's one less pervert in the world," she said.

"One *fewer*," Benny corrected. The pervading story seemed to be that Mr. Choi had drugged Brittany and locked her in the pom-pom closet so he could sneak into her mascot costume and watch all the cheerleaders undress. Some of the football players were now claiming they'd known all along that the mascot was Mr. Choi, and that they had in fact heroically *chased* him from the field that night to spare the girls from his pervy glances. Which made no sense, but no one seemed to care. Everyone's feelings were so jumbled and disorganized—the joy that Brittany was alive, the relief that they didn't have to be sad anymore, that they could return to their self-involvement, overshadowed the desire to understand what had actually happened.

Only Benny and Virginia knew how far it went—that Mr. Choi had not only been hiding in the costume, but had actually been videotaping the whole thing. There were still a lot of questions. Why had he run to the bridge? And who was that mysterious figure in the video, the one forcing him to jump?

"Someone must have caught him," Virginia said, trying to reanimate Benny. "So he ran from the field, but then got cornered at the bridge."

"If that were true, it would mean that this entire time that person knew Brittany wasn't really dead. They knew it was Mr. Choi."

"Can you think of anyone whose mourning seemed fake?" Virginia asked. It was getting quiet in the assembly hall as it emptied out.

"Everyone's mourning seemed fake," Benny said. "Mourning *is* fake. It's just a performance we carry out in society to signify grief and cope with our own mortality."

"Okaaay . . ." Virginia looked at him. "You can take off your tiara now. We're the only ones left."

Benny lifted his hand, but then dropped it, as if suddenly lacking the energy. His gloom made Virginia impatient. There was still a ton they didn't know. It wasn't like the mystery was over.

"The locker room," Benny said. "*That's* where it started—not the football field. I can't believe I made such a stupid error. We should have gotten to her first. Who knows what we could have found."

"We can still look around," Virginia said, but she knew it

was a lame suggestion. The pom-pom closet was cordoned off now, and no one could get near it. And questioning Brittany seemed like an unlikely proposition, at least until the protective wall of cheerleaders and their boyfriends withdrew from around her and things got back to normal.

"And anyway, it's good to make mistakes, because then you can learn from them," Virginia said, feeling stupid immediately. Had she ever said anything less interesting in her life?

"Don't try to pep-talk me," Benny said back. "Just let me beat myself up. It's part of my process."

"Okay . . . Do what you gotta do, I guess." Virginia got up and left Benny to his brooding.

The sophomore lounge, 10:00 a.m.

"Every time I think about it, I get goose bumps all over my body."

There was the crack and hiss of Coke cans being opened as Mrs. Hope passed them out to all the girls. The whole school had been separated into girl-only and boy-only groups so they could relax and be safe and talk about their feelings. The atmosphere in the school had changed in the hour since the assembly. Brittany had gone home, and it was like everyone's joy and excitement and relief had gone with her. Now they were glum and lost again, and the teachers were forcing them to talk about Mr. Choi, and how it felt to realize there had been a pervert in their midst.

"I mean, the locker room was our sanctuary," Corny was saying. "Like, our special private pep fortress."

I've seen your boobs, Virginia thought. It was hard to look at Corny without seeing the locker room footage playing before her eyes.

"I'm supposed to wear the wildcat costume this Friday," Kirsten Fagerland piped up. "But I refuse. I'm not going to do it. That mascot violated us."

I've seen your boobs too.

"That's fair," said Mrs. Hope, taking a long sip of her Coke. "No one's going to make you do anything you don't want to do."

Virginia felt lucky she'd ended up in Mrs. Hope's group. Mrs. Hope was one of the few cool teachers at Winship. She wasn't going to be awkward or creepy or tell the cheerleaders it was their own fault for being beautiful. Apparently Mrs. MacDonald was telling her group that if they didn't want perverts obsessing over them, they should ask the school to buy more conservative cheerleading uniforms.

"I think about all those times Mr. Choi asked me to stay late because my cello was out of tune," said Mandy Li. "It always sounded tuned to me. Now I'm thinking he was just trying to get me alone."

There was a collective shudder in the room.

"It's important to feel safe in your own school," Mrs. Hope said. "It's important to feel safe in your own body. But it's going to take time."

"If Mr. Choi weren't already dead, I think my boyfriend would probably kill him," Corny said proudly. "I always feel safe when I'm with Winn."

Next to her, Angie Montague sighed. "Brittany is so brave," she said. "But I'm not. I just want to wear a burlap sack and hide in my room forever." She folded her arms as if to protect her breasts from the leering world. Not that it made any difference. Virginia had already seen Angie's boobs and could see them now in her mind—naked and fresh and full, sparkling with glitter and jiggling as she laughed.

"What about you, Virginia?" Mrs. Hope said. "How are you feeling?"

"Um, I don't know," Virginia said carefully. She couldn't just blurt stuff out the way she used to—she had to protect Mystery Club and their information. "I'm not a cheerleader and I'm not in band," she said, "so I probably wasn't on Mr. Choi's radar. I don't think he even knew me."

Mrs. Hope nodded, giving her an appraising look. "But even if you didn't know Mr. Choi personally, you're still a part of the community he affected. . . . Do you feel safe?"

Virginia looked around. She didn't know what she felt. Creeped out, definitely, but something else too . . . *excitement.* Excitement that people weren't necessarily what they seemed. Because if everyone was what they seemed, Virginia was certain she was going to die of boredom and disappointment. She'd had enough disappointment in her life; it was like people just lined up to let her down, and then acted like it was her own fault for expecting anything else. If there was one thing she'd learned in Florida, it was how much people will resent you for expecting them to be anything but predictable and petty and passionless.

"I think it's a mistake to be obsessed with safety," she said to the group. "Safety is boring and it makes people weak. If people are always safe, they never have to learn how to stick up for themselves."

Everyone looked at her.

"Is that how you feel?" Mrs. Hope asked. "That people should learn to stick up for themselves?"

Virginia shrugged. "I dunno. In the Boarders we do it all the time. Sometimes they don't open the cafeteria, and we have to take the bus to the grocery store just to get food. But you never hear us complaining."

"It sounds like you're complaining right now," Kirsten said.

"Well I'm not," Virginia snapped back, unsure how the conversation had veered off in this direction. "I'm just saying that there are worse things than being looked at."

"Like what?"

"Like . . . like . . ." *Like not being noticed at all.*

Room 202, 10:15 a.m.

"Respect," Coach Miles declared, leaning confidently against the teacher's desk. It was weird seeing him in a classroom instead of on one of the sports fields. But everyone was mixed up today. Benny had ended up in a group with mostly jocks. He suspected he was there to provide diversity, both ethnically and intellectually, a responsibility that made him self-conscious and annoyed.

"Let's talk about what you can do to show the ladies respect. Imagine what it's like to be a girl. You got this smokin' bod that everyone wants to get a peep at. Can you imagine what that feels like? No, you can't, because you're dudes, and your bodies are disgusting."

Everyone laughed.

"I'm serious; no one wants to see that," he said, pointing a finger toward Chase Creevey's crotch. "No one wants to see your hairy chest or your veiny dick! You're lucky if a girl will look twice at you! But imagine, y'all—what if you had to go through life being ogled and stared at from dusk till dawn?"

"I don't think I'd care," Chase said, grinning. "Bring it on!" Chase was so stupid, he was always taking the bait like that.

"Well think again, asshole," the coach snapped. Benny tensed. Maybe the football players were used to hearing profanity in school, but he wasn't. Coach Miles plowed on. "Because what if the people ogling you were stronger than you, and faster than you, and could probably *rape* you."

The room was suddenly silent.

"Not so cool now, huh? And what you need to understand is that every one of you is a potential rapist. You've got the hardware." He made a crude, ball-cupping gesture. "And you don't have to be a big stud, either. Even ol' Scooby could be a rapist."

Everyone laughed. Benny froze, feeling like his cheeks were on fire.

"Scooby the rapist!" Chase cried, delighted.

"Do you need a Scooby snack, Scooby?" someone else asked.

"Okay, okay, you get the point," Coach Miles said quickly, realizing what he'd started. "So what can you do to make sure you *respect* the ladies and never rape them accidentally. Well first of all, throw out your dictionary. You need to learn *girl language*. And in girl language, everything means no. No means no; I don't know means no; maybe means no. Being drunk means no. Being a lot younger than you means no."

"Being asleep means no," Chase added. Everyone snickered and looked at Big Gabe, who had famously given cunnilingus to his girlfriend while she was asleep during the class trip to Washington, DC.

"Well what if they say *yes*?" Trevor Cheek spoke up, a huge smirk on his face.

"News flash, stud," Coach Miles snapped at him. "Sometimes even yes means no. So how can you tell? Well here's what you do, guys. If she says yes—and don't fuckin' count on it—if she says yes, you reach up her skirt and feel around. If she's nice and lubricated—"

Everyone groaned.

"Shut up, shut up. If she's nice and wet, then you go ahead and seal the deal. If she's not, then sorry buddy, yes means no, and you better seek other accommodations." He made a jerking motion with his hand.

Oh my God, Benny thought, staring at the floor in horror. If only he'd gotten into Mr. Rashid's group. They were probably just having study hall.

"Well what if she's wet but says no?" Chase asked, sounding genuinely curious.

"No trumps wet," Coach said authoritatively. "Sorry, Chase. Body and mind must be in agreement. I'm telling you this for your own good. I'm trying to keep you out of jail. So what else can we do to respect the ladies?"

Maybe not calling them "the ladies" as if they were some strange alien species, Benny thought, but he didn't say anything. There was no way he was participating in this embarrassing and debasing forum. What made it even worse was that half the guys were still wearing their tiaras.

"We protect them," Winn declared. Benny looked at him and felt a twinge of envy. Only Winn could look that manly and dignified in a cheap plastic tiara.

"That's right," Coach Miles said. "We use our bodies"—he made a weight-lifting motion—"to protect their bodies."

"We, like, open doors for them," offered Tyler Jeter.

"Yep, yep. You gotta imagine what it's like to be a woman. It's hard! No one cares about their sports teams.

They go apeshit on the monthly and can't even help it. They wake up at the crack of butt so they can do their hair and look nice for us stupid ogres. The least we can do is open the fuckin' door. Got it?"

"Got it!" all the football players boomed in unison.

"Got it," Benny joined in, a little too late.

Then Coach Miles clapped his hands together loudly, making Benny jump. "All right! That's that!" he shouted. "Now get outta here and be a force of good in the world. Respect the ladies!"

Wednesday
The sophomore lockers, 8:00 a.m.

A single long-stem rose with pale yellow petals was taped to her locker. Virginia stared at it, her heart speeding up. A *rose*? For *her*? She carefully took it down and sniffed the blossom. It was the familiar rosy perfume, but with a touch of honey and butter and earth. She tried to guess who it could be from. Benny? Skylar? A note was attached to the stem. Virginia unfolded it.

SORRY I WAS A DICK YESTERDAY. I WILL MAKE IT UP TO YOU, WITH SAID DICK (JUST KIDDING) YOUR THE BEST

Virginia scowled.

"Do you have an admirer?"

She turned around. It was Benny.

"No," she said sourly. "Corny Davenport does. This idiot person keeps mixing us up. They dumped her pom-poms at my door last Saturday. And they always spell 'you're' wrong."

"Can I look at the note?" Benny leaned in to read over Virginia's shoulder.

"I'd say it was Winn, but Winn should know where his girlfriend's locker is. Do you think Corny's cheating on him?"

Benny wasn't listening. His own locker, midway down the row with *F*s, had a little slip of white wedged into the door.

"Hang on."

He went over to the locker and pulled it out. It was a grubby index card with words scratched so deep into the paper it had almost torn in places.

DON'T GET SO CLOSE TO HER DO YOU HAVE A DEATH WISH SHE HAS A BOYFRIEND

"Oh my God. Is it *you*?" Virginia burst out laughing.

Benny quickly folded the note, not realizing Virginia had been looking over his shoulder too.

"Is what me?"

"The guy—the guy Corny's cheating with!" She was laughing so uproariously it was hard not to be insulted.

Benny looked around. People were staring at them. Why did Virginia always have to be so loud? "Gimme your note," he said. Virginia handed it to him as her laughter dissolved into breathless sighing.

"Benny and Corny, class couple!"

Benny ignored her, feeling his cheeks heat up. He compared

the two notes. It was hard to tell whether they could have come from the same person. Virginia's note seemed to have been written by someone normal, at least, while Benny's was written by a psychopath. The pen was the same—black ballpoint—but that didn't say much. Black ballpoint was pretty much the most common pen on the planet.

Don't get so close to her.

"Her" couldn't mean Corny, could it? Benny had hardly ever talked to Corny in his life. The only "her" he was remotely close to was Virginia.

"I think it's about you," he said, bracing himself for one of Virginia's loud and annoying reactions. But she just gawked at him, the rose hanging limply in her hand.

"Moi?"

"Well, is it true? Do you have a boyfriend?"

"No!" she snorted.

Benny looked at her.

"What? I don't! Do you think I'm lying?"

Benny shrugged.

"Stop looking at me like that. Come on, it's a small school. Don't you think if I had a boyfriend you would have heard?"

"I'm not exactly looped in, if you hadn't noticed," Benny said. "Do you have a boyfriend at home? In Florida?"

Virginia visibly stiffened. She didn't answer.

"Or from wherever," Benny amended lamely, feeling a flush of discomfort.

"*No,*" Virginia said finally. "I do not have a boyfriend. Anywhere."

"Okay!" Benny said, his voice squeaking.

For a second they stood there, avoiding each other's eyes. Virginia rustled around in her backpack, pretending to look for something. The stem of the rose bent and snapped, and one of the petals dropped to the floor.

"Well . . . the bell's about to ring," Benny said. "I guess we should go."

"I'm skipping homeroom," Virginia said. It was one of those things people weren't supposed to do, but no one ever actually got in trouble for. Benny couldn't picture himself skipping, though. He just wouldn't be able to relax, so what would be the point?

"I'm getting a muffin from the caf. You want one?"

Benny shook his head, giving her a quick look. She was already walking away.

"See you tonight," she called over her shoulder.

Benny opened the note and read it again.

DON'T GET SO CLOSE TO HER.

The Boarders, 7:00 p.m.

Virginia frowned at the pile of clothes on her bed. It was really frustrating when you had an idea of what you wanted to look like, but none of the pieces in your wardrobe added up to it.

"What are you doing?"

Virginia turned around. Zaire Bolo was standing in her doorway sipping coffee and holding a thick book under her arm.

"I'm trying to find something to wear to the Sapphire Lounge tonight," Virginia answered.

Zaire raised her eyebrows. "You're going to the Sapphire Lounge? Gosh. I'm impressed."

"Well don't be," Virginia said back. "I go to cool places like the Sapphire Lounge all the time."

"I wouldn't call the Sapphire Lounge *cool*, necessarily," Zaire said.

"You've been there?" Virginia asked.

Zaire shrugged noncommittally.

She's never been there, Virginia thought. Zaire just couldn't stand the idea of anyone being more sophisticated than her.

"You can come with us if you want," Virginia offered, less to be nice than to be cool. "Benny's mom's driving us."

"No thanks," Zaire said. "I don't really do moms."

Virginia turned back to her bed so Zaire wouldn't see her rolling her eyes. Zaire thought she was better than everything, including moms apparently.

"Do you want to borrow something of mine?"

Virginia whipped around. "Really?" Zaire had fantastic clothes, which seemed like a waste, because all she ever did was study. Who needed plush velvet skirts from Milan to read *Moby Dick* and do algebra?

"Sure. Come on."

Virginia followed Zaire across the hall to her room. Zaire's room was very tidy. Even the piles of books on the floor—too many to fit on the small standard-issue dorm bookshelf—were stacked in neat, perfect towers. Virginia sat on the edge of the flawlessly made bed while Zaire rummaged through her closet.

"Omigod, Wildcat!" Virginia squealed, noticing a small furry lump nestled among Zaire's satin pillows.

"Oh yeah," Zaire said casually. "He sleeps with me all the time."

"Seriously? He doesn't maul your face?"

"Wildcat loves me. Watch this." Zaire clicked her tongue and wiggled her fingers. "Wildcat, darling, hop up!" And in an instant Wildcat uncurled himself and trotted across the bed to Zaire, rubbing his whiskers against her outstretched fingers and purring.

"Wow," Virginia said. She'd never seen Wildcat acting so friendly. She reached out to pet him, but Wildcat immediately turned and hissed at her. "Okay, okay, jeez." Virginia snatched her hand back before Wildcat could scratch it.

"How about this?" Zaire carelessly tossed a beautiful black cashmere sweater and a gold pleated skirt on her bed.

"Oh my God," Virginia said. It was perfect. But she didn't love the idea of borrowing it from Zaire, because then it meant she'd have to be nice to her.

"Are you going anywhere for fall break?" Zaire asked.

"Probably not. Maybe Boca Raton if the schedule works out."

"Boca's . . . nice," Zaire said, as if struggling to compliment a trailer park or the site of a famous nuclear spill. "I'm going to Barcelona. You should come with me. My dad will buy you a ticket."

Virginia narrowed her eyes. "No thanks. I don't really do Spain."

Zaire looked at her. "I think you'll look great in that outfit," she said.

"Thank you," Virginia said back. "It's definitely better than anything I've got."

Zaire sat down next to her on the bed. She leaned back on her elbows and closed her eyes. "I can just imagine you walking into the Sapphire Lounge in that skirt. You know what people will see? Not some gauche fifteen-year-old. They'll see a confident, poised, mysterious female. Order a sidecar, not some nasty candy-flavored thing with an umbrella in it. Sidecars are ultra stylish. Just make sure they use Cointreau and not some low-shelf triple sec. Don't let them sugar the rim, and say you want it dry."

"Dry," Virginia repeated, hoping she'd remember. Her head felt kind of fuzzy all of a sudden.

"Confidence is everything. But I don't think you'll have any trouble, not in that outfit." Then Zaire stood abruptly. "Can you help me with the computer in the common room? I can't get the Internet to work."

"Um, sure," Virginia said, gathering the clothes in her arms. She reached out a hand to pet the cat, then thought better of it. The cat's eyes followed her as she left, as if daring her to try.

The Boarders driveway, 7:20 p.m.

The Boarders always looked creepy at night. One of the streetlamps blinked, and a pair of enormous magnolia trees cast mottled shadows on the gray stone. You never knew if Mrs. Morehouse would be there to yell at you, or if it would just be empty.

"I'll only be a minute," Benny said to his mom. He shut the car door and walked up the stone steps. He was about to press the call button to Virginia's room when he saw her through the window. She was sitting in the common room with Zaire Bollo. The window panes were made of old glass, the kind that's a little thicker and foggier at the bottom, perpetuating the myth that glass was a liquid. Old glass was rare in this region and highly prized, because General Sherman had scorched everything in his March to the Sea. Anything that hadn't been destroyed—glass, furniture, square dancing, family names, unburned tracts of land—became a precious symbol of survival. Benny found the enduring obsession with "Dixie Land" weirdly touching. It was like their Israel. Except rather than being a hope for the future, it existed only in the past. If it had ever existed at all.

What is Virginia doing? Benny peered through the window. Virginia and Zaire were sitting side by side at the computer. He tried to see what they were looking at, but the warped glass made it hard to tell. Was that the bridge? Was she showing Zaire the footage from Mr. Choi's camera?

Benny lunged to the door and started pounding on it. "Virginia!" he called. "I'm here!"

He heard movement inside, and after a moment Virginia opened the door. "What?" she said, giving him a weird look. "Why are you banging on the door like a freak?"

"I'm just . . . We have to go." He arched his neck to see if Zaire was still in the common room, but he couldn't see her.

"Were you just showing Zaire the bridge footage?" he whispered.

"What? No." Virginia stepped onto the porch and closed the door behind her.

"I told you not to show that to anyone else!"

"And I didn't!" she insisted.

Benny opened his mouth to argue, but was startled by Virginia's outfit. She was wearing an expensive-looking sweater and a very short gold skirt. It was hard not to notice her legs; he could see their entire shape, and his eyes felt commanded to look at them. He wasn't sure if he should give her a compliment. Sometimes compliments were tricky—like if you told a girl she looked nice, but sounded too surprised, she might end up being insulted.

"Good choice of clothes," he said carefully.

"Thank you! It doesn't look like a costume?" Virginia looked down at herself.

"No . . . You're a natural."

"Benjamin?" Benny heard his mom call from the car. "Are we going?"

"Yes, ma'am!" he called back. "Come on," he said to Virginia. As they walked down the porch steps, Benny glanced over his shoulder at the common-room window. There was no one inside. Like a ghost town, the Boarders was empty.

Peachtree Street, 7:30 p.m.

Virginia sat in the passenger seat of Mrs. Flax's car. Benny had insisted that she sit in the front. He probably thought he was being gentlemanly, but Virginia wished he would just be a normal guy for once. *It must be a Jewish thing,* Virginia thought. Benny was the most well-mannered boy in school; he was also the only Jew she knew. It seemed like there was probably a connection. In any case, Virginia wished Benny had just sat in the front with his mom, even if it wasn't the polite thing to do. Mrs. Flax was incredibly scary, and Virginia was having a hard time coming up with conversation points.

"So . . . Yom Kippur's coming up soon. . . ."

Mrs. Flax gave Virginia a quick, menacing look, before turning her attention to Benny in the backseat. "Shouldn't you be using this time to study for your science test?"

"I'm pretty sure the test is canceled," Benny said.

"They canceled everything," Virginia added.

Mrs. Flax frowned. "I thought Winship was a *serious* school."

"Well, everybody's pretty freaked out . . . ," Virginia said meekly.

Mrs. Flax pursed her lips, appearing to concentrate on the road. A cheerleader was dead, then not dead, then a teacher was dead, then revealed to be a Peeping Tom. The whole school was in chaos over it, but Mrs. Flax was clearly unimpressed.

"This is not a nice neighborhood," Mrs. Flax muttered as they pulled up to the huge public library on Margaret Mitchell Square. Benny had convinced his mom that he and Virginia were attending a Model UN meeting with some students from other schools. Benny didn't like having to lie; he preferred to conduct his investigations in as straight-forward a manner as possible. But he was willing to demonstrate a little moral flexibility when necessary. There was no way in a million years that his mom would drop him off downtown to go to a place like the Sapphire Lounge.

Benny and Virginia waved as Mrs. Flax pulled away from the curb. They watched the car until it turned a corner out of sight.

"Which way are we going?" Virginia asked.

"That way," Benny said, pointing to a deserted railroad

yard in the distance. It was clustered with seedy storefronts, illuminated by a huge neon light in the shape of a blue jewel.

The Sapphire Lounge parking lot, 7:45 p.m.

R.I.P. PERVERT, the sign read. SAYONARA MOLESTER, read another. They lay in a pile next to Gerard's car. It was "a night of jazz and remembrance" at the Sapphire Lounge, organized by Mr. Choi's bandmates in honor of their fallen sax player. Gerard had read about it in the paper and immediately sent an e-mail to the entire school announcing that he was staging a protest. He'd hoped Angie and the other cheerleaders would come. Maybe even Brittany would make an appearance, and the local news would send a camera team. He imagined himself on television surrounded by the most beautiful girls at Winship: *Local boy is hero to victims of Peeping Tom.*

Except no one showed up—no one but Gottfried the weird German exchange student, anyway. And it seemed like Gottfried had just come for the donuts. He'd eaten four already, and they'd only been there twenty minutes.

"Slow down," Gerard told him. "People could still come, and there won't be any donuts left. Look, there's someone now!" He pointed down the street, where he could see Scooby-Doo and some skanky girl. *Oh my God, is that Virginia Leeds?* What the hell was she wearing? It seemed really inappropriate for a protest against perverts. But whatever, better to have a skank at your protest than no girls at all.

"Hi, guys!" he said. "Thanks for coming! Grab a sign!"

"Hurrow," Gottfried said, his mouth full of donut.

"Hi, um . . ." Scooby was edging away from the signs.

"We're not protesting," Virginia explained. "We're attending."

"You're *attending*? You're attending a night of jazz for a lecher! No jazz for lechers!" He quickly rummaged through his pile of signs and produced one declaring NO JAZZ FOR LECHERS.

"Gerard, jazz is like the soundtrack of lechery," Virginia said back. "It's like saying no ukuleles for whimsical girls."

Gerard threw his sign on the ground. "Fine! Fine! Go celebrate the local pervert!"

"You're being embarrassing, Gerard," Virginia said. "Choi's dead. He can't visually assault anyone anymore. You need to chill."

"Leave him alone," Benny said. "Let's just go."

"Bye-bye!" Gottfried waved at them, wiping donut crumbs from his mouth.

Gerard scowled as he watched them walk away. He didn't need that pair of freaks anyway. Benny was just an uppity Jew, and Virginia looked like a slutty alien, her gold skirt shining and her pale legs glowing blue under the light of the neon sign.

The bar, 8:00 p.m.
Virginia crossed her legs, then uncrossed them. She hadn't realized exactly how short her skirt was until she'd tried to

sit in it. But she tried to stop squirming. She didn't want to seem like a child in front of all these scary people. Virginia had envisioned the Sapphire Lounge being full of jazzy flappers and cool lounge lizards. But most of the people here seemed grizzled and sad. She glanced at Benny. Somehow he was managing to look cool, despite his dorky mustard-yellow turtleneck. He was leaning against the bar, gazing intently around the club. There was a ring of shadowy booths against the walls, and a curtained-off stage. They could hear a drum kit being set up and a bass guitar being tuned. A handwritten sign in front of the curtain read *Asian Fusion Presents: Remembering Pat "Sax Machine" Choi.*

"So what are we doing?" Virginia asked. Benny was always so tight-lipped about their plans, like he assumed Virginia would ruin everything if he let her in on a scheme. It was annoying, but Virginia was used to it.

"Looking," Benny answered, scanning the room.

"You want a drink?"

Virginia swiveled around on her barstool, expecting to see a bartender. But it was Gottfried.

"Dey do not card me," he said. "I get you somesing?"

"Um, sure. I'll have a sidecar. Dry, please, with Cointreau."

Benny gaped at her.

"You got it," Gottfried said. "Scooby?"

"Me? Um, just a tonic water?"

The crimson curtains opened partway, then got snagged

on something. A slim, sad-looking Asian man came out onstage and yanked them the rest of the way open.

"Hey, people," he said, standing at the edge of the stage. "Welcome to Choi's night." There was a smattering of hesitant applause. "We're here to remember our pal Choi. Not because he was the greatest guy on earth, but because he was our friend. Nobody's perfect. But everyone deserves to be remembered. So we're gonna play some of Pat's favorite tunes tonight. And everyone gets a soju on the house, 'cause Pat made the bar stock it, and now there's like twenty bottles, but no one else will drink it." He paused.

"Is he crying?" Virginia whispered to Benny.

"The music will probably suck tonight," the guy onstage went on, "because we don't have a sax player anymore. It's just me and Lucius. So, you know . . . give us a break."

And with that, the other guy, Lucius, banged his drumsticks together and then started playing. The first guy picked up his bass and began soberly plucking the strings.

"Were you showing Zaire the bridge video? I saw you," Benny said loudly over the music. "I'm not going to yell at you. I just need to know. Your actions affect me."

"Benny, I swear I didn't. She asked me to fix the Internet, and I fixed it."

Benny looked at her. He didn't say anything. He kept seeing the weird note in his mind. *Don't get so close to her.* It was the second time in twenty-four hours that Virginia had been in the position of having to deny something—first with the boyfriend and now this—which was enough to raise a red flag in Benny's estimation.

"You don't trust me," Virginia said. It didn't sound like an accusation, just a statement. *You don't have any milk in the refrigerator. You don't trust me.*

"Well I mean, I barely know you. If you think about it."

"Um, if you think about it, we've gone to the same school since we were thirteen, and I've been in Mystery Club for a month," Virginia said.

"But this is our first case together," Benny shouted over the band. "You know what I mean. I don't know what I mean. Just . . . forget it. I think you should go look around backstage. You're less suspicious than me."

Virginia glared at him. Benny was in charge of everything, wasn't he? Even the conversation.

"Just go," Benny ordered. "Poke around. Maybe Mr. Choi left some stuff back there." He pulled out his phone and handed it to her. "Use the flashlight app if you need to. It might be dark back there." As soon as the phone was in Virginia's hand, Benny kind of wanted it back. It felt too personal, sharing his phone with her. But it was too late now.

"Okay," Virginia said, taking the phone. She slid off the barstool, but then hesitated. The bar was the only moderately well-lit area in the whole seedy place, and now she was leaving? It seemed willfully stupid. But she forced herself to move. She could almost feel the darkness on her skin as she stepped into it.

Backstage, 8:15 p.m.

Virginia stood motionless in the dark, cramped space. She was terrified that at any second someone would barge in and yell at her. She reminded herself that as long as she could hear the music, it meant Asian Fusion was onstage and couldn't catch her. And if a bartender or someone walked in, she could just pretend to be lost. But she was so nervous she hadn't even started looking.

Look, she commanded herself. She flicked on the flashlight app and shined it around. Dingy walls with water damage. Half-drunk drinks sitting on a plywood bench. Dirty carpet, a beige lamp. A large bass case on the floor. Virginia crouched down next to it and carefully opened the lid. The case was lined with green velvet, with some clippings stapled to the top. She moved the light across them. LOCAL JAZZ TRIO PLAYS 24-HOUR JACO PASTORIUS MARATHON. ASIAN FUSION VOTED BEST HAPPY HOUR LIVE ENTERTAINMENT.

Then she froze. The last clipping wasn't about the band. It was a photocopy of a print picture, like from a yearbook or a newsletter. A young, bright girl in a Winship cheerleading uniform. But it wasn't Brittany Montague, or even Angie.

Virginia stared at it, assuring herself that she was seeing what she was seeing. She didn't want to go back to Benny with bad information. The image was fuzzy, so Virginia leaned in close with the flashlight, her face inches away.

It's her. It's definitely her.

The bar, 8:20 p.m.

Gottfried sauntered over with two drinks in his hands. "For da lady," he said, setting down the sidecar, "and for da gentleman." He handed Benny the tonic water.

"Thanks," Benny said, reaching in his pocket for some money. He didn't know how much a sidecar cost, but he assumed it was expensive.

"*Nein*, no no no," Gottfried said. "Do not sink of it."

"Please," Benny insisted, but Gottfried shook his head. Benny let it go. He was awkward with money; all those Jewish stereotypes made him self-conscious. Mrs. Flax had always told him never to let his classmates pay for him, or else they wouldn't respect him or see him as an equal. But Benny had found the opposite to be true—the best way to blend in at Winship was to treat money the way they did, like it was pretend, and like there was so much of it, it was petty and pointless to keep track of the tab.

"So you're feeling better?" Benny asked him.

"Hm?"

"On Saturday you were quite ill."

"Ah yes. I am very sensitive. When I'm stressed, my body just falls apart, you know?"

"What are you stressed about?" Benny asked casually.

Gottfried cocked his eyebrow. "Hm? Stressed? No! I am having a wonderful night! *Wunderbar*, we say!" Gottfried slapped Benny on the back, hard, and then strode across the club to join a pair of heavily made-up women in a corner booth. They had to be at least forty years old. They squealed when he sat down, and pinched his cheeks. Gottfried looked completely delighted.

"Benny!"

Benny swiveled around on his stool. Virginia was sprinting toward him like a dog with a squirrel in its teeth.

"What?"

"There's a *picture* in his guitar case. Of *Corny*."

"Really?" Benny exclaimed, amazed that she'd found something so fast.

"I opened the case and it was there. Oh my God."

"People are stupid," Benny said excitedly. "They leave evidence everywhere. It's not like on TV where everyone's a criminal mastermind."

"Ooh, is this my drink?" Virginia grabbed the sidecar. She took a sip, wrinkling her nose. "It's good!" she said, unconvincingly.

Benny studied the bass player. He had long hair and looked younger than Mr. Choi by about ten years. His face was intelligent, but not very serious. Like the kind of guy who has a high IQ but sits around smoking pot all day.

"So what do you think?" Virginia asked.

"Maybe Mr. Choi's bandmates knew about his peeping

tendencies. Maybe he'd bragged about all the hot girls at Winship, and they wanted a piece of it."

"Couldn't they just watch cheerleader porn on the Internet?" Virginia asked.

Benny shook his head. "This would serve a different desire than porn. Porn *invites* you to watch; this would be the thrill of seeing bodies that are forbidden to you."

"Wow. Did you, like, read a book about perverts or something?"

Benny shrugged. "It could be him in the video," he said, nodding toward the bass player. "The person standing at the edge of the bridge." He stirred his tonic water, thinking. "This is going to be easy. All we have to do is dangle the video in front of him and see if he bites. I'll tell you exactly what to do."

Virginia took another sip of her sidecar. "God, look at Gottfried." He and the two older ladies were laughing uproariously in the corner booth. The fatter of the two appeared to be giving Gottfried an innuendo-filled palm reading. There were about ten drinks on the table in front of them.

"You know, I think he's still hooking up with Zaire," Virginia said. "Did you see his face earlier? He had a brown smudge on his cheek. Zaire wears a shit-ton of makeup. I think it smudges off on him when they make out."

Benny looked at her. The quality that made Virginia an amazing gossip also had the potential to make her an amazing detective: She paid attention. She *cared* what other people did. Which was kind of rare in a world where most people cared only about themselves.

9:00 p.m.

Virginia had seen enough movies to know how to hold a drink. That was easy: Pinch the stem, extend the arm lackadaisically, like you couldn't care less if it spilled. But of course it won't if you're holding it right. What was hard was knowing how to walk. She couldn't see what she looked like, she just had to feel it. "Flirt with them," Benny had said, as if it were a foregone conclusion that Virginia could just be a world-class flirt on command. As if her feminine wiles were a tried-and-tested asset. Which they definitely weren't.

"*You* flirt with them." Virginia had balked.

Benny had rolled his eyes. "Do you want to contribute or not?" he'd asked. "We use what we can use."

"You can't just flirt with people to get what you want!"

"Yes you can, if you look like *that*." He'd given a quick nod to her skirt, then shifted his gaze unnaturally to the ceiling. "You look great. Use it."

Virginia stood a little straighter, hearing that. Benny was always factual; if he said she looked great, it had to be a fact.

"Just remember, *you* control the conversation. Don't let them run over you like Angie did."

Control, Virginia repeated to herself. She walked up to the bar.

"Anyone sitting here?" Her voice was a little too high. But she reminded herself that they didn't know what her voice was supposed to sound like, so it didn't matter.

The two men gawked at her. Virginia hopped onto a stool next to them and set down her sidecar. It was her second one. "I loved your set," she said, trying to act like it wasn't weird that they hadn't said anything to her yet.

"Thanks . . . ," the one with long hair said. "You one of Choi's students?"

"Ha!" Virginia said. "Maybe ten years ago I was."

"So . . . when you were two?"

Virginia forced herself to laugh. "It's the light. It's very flattering. Even you two look pretty good."

The drummer laughed loudly. He was shorter than the bass player, with a round face and a trad, Republican side-part haircut that either his mother gave him or was supposed to be ironic.

"I'm Lucius," he said, waving.

"I'm Min-Jun," said the bass player.

"I'm Virginia," Virginia said, and then she immediately wondered if she should have chosen an alias of some kind. Oh well, too late now.

"You look like a *Virgin*ia," Lucius replied. The other one, Min-Jun, punched him in the chest. "Ow!"

"So do y'all have a lot of groupies?" Virginia asked, opening her eyes really wide, trying to look fascinated.

"Um, no. Big no," Min-Jun said.

"Well you do now," Virginia said back.

Lucius and Min-Jun exchanged a look.

"Just kidding," Virginia said, seeing that they were laughing at her. *Damn it,* she thought. She took another gulp of her sidecar, finishing it.

The bartender, an old man with an Afro, pushed three glasses across the bar. "Soju, on the house."

"Have you ever had soju?" Min-Jun asked her.

"No," Virginia said, happy he was talking to her. She could feel Benny watching her from across the bar, and she didn't want to disappoint him. "Do you sip it, or down it like a shot?"

"Sip it," Min-Jun said. "Actually there are a lot of rules for drinking soju. Like, you hold the glass with two hands, like this." He reached for Virginia's hands and gently arranged her fingers around the glass. His hands felt warm but tough, his fingers calloused from the bass strings.

"And you bow your head to your elder," Lucius added. "How old are you again?"

"Ignore him," Min-Jun said.

"And you never pour a glass for yourself. Everyone pours for everyone else."

"That's nice," she said, taking a sip. "Wow. Very . . . alchoholy."

Min-Jun nodded. "You clearly have a refined palate."

Virginia sipped again. Her head was starting to feel sort of cloudy. She caught Min-Jun glancing at her legs, and she uncrossed them slowly. She leaned back and took a long look at him. Suddenly she didn't feel like she needed to talk anymore. It was as if the arrival of the soju had reorganized the power somehow. Like the moment in a game when you realize you're going to win.

"So you like jazz?" Min-Jun asked her.

"I adore jazz," Virginia said.

"We need a new sax player."

"Hopefully one who doesn't turn out to be a child molester," Lucius chimed in.

"Christ, Lucius don't bring that up."

"Well I'm devastated about Mr. Choi," Virginia sighed. "He was such a promising talent. Did you know about his burgonine—bourgenineg"—she was having trouble pronouncing the word—"*emerging* interest in documentary filmmaking?"

The two men stared at her. Min-Jun had frozen, his soju glass halfway to his lips.

"I have the pleasoore—Jesus—*pleasure* of being in possession of his final cinematic work."

"Whaaa . . ."

"It's very artistic. Do you want to see it?"

Neither of them moved. "Um, who *are* you?" Lucius asked carefully.

Virginia smiled brightly. "It's okay! I'm Choi's little helper."

"You're his little helper," Min-Jun repeated.

Virginia leaned in and poked Min-Jun's chest. "And maybe you could be my *big* helper. There's a character in the film that I don't understand. I call him Mysterious Person at the Bridge." She tried to read Min-Jun's face, but it was expressionless. "I'd love to sell it to you. You could watch it, or maybe just throw it on a bonfire. Whatever suits you."

"What price?" Lucius asked in a flat tone.

"I'm thinking . . . five hundred dollars."

Lucius scoffed loudly. "I'm thinking you're a little crazy, little girl," he said, swallowing the rest of his soju and slamming the glass down. "Whatever weird thing you're up to, please leave us out of it. Come on, Min-Jun. Let's go."

Lucius pushed back from the bar and started walking away. Min-Jun downed the rest of his soju and followed him. But before he disappeared backstage, he turned and looked at her. His long black hair half hid his eyes, so Virginia couldn't tell what the look was saying.

The corner booth, 9:45 p.m.

"We love your little German friend! Nothing *little* about him, you know!"

Benny watched, slightly horrified, as the woman opened her jaws and smothered Gottfried's face with a long, messy kiss, her tongue extending like a wet pink tentacle to invade Gottfried's lips. The woman's friend cackled with laughter, which made Virginia laugh, which made her sidecar (her third one) slosh on her sweater. Benny reached for a napkin and handed it to her.

He wasn't completely sure how he and Virginia had ended up in the large corner booth with Gottfried and his random middle-aged lady friends. Their names were Sabrina and Pearla, and though they were very different physically—one was lumpy and orange-skinned, the other horsey and muscular—they projected an air of being interchangeable as they traded equally unimaginative innuendos and guzzled each other's cocktails. One of them had insisted on reading Benny's palm, but was so drunk all she'd managed to say was that Benny had a "heart of mold."

The one kissing Gottfried, Sabrina, finally came up for air, her lips making a loud smack. Gottfried looked embarrassed but thrilled. "Hubba hubba!" he exclaimed.

The women laughed hysterically. Virginia was laughing too, but she didn't seem aware of what she was laughing at. Benny wanted to take her sidecar away, but it didn't seem like his place somehow.

"I have *two* life linessss," Virginia declared, staring unfocusedly at her palm.

"Honey, you're buzzed, with a capital Z," Pearla said. Then she seized Virginia's hand. "Oh my God! You *do* have two life lines! Sabrina look here!"

But Sabrina was entranced by Gottfried's bottomless blue

eyes. "Sheesh, you kids are trouble," she purred to him. "No wonder Patty went nutty on us!"

At the edge of the booth Benny snapped to alertness. "Were you friends with Pat?" Benny asked. "Did you know him?"

"Always the istavigator, never the ivesti-vavigated-ed," Virginia slurred, giving Benny a weird wink.

"Oh sure," Sabrina cooed. "We were best friends! Poor old Patty. You know what's spooky is that I saw him that very night. The last time I ever saw my Peppermint Patty."

"Last Friday night?" Benny asked. "You saw Mr. Choi? What time?"

"I don't know, some time."

"That was Thursdee," Pearla said, wagging a finger. "Thirsty Thursdee."

"It was couples' night, which is Friday."

"No, it was two-for-one-shots night."

"That *is* couples' night! That's why they're two for one, you drunk duck!"

Benny thumped his fingers on the table to get their attention back. "Wait, wait. Answer this: Was the band playing? Was Asian Fusion playing?" He knew Mr. Choi's band only played Monday through Thursday, so hopefully that would resolve the confusion.

"No," Sabrina said, sounding certain. But then two seconds later she exclaimed, "YES! Yes. They played 'Fly Me to the Moon'!"

Benny rubbed his temples. He had never felt so foolish in his life, trying to conduct an interview at a cheesy
nightclub with four drunk people. *They* were the fools, he
tried to convince himself, but it wasn't working. He didn't
feel superior; he just felt left out. And frustrated. Nothing
was adding up. Before becoming so drunk she could barely
form words, Virginia had given him a full report of what
had gone down at the other end of the bar. She'd dangled
the tape, but neither of Choi's bandmates had gone for
it. Which meant it probably wasn't either of them at the
bridge. And now a crazy lady was saying she saw Mr. Choi
on Friday night, or maybe it was Thursday. All this on
top of the fact that his mother was picking them up at the
library in twenty minutes, and if she realized Virginia and
Gottfried had been drinking, she'd never let Benny leave
the house again.

Virginia didn't worry him nearly as much as Gottfried.
Drunkenness just seemed to make her laugh at everything,
but not in the mean, coarse way she usually laughed at
everything. In fact, rather than making her more bellig-
erent, inebriation seemed to make Virginia temporarily
benign and introverted. Gottfried, however, was a potential disaster. Gerard Cole had packed up his lame protest
and abandoned Gottfried at the club, which made Benny
responsible for him now. Benny hoped Mrs. Flax would
simply mistake Gottfried's drunkenness for Europeanness,
but this was a huge risk. It was a twenty-minute drive back

to the Boarders—what if Gottfried threw up or started bellowing German drinking songs? Benny both scorned and envied people like Gottfried—carefree goofballs who only survived because dependable suckers like himself were willing to take responsibility for them.

Suddenly an amber-colored drink appeared on the table. The Afroed old bartender set it down unceremoniously and said, "Compliments of the gentleman at the bar." Then he left.

Benny squinted across the dark room. At the bar, the bass player from Asian Fusion was staring at them. Not at them—at Virginia.

Virginia reached for the glass. Benny quickly reached out and grabbed it before she could.

"Hey!"

He sniffed it. Did roofies have a smell? He didn't know.

"Gimme please," Virginia demanded.

Benny glanced at the bar. The long-haired guy had narrowed his eyes. He was getting up from his stool.

"Come on," Benny said, setting the drink down and scooching out of the booth. "It's time to go."

"Nooooooo!" the old ladies moaned, each clutching one of Gottfried's arms.

Virginia stood up, wobbling. "Say alf-veeder-shane, Gottfried." She reached over the horsey woman and yanked Gottfried by the collar of his shirt. Gottfried laughed and allowed himself to be pulled out of the booth.

The fat one trailed after them, planting glossy kisses on Gottfried's face.

Benny felt an arm curl around his waist as Virginia steadied herself against him. She was leaning on him, and Gottfried was leaning on her as Benny led them awkwardly out of the club.

"Not one more drink? For da road?" Gottfried asked, sounding sad.

Then Benny felt Virginia slipping, and he heaved her up by the arm before she could fall.

"Thanks, Dad," she said absently.

Benny looked at her. Gottfried roared with laughter. "Shut up, Gottfried," Benny said, not wanting to draw attention.

As they approached the public library, he saw his mother's car already parked in the lot. She was always ten minutes early. Benny dragged Virginia and Gottfried around the back so she wouldn't see them coming from the street.

"Wheeeeee!" Gottfried cried as they circled around.

"Gottfried you have to be quiet," Benny said. "When we get to the car, neither of you say a single word."

"What if she . . . inquires about the United Nation?" Virginia asked, obviously straining to articulate.

"You say nothing. Gottfried, are you listening? When you get in the car, what do you say?"

"I shall say *guten Tag*, Merssus Fleck!"

"Oh my God, no, Gottfried. You say nothing. You are silent. Do you understand? My mother will kill me. She'll pull me out of school."

Gottfried nodded stupidly. Benny couldn't tell if he really understood, but there was nothing to do but get in the car. *This is the end,* Benny thought. *This is the end, and I'm just walking right into it.*

The Boarders, midnight

It was hard to describe what she was feeling. She felt like she was on a tire swing, or in one of those dreams where you can't walk properly. It was like time dragged for long moments, and she'd be staring at photographs on the bulletin board, but then time sped up again, and she suddenly couldn't remember what she'd been doing. And she kept missing things, like in a play where all the action happens offstage. Benny had been right there, and then he was gone, but she couldn't remember him leaving. Gottfried had been there too, but now she couldn't find him, either.

"Gottfried?" she called.

She heard a murmur coming from the common room. She stumbled back toward it and found Gottfried slumped on the sofa. "My first real American girlfriend!" he exclaimed, looking wasted and ecstatic.

"Whaaaa?" Virginia said, and burst out laughing. Did Gottfried think she was his girlfriend now? They'd sort of held hands for five seconds when Virginia had grabbed him to keep from falling down. *Oh my God,* she thought, feeling a weird giddiness tinged with dread. But then she realized Gottfried was talking about his low-class old lady at the Sapphire Lounge. He had a piece of paper with her phone number on it and was kissing it over and over. Virginia started laughing even harder.

"Amerikanische Frau!" Gottfried cried. "I shall never go home again!" And then he closed his eyes and fell over on the sofa, presumably to dream of fake blondes with two-inch roots and streakily tanned bosoms.

Virginia's laughter trailed off, and she stared at him, wondering if he was really asleep. Gottfried was famous among the boarders for being an extreme insomniac. Apparently back in Germany he'd had a personal sleep therapist or something, but he couldn't find one in America. Which meant that no matter what time of night, you could usually count on him being awake and padding around the Boarders in his slippers. He seemed thoroughly conked out now, though, unless he was faking. But Virginia didn't think Gottfried was the type to fake anything. He seemed incapable of the artifice required to act like a normal person.

"Gottfried?" Virginia said quietly. "Gottfried?" He didn't move. She eyed the pink piece of paper still loosely clutched in his hand. She heard Benny's voice in her mind: *Do you want to contribute or not?* She focused her bleary eyes on the paper, then reached over and grabbed it.

Then she was in her dark, quiet room, with no memory of how she got there. She sat up on the bed. She was uncomfortable. The gold skirt had been rubbing against her waist all night and it felt like she had a rash. Had she been sleeping? She looked at her clock. It was one in the morning. She felt dizzy in a way that alarmed her, not like the pleasant, airy, oblivious dizziness she'd felt earlier.

She found herself staring at the window. It was pitch-black outside, the black outlines of trees against a starless black sky. But as her eyes adjusted, she noticed a pale shadow standing against the background, almost like a ghost. It moved toward her window, like it knew she had seen it.

And then Virginia was screaming.

1:00 a.m.

"BENNY! BENNY! BENNY! BENNY!"

The screams were hysterical, like they were coming from an unhinged lunatic or someone waking up from a nightmare.

Zaire had been awake for an hour, listening to Gottfried crashing around the common room sounding drunk, which was pretty weird for a Wednesday night. She'd been waiting for Virginia to go to bed so she could see what the hell he was up to. But Virginia just kept hanging around, wandering the hall and giggling idiotically. What were they even doing hanging out together? Since when were Gottfried and Virginia Leeds friends?

The screams didn't stop. Zaire flung her door open and saw Virginia on the floor. She was backing away from her room like a deranged crab.

Other doors opened. "What's going on?" Chrissie White asked, rubbing her eyes.

Zaire knelt down next to Virginia. "Bloody hell, what's wrong?" There was a rip in the gold skirt she'd loaned her, she couldn't help noticing.

Virginia pointed to her room. Her face was completely white. "He was there. He was watching me."

"Who? Benny?"

"NO!" Virginia shouted. "I need to call Benny!"

Zaire got up and flicked on the light in Virginia's room. She looked around. "There's no one here," Zaire said. "You were having a dream."

Virginia sat pressed against the wall, breathing heavily. After a moment she started to calm down.

"See? You're waking up now. You're fine. Go to bed, guys; she's fine," Zaire said to Chrissie and the other girls. She turned back to Virginia. "So . . . wild night with Gottfried, huh?"

Virginia was holding her head in her hands. "Huh?"

"I heard you coming in with Gottfried. What were you two doing?"

"I don't know," Virginia said. She sounded like she was about to cry. "I don't feel very good."

"Well yeah, you're clearly trashed. Come on." She helped

Virginia get up. "Go back to sleep. Nighty-night. Bye." She pushed Virginia into her room, turned off the light, and shut the door. Zaire knew she was being brusque, but she was eager to get rid of her so she could get Gottfried alone. Zaire had assumed Virginia liked that Scooby guy she was always lurking around with. But maybe Scooby was gay like everyone said, and Virginia had given up on him and set her sights on Gottfried. If Zaire had known that, she definitely wouldn't have picked out her hottest skirt to lend her. She would have picked something ugly and beige.

Zaire listened at Virginia's door for a moment to make sure she wasn't coming back out. Then she dashed back to her room to smear some concealer under her eyes and do some contouring. She brushed her hair, tightened the belt of her blue satin robe, and snuck down the hall to the common room. As she peeked in the doorway, she expected to see Gottfried flopped on the sofa, maybe with that cute, spacey look on his face, his beautiful limbs sprawled out in all directions. But the common room was empty.

"Hello?" she said. No answer. *Where did he go?* Zaire was sure she hadn't heard him going up the stairs to the boys' hall. She walked around the room to make sure he wasn't lying on the floor or something. There was no one. She shouldn't have been surprised. Even when they were dating, he'd been impossible to predict, and impossible to control.

Thursday
The fountain, 8:00 a.m.

The sun had just risen over the top of the building when he saw Virginia. She was eating a banana and drinking a hot chocolate and reading the newspaper. Benny was surprised—he'd told Virginia she should read the newspaper every day to keep up with local crime coverage, but he hadn't expected her to actually do it. He also hadn't expected to see her looking so normal after last night.

The twenty-minute ride from the public library to the Boarders had been possibly the most stressful of his life. Trying to keep Gottfried upright in his seat, trying to keep up a steady stream of chatter so neither Gottfried nor Virginia would have a chance to drunkenly open their mouths. "I heard that reading aloud can enhance memory retention," he'd announced to the car. "So I think I'll read aloud from my history book in preparation for my test next Monday. 'Tokugawa Yoshinobu was the last shogun of the Edo period of Japan.'"

"TO-KU-GA-WA!" Gottfried had boomed in a cartoonish

Japanese accent, while Virginia giggled in the front seat. Benny had continued reading, making his voice even louder. At which point Gottfried started barking random observations about whatever they passed on the road. "That house has a large door. This red light is very long for no traffic. In *Deutschland* we use the kilometer. Should the world not be in agreement of its measuring?" He was particularly upset by a Waffle House whose sign was not fully illuminated, reading AFFLE HO SE. Mrs. Flax had said nothing, her mouth pressed in a tight, disapproving line as she drove.

Virginia had been so out of it Benny had been forced to walk her to the door with his arm wrapped around her. It felt weird. He and Virginia had barely touched before, and now he was practically carrying her, her whole body leaning against him and his arm enclosing her waist. He'd even felt her skin a few times as her sweater bunched up. And now his mother probably thought they were in love or something. He'd dreaded getting back in the car and braced himself for one of his mother's scary lectures. But all she'd done was give him a deeply disapproving look and say, "I thought the Model UN was for *serious* students."

And now here was Virginia, reading the *Atlanta Journal-Constitution* and eating breakfast as if it were an ordinary morning. A breeze rustled the pages of Virginia's paper and created a thin, cool mist from the fountain's streaming water.

Benny came up behind her. "Hey."

Virginia jumped, almost sloshing her hot chocolate. "Benny, hi. You surprised me."

"How are you feeling?" he asked her.

"Oh, not too bad. Gottfried's dead to the world, though. He fell asleep on the common-room sofa and wouldn't even get up." She lifted the paper. "Did you know Mr. Choi had a wife and a daughter? They live in *Gainesville*." Everyone made fun of Gainesville, a sad suburban dump whose water tower desperately proclaimed WHERE SUCCESS LIVES!

"It's a closed funeral," she said, "at some Korean church. Maybe we could sneak in, except I don't know how we'd get all the way to Gainesville."

Benny sat down next to her at the edge of the fountain. He looked at the photo in the paper. Mrs. Choi looked so normal. Like a nice vice principal or a bingo caller. Had she known she was married to a pervert? Did she have enough money to get by? When Benny's dad had his accident, the family got compensation from the company, enough to pay for Rodrigo and physical therapy and making the whole house wheelchair accessible during the months when Mr. Flax couldn't walk. What would Mrs. Choi get? Anything?

Benny blinked, snapping himself out of it. *Lift off*, he told himself. Whenever he found himself getting bogged down in the human element of a mystery, Benny tried to imagine himself lifting off in a plane and flying far above it. You had clearer perspective at thirty thousand feet.

"Wildcat's been glaring at me for fifteen minutes," Virginia said, nodding toward the bench under the magnolia tree. Benny saw the scruffy brown cat hunched in the shadows under the bench, looking cranky. *Poor Wildcat,* Benny thought. He had probably been a nice, normal cat at some point but had grown violent and prone to hiding after years of being chased and smothered by gleeful sixth-graders. Now he was practically feral and wasn't allowed inside anymore. They had created a brute, and then punished him for behaving like one.

"Did you know Wildcat sleeps in the Boarders sometimes? On Zaire Bollo's bed?"

"That's hard to believe," Benny said.

"I wouldn't have believed it either, but I saw it. Oh, and look what I got." Virginia handed Benny a piece of paper. It had a phone number and a pink puckered kiss mark on it. "It's that lady's number. Serena or Ruby or whichever one was sucking Gottfried's face. I stole it from him while he was sleeping. We should call her when she's sober and ask about Choi."

Benny examined the paper. "You should have copied the number and then put it back, so Gottfried wouldn't notice it was gone."

"Oh . . . I didn't think of that."

For a moment they sat there not talking. Virginia ate the last bite of her banana and tossed the peel in the bushes.

Benny frowned at her. "There's a trash can right over there."

"It's *organic matter*," Virginia snapped at him. "It's good for the earth. Will you stop criticizing everything I do? You're so annoying."

"Sorry, sorry," Benny said, standing up.

"You don't have to leave," Virginia sighed. "I just have a headache."

"The bell's about to ring," he said lamely. "See ya." He took the long way around the fountain so he didn't have to cross in front of Virginia. As he passed the bench, Wildcat hissed and lunged at him. "Wildcat, leave me alone," he snapped, but then he felt bad. "Sorry," he said, turning back. But Wildcat just hissed again and ran.

Room 300, 11:30 a.m.

"I feel eyes on me all the time. Even in an empty room."

"In the locker room, we all change in the bathroom stalls now. It's like the age of innocence is over."

Virginia rubbed her temples, wishing she could go back to the Boarders and get into bed. She was so sick of watching PSAs about predatory teachers and listening to the cheerleaders moan about the sanctity of their boobs. Winship always went overboard with this stuff. Like in the eighth grade when FCA tried to convert Benny to Christianity, and the principal reacted by making the whole student body watch *School Ties* and read *The Chosen*, which was supposed to make them learn acceptance but had pretty much doomed Benny forever.

Virginia noticed Zaire Bollo sliding a note across her desk. Virginia picked it up and unfolded it. Right away she noticed a Smythson watermark on the paper. That was so Zaire, to write notes in class on expensive British stationery.

You OK? You were pretty demented last night. Btw I didn't know you and Gottfried were drinking buddies. Invite me next time!

Virginia crumpled the note, but the paper was so thick it was difficult. Was Zaire trying to get her expelled? If a teacher saw that note, they'd all be done for. She put it in her backpack to rip up later. Then she got a regular piece of notebook paper and wrote:

I did invite you.

Zaire looked at the note and quickly wrote back:

I thought you were going with Benny.

I did go with Benny.

Then why did you come home with Gottfried? Just asking cuz I'm confused.

Because home is the dorm where we both live. Obviously. Where did you expect us to go?

Zaire frowned, folded up the note, and stared ahead. Evidently the conversation was over.

Mrs. Turner was turning on the classroom TV. "This video is called *Crossing the Line*," she said. "Young girls make easy targets for sexual predators, because you haven't learned boundaries and can be easily confused. This video will outline what is appropriate versus inappropriate behavior, and how to ask for help when someone crosses the line."

Virginia felt annoyed. They shouldn't be learning how to ask for help; they should be learning to help themselves. She raised her hand to say as much, but Mrs. Turner pretended not to see her. Mrs. Turner always pretended not to see her, because it made her lame job easier.

Virginia looked out the window. There was a police car parked in the driveway right outside. She didn't know how long it had been there.

"That janitor? He just CROSSED THE LINE." The video boomed.

Virginia squinted at the car. There was a cop in the passenger seat staring vacantly out the windshield. *Don't people realize how dumb they look when they sit there doing nothing?* Virginia thought. But some people just didn't seem to care if they looked dumb. They didn't care what anybody thought about them at all. Which was disgusting and low class, in Virginia's opinion.

"That tennis instructor? He just CROSSED THE LINE."

Then the cop got out and opened the back door of the car. A second cop was approaching, with his arm around a kid's shoulder. She couldn't tell if the kid had handcuffs on or not. She couldn't even tell who it was, because the cop was in the way. But then he stepped aside to open the car door, and Virginia saw his face. *Oh my God.*

She wasn't the only one who'd seen it.

"Whoa, did you see that?" someone was asking.

"Are they arresting Gerard?"

"The water boy? They're arresting the water boy?"

Everyone got up from their desks and pressed against the window to watch. The cop had placed his hand on Gerard's head to push him into the backseat, just like cops on TV.

"That ice cream truck driver? He just CROSSED THE LINE."

"Everyone sit back down!" Mrs. Turner said. "Please, I'm sure there will be an explanation."

Virginia pushed away from the window. Obviously she had to find Benny immediately. She was pretty sure he had a free period right now, which he usually spent in the library.

"I have to go to the bathroom," she called back to Mrs. Turner. But she didn't get far. In the hallway there was a tall man in a suit and tie wearing a severe look and

standing next to Principal Baron. The principal was pointing at her.

"That's the girl you want. That's Virginia Leeds."

The principal's office, 11:30 a.m.

STUD DATA SOFT.

Benny clicked. It took a few seconds for the program
to load, which was just enough time for Benny to go into
a full-blown panic. *What am I doing? What the hell am I
doing?*

He was in the principal's office. He'd been walking
past the administrative annex when he saw Principal Baron
step into the conference room with a formidable-looking
man in a dark suit. The secretary must have been at lunch,
because her desk was empty. And the door to the principal's
office was wide open. Without thinking about the possible
consequences, Benny had slipped inside.

Leeds, Virginia, Benny entered into the search field.
He scanned the file. A phone number, an address in Boca
Raton. A transcript from an elementary school in Jackson-
ville, Florida. Immunizations. Medical records.

Personal background.

He clicked. The little hourglass icon turned over
and over as the page loaded. Benny looked up from the
computer and glanced at the door. His face was hot,
and he could feel his heart slamming in his chest. What
did he think he was doing? Logging into the principal's

computer? Rifling through private student data? He'd be expelled in a second if he were caught. And what did he expect to find, anyway? Boyfriend records? An answer to whether or not Virginia showed Zaire the video? It was absurd.

Will you stop criticizing everything I do? Benny kept hearing Virginia's voice snapping at him in his mind. Did he really do that? Criticize everything? He didn't mean to, necessarily, it just seemed like Virginia didn't think things through half the time. What was he supposed to do, just let her overrun his investigation with bad ideas and clumsy follow-through so he didn't hurt her feelings?

Except it wasn't Virginia's feelings that were smarting right now, if Benny was being honest. *You're so annoying.* Virginia was calling *him* annoying? Annoying people found other people annoying? The idea was baffling. It made him feel agitated and uncertain of himself. Which was doubly annoying because *Virginia* was the one he hardly knew anything about. He should have been feeling insecure about her, not himself. Yet here he was in the principal's office searching her student records . . . why? To get back at her in some meaningless, oblique way?

He clicked on a thumbnail of a legal document in Virginia's file, dated July two years ago. Virginia must have been thirteen. Benny scanned it, reading so fast he realized he wasn't absorbing any of it. He scrolled to the top and started reading again.

Notice of Hearing and Court Order. In the
matter of <u>Virginia Leeds</u>, minor(s), it is repre-
sented that <u>Stephen Kroll</u>, in the petition for
Personal Protection from the state of Florida
regarding the minor(s) listed above, which is
necessary in the best interest of the minor
due to ongoing harassment and repeated
attempts on the part of the petitioner

Benny stopped reading. It was a restraining order.

Virginia has a stalker? Benny thought, his heart pounding. How could she not have mentioned that? Virginia
was famous for not being able to keep a secret. But apparently she could, as long as it was her own. Virginia had
a secret. It creeped Benny out, but more than that, it
impressed him.

He scrolled through the rest of the court order, reading
it as fast as he could. But it started to get confusing. The
legalese was convoluted and a little over his head. He went
back to the beginning again and read more carefully.

On behalf of the petitioner . . . in immedi-
ate and present danger of further harassment
on the part of the adverse party . . . a person
who commits a felony in violation of the Order
of Protection shall be punished by imprison-
ment, or in the case of the minor(s) directed to

a juvenile detention center at the discretion of
the state. . . .

"Wait . . . ," Benny said out loud. Who was the petitioner here, Virginia or the other guy? Was the restraining order against . . . *her*? He read it again. Why did they make this stuff so impossible to understand?

"I'll grab a student worker to find Ben Flax," Principal Baron's voice boomed suddenly in the hall.

Benny froze. Had he just heard his own name? Frantically he clicked out of the data program. The little hourglass spun around. "Oh my God, *close*," he hissed at the screen.

"Caroline?" Principal Baron was calling.

The program finally closed, and Benny lunged toward the door. At the last second he grabbed a random piece of paper from a stack on the principal's desk. He slid out the door just as Principal Baron was making his way in.

"Ben!" the principal said. "Just the man I was looking for. What are you . . . doing in my office?"

Benny held up the paper. "Sorry, sir. I just needed an excused absence form." He held up the paper.

The principal looked at it. "Well this is a course transfer form. And you ask Caroline for those things—you don't just barge on in."

"Yes, sir. I'm very sorry, sir." The paper was getting moist from his sweaty hand.

Behind Principal Baron was the man in the suit, leaning against the doorway and looking at Benny with a pair of cool, expressionless eyes. His suit was crisp but not tailored—clearly off the rack. The jacket was loose and unbuttoned, ideal for concealing a holstered gun. He held a slim tape recorder under his left arm. He was a detective, it was suddenly obvious. A real-life, adult detective from the police department. And the way he stared Benny down, it was like he could read every thought he'd ever had.

The library conference room, 12:00 p.m.

I chowed a great wad of pizza sauce. No one saw me chomp the wad of prawns.

Virginia frowned. She was pretty sure she couldn't read lips. She squinted at Benny's face through the small gap in the blinds. He was sitting at the immense conference table across from Detective Disco. Detective Disco—that was actually his name. Virginia wondered how often he knocked on people's doors and they thought he was a male stripper. She imagined him peering through a comically huge magnifying glass at some bachelorette's boobs, declaring, *Aha! A clue!* Then "Funkytown" would start playing, and he'd rip his clothes off. Through the window, Virginia gave the detective a once-over, wondering what he would look like naked. Probably pretty good, she decided, though the thought wasn't especially titillating. She'd seen a Lifetime movie about male strippers once and found all their bulging and gyrating to be pretty ridiculous. That was the thing about trying to objectify men—it just didn't work for some reason.

"Virginia, could you stand over here with me please?" said Principal Baron, who was waiting with her in the library. Virginia knew what he was doing. She wasn't being allowed to see Benny or communicate with him in any way, so they had no time to get their stories straight. She didn't even know what was going on. Were she and Benny suspects now? Suspects of what? Maybe someone had reported her underage drinking at the Sapphire Lounge, and now she and Benny were about to be expelled. The thought made her cheeks flush with panic. Where would she even go if she got expelled? Who would she call? Her stepdad's phone had been dead for weeks; she was pretty sure he'd moved to Cuba. And there was no one else she'd want to call in a million years.

The door opened, and Virginia could hear the detective's voice. "Thank you, Benny. We'll let you know if we have any further questions."

Benny emerged from the room, head down. As he passed Detective Disco, he shot Virginia the quickest look, mouthing a single word: *Go.* Or was it *don't*? Virginia couldn't tell. And now Benny had looked back down and was walking away, and the detective was saying, "Virginia Leeds? If you would join me?"

"Okay," she said in a tiny voice. He was towering in the

doorway, and Virginia slinked past him. She felt so over-powered by his authority all of a sudden, it was like being five years old again, back when adults seemed actually scary, and not just like pathetic old people.

She pulled out the chair and saw a piece of paper on the seat. She started to brush it onto the floor, but then she stopped. She sat down, quickly crumpling the paper in her fist and looking up at Detective Disco to see if he'd noticed. If he had, he didn't show it. He stared at her, leaning back in his chair. Virginia unclenched her fist and glanced down at the paper in her hand. There was writing in Benny's sloppy handwriting, but she couldn't look down long enough to read it without being conspicuous.

"See that?" Detective Disco was pointing to something behind her. Virginia twisted in her chair, still clutching the note. On the wall there was one of those READ posters, this one featuring Queen Latifah reading a novelization of *Ice Age*. The frame had a huge crack in the glass, and there was a brown stain running down the wall.

"Gerard Cole threw a Coke at the wall. Give a guy a nice can of Coke, and he throws it at the wall. Don't you think that's a little rude? Don't you think that's a little crazy?"

Virginia nodded.

"If I gave *you* a Coke," the detective said, "would you throw it at the wall, or would you drink it like a normal, mature young lady?"

"I'd drink it," she said.

"Promise?" It almost could have been flirtatious, but it wasn't. His gaze was stony, and his voice was flat.

Virginia nodded.

Detective Disco leaned back in his chair and banged on the beige door of the conference room. "Gimme a Coke!" he boomed. Seconds later Principal Baron opened the door a crack and passed the detective a Coke. It was weird to see the principal being bossed around like that. But Detective Disco seemed like the kind of guy who could boss anyone around.

He slid the Coke across the table. Virginia grabbed it with one hand and opened it awkwardly, not wanting to show the paper held tight in her other hand. She took three long gulps in a row, watching the detective watching her, their eyes locked on each other. Then, lowering the can from her lips, she made a quick motion as if she were about to fling it across the room.

"Just kidding," she said, smiling and setting the can down.

Detective Disco smiled too, and the smile transformed his face so completely that Virginia was startled by it.

"I think it should be a crime to throw a Coke in this city," Virginia said casually.

"I agree," Detective Disco said. "Don't throw a Coke in the ATL."

"I mean, throw a Pepsi for Christ's sake," Virginia said, and Detective Disco laughed. *Where am I getting this banter?* Virginia thought. She was freaking herself out a little. Then she realized—she was being the Virginia from the Sapphire Lounge. It was weird to discover she could do it even without the miniskirt and sexy sweater.

"Ha! You're damn right—throw a Pepsi."

Virginia took another sip, slowly, giving herself time to come up with something clever to say next. But the detective spoke first.

"So. Let's talk about Gerard."

"Must we?" Virginia said coquettishly. But it was immediately apparent that the flirting was over. Detective Disco's face was expressionless again.

"Gerard tells me you have a video? A video I should see?"

Virginia felt her eyes go wide, and immediately tried to readjust her face to be inscrutable. But she knew it was too late. She remembered the paper in her hand, and wished the detective would stop watching her so intently so she could read it. She picked up her Coke and took a sloppy sip so that just enough spilled on her front, giving her an excuse to look down.

"Ah damn," she said.

"Need a napkin?" The detective offered.

"No, it's okay," she said, dabbing at the spot with her sleeve. With her other hand she quickly scanned the note. The words were hard to read and crooked, like Benny had written it without looking where he was writing.

DENY TAPE NO TAPE

She tucked the note into her sleeve and looked up. "Sorry! Coke makes me spazzy. What were you saying?"

Detective Disco was looking at her. "I was saying, can you tell me about this video?"

"Right. Well, Gerard's a nutcase," she said, feeling her cheeks get hot. "I mean, who throws a Coke? Like you said." *Get it together,* she commanded herself.

"Not your first nutcase though," Detective Disco said. His lip twitched.

Virginia stared at him. "Excuse me?"

He held up a piece of paper. It was a crappy photocopy of a legal document with the Florida state seal. It was stamped DEFENDANT'S COPY.

Virginia squinted at it. "What is that?"

The detective's eyebrow raised. "Your name's on it. You should know."

"My name?" She scanned the page looking for it, but the print was small and the ink was smudged. Was this some kind of trick? To psych her out?

"Anyway!" The detective slapped the paper facedown on the table and slid it away. "Can you tell me about this little club you're in? This little mysterious club?"

"*Mystery* Club," Virginia corrected. "We study mystery solving."

"What kinds of mysteries?"

"Um, existential mysteries. The mystery of life. The mystery of death."

"Hm. Interesting. Cute."

Virginia smiled cutely.

"Well tell me, Virginia, does your club ever dabble in more concrete stuff? You know, real whodunits?"

"Not really. Mostly it's like . . . whodunit . . . in your soul." *Oh my God,* she thought, hoping she didn't sound as stupid as she felt.

"So no tape, then," he said, not a question.

Virginia shook her head. It was easier to lie knowing that Benny had lied too, and that he must have lied pretty well or they wouldn't have let him leave. They would have charged him with withholding evidence or something.

"Honestly, Gerard is a freak. I wouldn't believe anything he says."

"Hm. Is that your opinion? Your teen detective opinion?"

Virginia frowned, annoyed that he was treating her like a child all of a sudden. She wanted to go back to their flirty Coke banter. "Yes," she said in a flat voice.

"Well, okay then!" he said abruptly. "That's all I need from you, Miss Teen Detective! We know where to find you if we have any more questions."

Virginia stood up, checking to make sure Benny's note hadn't dropped out of her sleeve. The detective was watching her, making her self-conscious. "Um, can I ask you something? One detective to another?" She was trying to be flirtatious again.

"Sure," he said, not looking at her but at a form he was filling out.

"Why is Gerard being arrested?"

The detective looked up. "Well, he tried to punch me, for one thing."

"Oh, Gerard tries to punch everyone," Virginia said. "That doesn't mean he's dangerous, does it?"

The detective looked at her. "Isn't that exactly what it means?"

"Well, no," Virginia said. "He's weak. His punches don't have any power."

"That doesn't matter. What matters is that he keeps trying."

"Oh . . ." Virginia smoothed her skirt down and started to leave.

"Hey, don't forget your Coke now."

Virginia looked at it. She didn't really want it anymore. She only liked the first few sips of Coke, when it was super cold and fresh and the carbonation sparkled. But she didn't want to offend Detective Disco, so she turned back. And as she reached for it, she saw the detective's eyes drop to the floor.

Immediately she knew what had happened. She dove down and spotted the little slip of paper that had escaped her sleeve and fallen, faceup, onto the floor. She slammed her hand down on it, covering the words, and looked up at the detective to see if he'd read it.

It didn't take a second look to be certain that he had.

The cafeteria, 12:35 p.m.

Benny sat alone at a table for six, staring at his lunch tray. Every day he ate a turkey sandwich with two cartons of orange juice. But now he couldn't stop thinking about what Virginia had said about all the sugar in juice and how you may as well drink a soda. He turned the carton over and read the nutrition facts label: thirty-five grams of sugar. Was that a lot? He checked the Coke can Detective Disco had given him: thirty-nine grams. So Virginia was right—you may as well drink a soda.

"Can we have this table?" Two tall boys and their girlfriends appeared, hovering with their trays. It was the third time someone had asked for Benny's table.

"Um, I'm waiting for someone," he said, looking down.

"Well can't you wait over there?" Winn Davis, obviously the leader, pointed to a smaller, two-person table across the room.

"I'm afraid not," Benny said, feeling awkward and flushed. He knew he was being rude, taking up an entire table and refusing to move. But this particular seat had a view of the library doors, and he needed to stay put so he could wait for Virginia to come out. *Why is she taking so long?* he thought, trying to contain his growing panic. Detective Disco had only questioned him for ten minutes, but Virginia had been in there for half an hour.

"It's just that, there are four of us, and only one of you," Corny said. Her voice was tiny and sweet and plaintive but carried the harsh underlying message: *And we're better than you.*

"You're welcome to join me," he offered. Corny and Winn and their friends looked from Benny to the empty seats, obviously debating whether it was worth being able to sit together if it meant they had to sit with him, too. Finally Winn set his tray down, and the rest followed. They started talking about some "crazy" thing Trevor Cheek had done at a party last week, ignoring Benny. Corny flashed her twinkling smile at him a few times, but other than that, they pretended he wasn't there. Benny sipped the rest of his Coke, now lukewarm and flat.

"Sweetie, you're spilling."

"No I'm not."

Winn was trying to drink his orange juice, but it kept dribbling down his chin.

"Stop making a mess!" Corny said, giggling and dabbing his face with a napkin.

Benny felt someone looking at him. He'd always been good at feeling people's eyes on him, maybe because it hardly ever happened. If you were someone like Brittany or Corny, someone people stared at all the time, you probably became desensitized to it. He turned in his seat, careful to look away from the library doors for only a second so he wouldn't miss Virginia coming out. It was Zaire Bollo, sitting alone two tables away. She was eating a baked potato in front of a large stack of books. Zaire always carried her books around like that—she was one of those people who never used their lockers. Her eyes glanced from Benny to

Winn, who had just dribbled more juice down his shirt.

"You did it again!" Corny squealed.

"Okay, whatever, so what," Winn was saying, sounding annoyed.

Benny looked away from Zaire and continued to concentrate on the library doors. He was so anxious, and wanted Virginia to appear so badly, it was almost like he could smell her, that overly florid punch of rose and musk. He inhaled. It really was uncanny. He could have sworn it was Virginia. Were olfactory hallucinations a thing? He sniffed a few more times. Then he realized it wasn't a hallucination—it was Corny.

"Are you wearing perfume?" he asked without thinking.

Everyone at the table stared at him. Benny felt his face going red.

"I am, actually!" Corny exclaimed, obviously trying to pretend it was normal for Benny to attempt to talk to them. "You're such a sweetie to notice. Winn bought it for me; isn't he the best?"

Winn gave a tight smile, and Benny nodded at him idiotically. *Winn sure is the best!*

After an awkward interval, Benny went back to staring at the library doors, and the others went back to ignoring him. At one o'clock the bell rang. It was the usual routine of everyone groaning and picking up their trays and feeling depressed that lunch was already over. But Benny didn't move. He continued to stare at the doors, waiting for

Virginia to come out. The second bell rang; classes were starting. Finally a janitor asked him to leave so he could wipe down the table. Benny dumped his tray, keeping his eyes on the library doors. Not that his vigilance was rewarded; it was five and a half hours before Virginia came out.

The Boarders, 5:30 p.m.

The room had been ransacked.

The drawers were flung open, their contents strewn across the floor. The bed had been unmade and the sheets tossed in a tangled heap on the floor. Every book had been opened, shaken out, and dumped in a mess of cracked spines and bent-up pages. Virginia stood in the doorway, her mouth hanging open.

"Oh my God."

A lady officer with a severe ponytail and a pantsuit noticed Virginia standing there and handed her a clipboard. "This is a list of everything we're taking in for evidence. Please look it over and sign here."

Virginia scanned the list. It was a bunch of stuff she didn't even care about, like her organizer and assignment books. So Benny was right. The police were morons.

"Wait, you're taking my candy stash?" Virginia said.

"I'm taking whatever's in this Amazing Box of Secrets."

"Oh my God, I made that in, like, seventh grade. It's just Snickers bars and collages of Christian Bale."

The officer shrugged. "We'll see."

"Come on, just let me keep one Snickers," Virginia demanded. She was starving because Detective Disco had made her miss lunch. And she knew for a fact there was nothing in the common-room refrigerator except condiments and a gross old fruitcake Mrs. Morehouse had gotten for the September birthdays knowing she'd be the only one who'd eat it.

"Sorry," she said, sounding totally not sorry.

Virginia frowned, handing back the clipboard. "Don't you get a headache wearing your ponytail that tight?"

The officer checked the signature. "I get a headache being around teenage girls who wear too much perfume. We'll call you in seventy-two hours to arrange for the return of your belongings. Here's my number if you have any questions. Thank you for your cooperation." She walked out into the hall, carrying a plastic bag of Virginia's stuff.

"Um, excuse me. Does someone want to clean this up?" Virginia called after her.

"Not my job," the lady said back.

"Well whose job is it?" Virginia yelled. But the officer just strode down the hall, leaving her alone with the mess.

6:00 p.m.

"Hello?"

Benny heard a muffled moan. The room was such a disaster, it took a second for him to realize Virginia was lying in the middle of the bed, facedown in a pile of clothes.

"Whoa, what happened in here?" he asked. "Are you okay?"

"I screwed up," Virginia said, her voice barely audible. "I dropped your note and Detective Funkytown saw it."

"WHAT?"

"So he made me wait with him in the library for hours while they searched my room. It was so boring!"

"They—they can't do that!" Benny shouted. "They need a warrant!"

"That's what I said, but he said they didn't, because I live on school property."

"So you have no rights? That's preposterous!"

"Ugh, stop shouting. I have a headache." She burrowed her face deeper into the pile of clothes.

"So they have the video now," Benny said. *Damn it, Virginia.* He should never have let her keep that flash drive. He'd thought it was smarter to leave it with her than keep it himself. As the president of Mystery Club he attracted attention, while no one would suspect dotty Virginia Leeds of harboring important evidence. But that same dottiness made Virginia a liability. She was impulsive and careless, and if her file was any indication, there was a lot about her that Benny didn't know. From now on Benny would do everything himself, and that included custodianship of all case-related materials. Virginia could stay in the club, but he wasn't giving her any more responsibilities. He was trying to come up with a tactful way to tell her this when Virginia said:

"Do you think I'm stupid?" Not in a caustic way, exactly, but more like she was genuinely asking.

"You're not stupid," Benny said generously. "It wasn't your fault. It was my fault for being disorganized, and for not predicting that Gerard would inform the police about the tape."

Virginia rolled onto her back. "No, I mean, you must think I'm stupid if you think I'd keep the video in my room. I assumed you thought I was smart, or else you wouldn't have let me join Mystery Club."

"Uh . . ." Benny didn't know what to say. Did Virginia think she'd been specially selected from an eager and highly qualified bunch of candidates? The truth was that Benny would have let anyone join Mystery Club—he didn't believe in excluding people. But no one except Virginia had been interested, which he obviously couldn't tell her now without insulting her.

"Wait," he said. "So they don't have the video?"

"I have a hiding place. We all have hiding places."

We all have hiding places. It was kind of deep and ironic, Benny thought, Virginia saying it in this raided room with her stuff everywhere.

"Gottfried keeps cigarettes above the rafters. Piper keeps condoms in a pineapple can in the pantry. Everyone has shit everywhere."

Everyone has shit everywhere. Benny was so excited all of a sudden, everything she said sounded profound and miraculous. The video was safe? Virginia maybe actually kind of knew what she was doing?

"Show me," he said.

Virginia sat up. Without looking at him, she walked out of the room, down the hall, and into the empty common room. She flicked off the lights. It was surprisingly dark— every day the sun set a little earlier than it had the day before.

"I turn the lights out in case someone sees through the window."

"Smart," Benny said, hoping he sounded impressed but not too impressed. He was embarrassed for being so condescending earlier, but he didn't want to go overboard sucking up to her to make up for it.

In the darkness he watched Virginia hoist herself up on the countertop, and then crawl onto the refrigerator.

Not the ceiling tiles, please not the ceiling tiles, Benny thought, starting to lose faith again. Ceiling tiles were pretty much the most obvious hiding place ever to be discovered by man.

"It's disgusting up here," Virginia was saying. "It's like twenty years of grime." Benny could see her dim outline reaching behind the refrigerator. "For a while I kept it in my pocket," she whispered. "But that seemed dumb. The cables back here are covered in duct tape, so I just picked a spot."

Benny heard tape ripping, and Virginia passed him the

drive. Her hand felt greasy and dirty, and the drive was cold in her palm.

"That's a great spot," he said. "Really."

"Do I get a merit badge?" Virginia asked. He couldn't see her face, so he couldn't tell if she was trying to make him feel bad, or if she was just joking. "Do you want to keep it at your house?"

"No," Benny said. "Keep it here. They might search me next."

Then there were footsteps coming up the walk toward the Boarders. "Put it back, put it back," Benny said quickly.

Virginia scrambled around, then hopped from the refrigerator with a thud. Just then the lights flicked on. Benny whirled around. Zaire Bollo was standing in the doorway.

"Well. Hello." She was carrying a Whole Foods bag and smirking, like she was certain she'd just caught them making out in the dark.

"Hi, Zaire," Virginia said, walking to the sink to wash her hands. She glanced at Benny as if to say, *Say something.*

"Uh . . . you have a car?" he asked.

"Hm?" Zaire said, still standing in the doorway. Then she looked down at her shopping bag. "Oh no. I begged Mrs. Morehouse to drive me."

Virginia whispered, "Is she here?"

"No, she went home, thank *God.*"

Benny didn't know exactly what the deal was with Mrs. Morehouse, except that she was universally loathed.

"Her car smelled like unwashed hair," Zaire was saying. "And would you believe she hit me up for petrol? God. But I just can't live without mozzarella di bufala. Here, try some." Zaire thrust a pinch of white cheese in Benny's face. He ate it.

"Awesome," he said. *Awesome?* he thought, horrified. *Since when do I say "awesome"?*

Virginia burst out laughing. "Mozzarella di bufala is the awesomest!" She was laughing so hard she grabbed the counter, evidently to keep from falling over. Benny stared at the floor. Why did she have to make everything so awkward?

Virginia stopped laughing eventually, and Benny caught her eyeing Zaire's food.

"Want one?" Zaire offered, holding up a beautiful-looking tomato. "It's heirloom."

Virginia considered it. She was obviously hungry, but Benny noticed her chin was tilted slightly away from Zaire, exerting a tiny physical resistance. *Virginia doesn't like her,* Benny realized.

"Don't ruin your appetite," he said, lightly brushing Virginia's hand away from the tomato. "We're going out, remember?"

Virginia looked at him. "We are?"

"Yeah, come on."

"Mom picking you up?" Zaire asked, still smirking as she began slicing the tomato.

Neither of them answered. Benny walked out the door, and Virginia followed him. Outside, the sky was violet and the air was cool and brisk. They were ambling. Virginia seemed to be waiting for him to say something.

"We're not really going out," Virginia said finally, with just the smallest trace of a question left in her voice.

Benny shrugged awkwardly. "Uh, well . . ."

"Not that I *care*. It's just that I'm starving. I have to organize my life, you know? I have to know whether I'm going out, or whether I have to make my own plans."

"I guess . . . make your own plans."

"Yeah, I mean, that's what I figured."

The cafeteria, 7:15 p.m.

They ended up at the cafeteria. Virginia didn't ask if Benny wanted to go in; she just swiped her meal card twice and said, "You can eat on my tab." He'd only walked her there to be polite, but now he'd missed his chance to say he was going home. He could imagine the scene: Rodrigo having his bourbon, Mr. Flax saying exciting, all-new words, Nana cooking a hot, delicious chicken pot pie in their bright, nice-smelling house. Meanwhile the cafeteria felt dank and depressing. The lighting clearly hadn't been designed for use after dark—the ceiling lamps were weak and greenish without the sun to supplement them. The heat lamps buzzed over neglected-looking food.

They must always buzz like that, Benny realized, except

during the day the sound was smothered by the genial loudness of three hundred students. It was creepy—six hours ago this building had felt like a completely different place. Benny believed in the concreteness and the intransigence of human character—the idea that, fundamentally, people never changed. People were who they were, day in, day out, sunrise, sunset, forever. But places weren't like that. They morphed and transformed based on the people and light inside them—or lack of people and lack of light.

The resident kids were scattered across the room at different tables, not many talking to one another. The boarders were cooped up so much, Benny figured they were sick of one another at this point. He and Virginia sat near the windows, which reflected dingy images of themselves as the sky outside turned black. They ate tacos and drank milk. Benny checked the nutrition facts on the milk carton. Only twelve grams of sugar.

"I didn't even tell you the weirdest thing he did," Virginia said. Benny knew she was talking about the detective.

"What?"

"He had this legal document that he waved in my face, and it had my name on it, but he wouldn't let me read it. Is that, like, some interrogation tactic?"

"Um . . ." Benny looked from Virginia to his tray and back to Virginia. Her face was blank. Was this a trick? Was she interrogating *him*? Did she know, somehow, that he'd read her file? "They'll do anything to throw you off," he said finally.

"Huh." Virginia went back to her dinner.

Benny kept glancing at her, expecting her to suddenly seem mysterious or something. But she was just Virginia as usual, scarfing food, pointing at people and talking about them way too loudly, her face a total open book. Was it possible she didn't even know about the restraining order? Either she didn't know, or she was a more masterful faker than Benny could have ever predicted.

He wished he could just ask her about it, but he knew he couldn't. First, he couldn't explain how he knew about the restraining order without admitting that he'd sleazily invaded her privacy and investigated her behind her back. Second, he didn't want to force Virginia to discuss what was probably a very personal and embarrassing matter. To Benny, friendship meant allowing your friends to maintain their dignity even when you knew weird shit about them.

Friendship? The word stuck out in his mind. Were he and Virginia *friends?* They were supposed to be colleagues. Maybe friendship was inevitable when you hung out with someone so much. Benny didn't know. He'd never been great at keeping friends. To him, it always ended up feeling like *work*—the conversations, the commitment to another person's interests and feelings—eventually it became draining. It didn't feel that way with Virginia, though. She was weirdly easy to be around. But he didn't want being friends to screw up their work relationship.

"Look at Gottfried," Virginia said, pointing. He was asleep at a table across the room, his hair falling into his taco.

"Have you noticed how wherever we are, he is?" Benny asked in a low voice he hoped didn't carry.

"Not really . . . ," Virginia said. "But I guess it always feels like that in the Boarders. People are always in your face."

"The football field Saturday morning. The Sapphire Lounge last night . . ."

"He wasn't at the game on Friday, though," Virginia pointed out. "If he were there, I would have noticed."

"Unless he was hiding," Benny said, remembering the cigarette butts he'd found under the bleachers. "Do you know what brand of cigarettes he smokes?"

"No . . . They come in a blue box. Or green maybe."

"Do you think he imports them from Germany?"

"No, he just goes to gas stations."

"Parliaments maybe? Newports?"

"I don't know. I just know Camels have the camel, so not those." Virginia shoved another taco into her mouth. Then she swallowed a huge bite and asked, "What do you think'll happen to Gerard?"

Benny shrugged. "He's not our responsibility. But I hope this whole thing has proven my point about sharing information. Imbeciles like Gerard can't handle themselves. The fewer people whose idiocy we have to deal with, the better."

Virginia nodded, dumping hot sauce on a third taco.

"You did fine today. It would have been better if you hadn't dropped my note, but all circumstances considered, you did fine."

"Fank woo," she said with her mouth full.

Benny leaned back in his chair and examined Gottfried across the room. He had moved in his sleep, his face smushed into a taco like it was a pillow. Benny would never understand the way some people lived. If he were caught sleeping in a taco, he would probably die of shame. But Gottfried just didn't care. Sleepy? Go ahead, rest yourself upon this comfy taco. Nighty-night!

Next to him, Virginia wasn't that much better. Her table manners were atrocious, and she was scarfing her food like one of the orphans from *Oliver!* Maybe it was the lack of adult supervision. The boarders had all gotten used to the idea that no one was watching.

I'm watching, Benny thought. But he knew that, to most people, he didn't count.

The road, 8:00 p.m.

It was dark now. Their steps crunched along the gravel road toward the Boarders. Gottfried's hand kept brushing against hers, holding it for a second, then dropping it. *What is wrong with him?* Virginia thought. It was like he could barely stand. He was shuffling along, leaning against her occasionally, like he was still drunk from last night. If Virginia hadn't bothered to wake him up and help him home, he probably would have slept all night in a plate of tacos.

"Walk straight, Gottfried," she said, steadying him with her arm.

"I am so tired," he moaned. "And so sad."

"Aw, there's no reason to be sad, Gottfried," Virginia said.

"But I'll never see that woman again. The beautiful woman in cheetah skin. I lost her phone number!"

"Oh, I have it," Virginia said, fishing in her pocket. "You dropped it last night in the common room."

Gottfried's face lit up instantly. "Oh, *danke!*"

He kissed the paper, and then kissed Virginia's cheek. Virginia stumbled a bit, surprised, and Gottfried's lips slid across her face and sort of landed in her hair. Virginia looked around in case anyone was watching. The way Gottfried was acting, it would seem like they were together or something. Which maybe wasn't the worst thing, considering. Gottfried was by far the most exotic guy in school. But he was too handsome, in Virginia's opinion. People would think she was superficial if it seemed like she liked him.

THWUMP!

Gottfried tipped forward. Virginia half fell trying to catch him. He was holding his head, like something had hit him. Then Virginia saw it rolling in front of their feet: a half-deflated football.

"Hey! Who's there?" Virginia shouted, whirling around. "Who just threw that?"

"Aww . . . ," Gottfried groaned, holding his head.

"Shhh!" Virginia said. "Listen."

She heard someone running in the woods. Virginia trained her ears for a second, then bolted into the trees. Branches scratched her arms as she flew between their black silhouettes. Within moments she'd passed the reach of the streetlamp. The darkness was sudden, and Virginia felt swallowed by it. Almost immediately she had to stop running. She couldn't see anything, and she couldn't hear anything either, not over the sound of her own pounding feet.

"Hey!" she shouted.

They were still running, whoever it was. Virginia could hear leaves crunching, but only faintly. They were far ahead of her now. Then the sounds stopped; they were gone. Or hiding. What was she supposed to do, stand there all night and wait for them to come out? She sighed and started trudging back.

"Gottfried?" she called, stepping out of the trees. She looked around. The street was empty; apparently Gottfried was gone too. The puckered football lay in an orange circle of lamplight. Virginia went over and picked it up. It was old—the leather was hard and misshapen. She gave the ball a throw. It bombed to the ground with zero spiral, landing about a foot from where she'd aimed. She stared at it, feeling weirdly certain it had been meant for her head.

The Boarders, 2:00 a.m.

This is the last time, Zaire told herself. *I swear to God this is the last time.*

She sat up on her bed and started putting on her slippers. She knew Gottfried was awake. She'd heard the soft squeak of his desk chair in the room above. Gottfried was an insomniac. It was different from what Zaire was, which was a night owl. Night owls stay up late because it's what feels natural to them. Insomniacs do it because they can't control the way their brains switch off and on.

She slipped silently up the stairs and knocked softly on Gottfried's door.

"*Ja?* Come in."

He always let her in. A lot of guys wouldn't do that with their exes. Or whatever she and Gottfried were. There was an unspoken rule among the boarders: Never date other boarders. And now Zaire knew why—because when you break up, there's no escape. Regular kids got to go home at the end of the day, but at the Boarders all they went home to was each other. And emptiness. Zaire used to like the quiet. It helped her study, and since studying was her main focus in life, she had no reason to complain. But now the quiet made her insane, because it meant she could hear every move Gottfried made.

Zaire pushed the door open. Gottfried was at his desk, half-hunched over a drawing pad. There was a bowl of canned pineapple chunks with a blob of mayonnaise on them. Gottfried would eat anything, like seriously anything. A week-old sandwich with mold on it, or an entire barrel of cheese puffs. He even drank Tab, which Zaire had only ever seen old-lady teachers drink.

"Can't you sleep?" she asked him.

He shook his head.

"Do you want us to . . . ," she started awkwardly, "you know . . ."

Gottfried shrugged good-naturedly. "*Ja*, sure . . . I mean if you want to; if you are okay wiss it. . . ." He pushed back from the desk, the chair's wheels bumping on the uneven wood floor. He arched his back a little, stretching. His knees spread open. Zaire's eyes ran hungrily up and down the long, lean shape of his legs. Gottfried was the only boy in school who wore jeans. All the other guys wore khakis and corduroys.

Zaire sat on the bed across from him. "Are you relaxed?"

"No," Gottfried said. "People are all driving me crazy today."

"God, me too," Zaire said, thrilled. Gottfried usually liked everyone—it had been the main point of conflict in their short-lived relationship. Zaire had wanted to spend all their time making out in his room and planning for the day they'd escape this clubby preppy shit-hole and return to Europe where they both belonged. But the more they were together, the more it became evident that Gottfried actually *liked* it here. He liked playing lacrosse and going to dances and eating hot dogs. He liked American cigarettes and American movies and American girls. He'd actually said that when they were breaking up, unbelievably—that he liked American girls.

"American girls?" Zaire had said back, appalled. What the hell did that mean? What was so great about American girls?

"Not American girls . . ." Gottfried had tried to explain. "You know . . . happy girls."

Happy girls? American girls weren't *happy*; they were *fake*. Corny Davenport wasn't *happy*; she was a pathological ditz who needed everyone to love her. Virginia Leeds wasn't *happy*; she was an insecure attention whore who had no life. American girls were vapid and asinine and fatuous, especially the ones at Winship. No Winship girl could come up with three synonyms for "stupid" that quickly, if they could at all.

"You're being very insulting," she'd said to him, her voice shaking. At which point Gottfried had apologized and began aggressively complimenting her to make up for it, saying she was beautiful and smart and that her name "rolled off the tongue very pleasing." And after that the conversation became such a humiliating nightmare that Zaire could hardly bear to remember it. Zaire demanding to know why, if she was so beautiful and smart, he didn't want to be with her. Gottfried awkwardly insisting that he didn't know; he just didn't want to be her boyfriend anymore. The relationship had only lasted a month. Zaire had expected dating Gottfried to be challenging—he was aloof and inarticulate and strange and hard to read—but she hadn't expected to fail quite so miserably.

That had been six months ago, and now they were supposedly friends. But Zaire was still in love with him. It was so stupid. She hated herself for it. And her self-hatred made it even harder to get over him. If only she could siphon some of that love back to herself, recover a bit of her self-esteem. Gottfried didn't need her love; he'd certainly made that clear. But there was something else he needed, and she was the only one who could give it to him. Only he wasn't aware of the price he was paying for it.

"Just close your eyes," she breathed. "Let me help us both relax."

2:10 a.m.

Virginia awoke with a jolt and trained her ears.

Whoooo . . . Shhhwhooooo . . .

It was the ghost.

During the day it was easy to joke about the ghost. *Ha-ha, the Boarders is haunted! Spooooooky!* But at night it wasn't funny anymore. It was a low, soft whistle that came from above their heads, always after the sun went down.

Virginia had tried to get Benny to investigate it, but it

was hard to get him interested. He hadn't experienced its eerie crooning waking him up in the middle of the night, the way its signal traveled through the dead dorm like an invitation. *Come out, come out.* If he could hear it now, he wouldn't be so dismissive.

"Why don't you just follow the sound and find out what it is?" That was always Benny's impatient suggestion, like it was the simplest thing in the world, and Virginia was a moron for not thinking of it herself. She *had* thought of it herself. But every time it happened, she would lie in bed, frozen with dread, telling herself, *In ten seconds I'll get up. Ten . . . nine . . . eight . . .* Then, *In twenty seconds I'll get up. Twenty . . . nineteen . . . eighteen . . .* At a certain point the ghostly noise would just stop, as if summoned back into its nocturnal realm. And only at that point would Virginia's courage uselessly reappear. She'd berate herself for being such a stupid coward and vow that next time she heard it, she'd get up and face it once and for all.

What made this night different from the others, Virginia didn't know. Maybe it was the way she'd jolted awake. Usually the sound woke her gently, like soft fingers pulling her from a dream. But this time, as soon as her eyes were open, her feet were on the floor and she was darting across the room to fling open the door, no countdowns or psyching herself out.

Whssshooooooooo . . .

Virginia looked up at the ceiling. Her eyes adjusted to

the darkness, and she found the stairs leading up to the boys' hall. She took them two at a time, on silent feet, then listened at the top of the landing.

Wwwwwhoooooo . . .

She crept out into the boys' hall. It was dark except for one small bit of light coming from a cracked-open door. She immediately knew whose room it was. Everyone kept a mental map of the rooms, particularly who lived above who. It was a weirdly intimate relationship, sharing the same vertical space with someone. You knew when they were out and when they were in; you heard their footsteps; you heard their phones ringing. If you got stuck with one of the younger kids above you, sometimes you'd hear them crying. The upper schoolers were supposed to reach out and mother the younger kids, but no one ever bothered. Virginia couldn't remember anyone bothering when she first came. You either learned to keep your misery inside, or you begged your parents to bring you home and no one ever saw you or thought of you again.

Virginia was lucky, because the room above her was empty. The one across from it, above Zaire, was Gottfried's. She stepped toward the light, slowly inching her way down through the darkness so the ancient floorboards wouldn't creak. She flattened herself against the dark wall and tilted her head. The door hung open a crack, just enough to see a slice of Gottfried's room.

Wssshhoooooo . . .

Zaire and Gottfried were staring at each other. Gottfried was at the edge of the unmade bed, Zaire facing him in his desk chair. In her hands she held an old-fashioned Coke bottle, and she was blowing across its lip, making a hollow, ghostly whistle.

It's Zaire! Virginia thought, partly relieved and partly annoyed. What was she doing, blowing in a Coke bottle at two in the morning? And why did she do it all the time? Didn't she know it creeped everyone out?

Zaire set the bottle down on the desk. "Are you relaxed?" she asked.

Gottfried sighed contentedly and nodded.

Then Zaire stood up and lifted her silky nightgown over her head. She posed in front of Gottfried, naked except for a pair of expensive-looking underwear. The lamplight reflected off the curves of her brown breasts with an unnatural sheen. Shimmery body lotion, Virginia decided. Her nipples were so dark they were almost black, sitting haughtily high on each plump mound. Virginia had seen so many boobs lately she thought she was immune to their allure. But Zaire's were incredible, she had to admit. And obviously Zaire knew it.

Virginia watched as Zaire straddled Gottfried on the bed and kissed his pale neck. Gottfried's hands reached for her ass, and his fingers dug into their round cheeks. Soon they were making out really intensely, Gottfried fully clothed and Zaire almost naked.

He shouldn't take advantage of her like that, Virginia thought. Maybe they were trying some post-breakup friends-with-benefits thing, but who did Zaire think she was kidding? Herself? She obviously still liked him, and if she kept throwing herself at him, she'd just drag the whole thing out. Maybe if she'd been the one to dump him instead of the other way around, they could still hook up without it being a disaster. But everyone knew Zaire had pressured him into the relationship in the first place.

They flopped over Gottfried's bed and were rolling around in the tangled sheets. Gottfried's hands pawed Zaire's smooth body, and Virginia could hear their soft moans. She held her breath, feeling weirdly transfixed. Gottfried was such a weirdo and a goofball, but all of a sudden he seemed brutally sexy. Maybe even the biggest goober in the world would seem sexy if you stuck a naked, shimmering, big-boobed girl on top of him, Virginia decided.

Zaire squirmed beneath Gottfried to wrap her legs around him, and in doing so, they rolled out of Virginia's view. She craned her neck a little but couldn't see them without stepping perilously close to the light and possibly exposing herself. She knew she'd better leave and was embarrassed to realize that if her view hadn't been blocked, she probably would have stood there endlessly like a peeping blob, watching until they'd moved way past making out. It made her shudder, realizing how easy it was to become a pervert if you didn't stop yourself in time.

Friday
Backstage of the assembly hall, 11:30 a.m.

A huge neon-pink banner hung above the stage: GATORADE PRESENTS: HONORING OUR CHEERLEADERS, A DAY OF SPIRIT AND GRATITUDE.

Backstage, Gerard did a few lunges to warm up. Then he flexed his biceps and checked them out for the hundredth time. *Not bad!* he thought, nodding to himself. The thing people didn't realize about Gerard was that he actually had a pretty great body. Maybe he wasn't as ripped as some of the guys at Winship, but he was lean and toned and had nice arm muscles from lugging fifty-pound water jugs all the time. Unfortunately, the only person who ever noticed was his mother, who always squealed, "Don't crush your poor mama with those big manly muscles!" whenever they hugged.

But today everyone was going to notice. Gerard was wearing a skintight black shirt with the buttons undone halfway down his chest and a pair of equally tight black high-waisted jeans. His hair had been carefully disheveled and then glued in place with his dad's pomade. The look verged on being seriously queer, Gerard knew, but he was confident he had the masculine prowess to pull it off. And besides, it was for Brittany. He'd have dressed like a clown or a transvestite or Curious George if he thought it would impress her.

Gerard was proud to say he knew Brittany's favorite movie, which was *Dirty Dancing*. He felt this knowledge was very intimate, and wasn't aware that it was true for half the girls in America. Nor was he aware that Brittany had about five hundred "favorite" movies, which changed depending on whatever movie anyone happened to be talking about at the time. "That's my *favorite* movie!" she gushed indiscriminately. But Gerard had seized upon this nugget of *Dirty Dancing*, and in his mind Brittany's love for it had ballooned into obsession. Brittany was *obsessed* with *Dirty Dancing*! Patrick Swayze was her god!

Which was why he was standing backstage in an uncomfortably tight Patrick Swayze outfit, preparing to perform a feverishly practiced solo dance to "The Time of My Life" in front of the whole school. It was all in honor of Brittany Montague, the unfallen mascot of beauty and innocence and joy.

Gerard knew he had to do something dramatic to erase the image in everyone's minds of him being hauled away in handcuffs, all because that Detective Douche Bag was a power-tripping asshole. Just remembering it filled Gerard with fresh humiliation. Everyone probably thought he had something to do with Mr. Choi's perverted demise now, when really he'd just been defending the cheerleaders' honor. "Hot little numbers" that macho dickhead detective had called them. Hot little numbers! Gerard had wanted to punch his big, smug chin, and had in fact tried to but just ended up getting himself thrown in jail for five hours. Which, besides being a total indignity, showed that this detective had no idea what the fuck he was doing. Arresting *Gerard*? Gerard, lover and respecter of all cheerleaders? Organizer of the protest against perverts? Devoted provider of strawberry-kiwi Gatorade? It was like the police department had especially chosen their biggest moron to put on the case.

Let it go, Gerard told himself, taking a deep breath to clear his head. He bounced on his toes to loosen up, and then admired his biceps again. Today wasn't about stupid detectives or perverted, dead band teachers. It was about Brittany. It was about joy and spirit and honor. It was about having the time of their lives.

The assembly hall, noon

The cheerleaders scurried around the assembly hall, happily passing out ice-cold bottles of strawberry-kiwi Gatorade to anyone who wanted one. Everyone was talking excitedly as they filled the hall, the pink bottles popping brightly against the blue of the cheerleaders' uniforms. The "Cheerleader

Survival" story had made national news, and Gatorade had donated a thousand bottles of Brittany's favorite flavor to the school, plus a ton of money to restore the old bridge and build safer rails. It was easier to fix the bridge than to fix the real problem, which was that sexual predators looked the same as everyone else and hid in plain sight.

Benny and Virginia sat in the front row. Benny was looking at his Gatorade, deciding whether to open it. He disliked commercialism, but a free drink was a free drink. Virginia was already gulping hers down, like someone might steal it if she didn't drink it immediately. She swallowed loudly and said, "Hey, guess what? I solved the mystery of the ghost."

"What ghost?" Benny said.

"The *Boarders* ghost. I told you it wasn't the wind. It's Zaire Bollo blowing on a Coke bottle. I think she and Gottfried have, like, a sex ritual they do."

Benny looked at her. Was the Coke bottle related to the sex ritual, or was she just making a random comment? Virginia knew so much crap about everybody and lacked the ability to discern what was relevant.

"So the next time I say I have a mystery, will you believe me?"

"Sure," Benny said, resisting the urge to roll his eyes.

The lights dimmed, and everyone clapped excitedly. Benny's clapping was spiritless and mechanical. You knew what to expect at these things—a succession of inane skits full of inside jokes that only the cheerleaders and jocks could appreciate or understand. Then, invariably, an act where the football players dressed up like cheerleaders and performed an inept dance routine, which the cheerleaders would find hilarious despite the fact that the guys were making a mockery of their sport.

"Welcome to this year's spirit show!" the principal boomed into the microphone. "We need spirit now more than ever. So without further ado, let's get started with a Wildcat roar!"

The crowd erupted in a mighty roar that filled the hall and made Benny want to cover his ears. School spirit was a mystery to him. The idea was that because they had all been randomly born, and then, due to circumstances beyond their control, happened to attend a particular school, they were better than everyone else?

"Our first act has requested the presence of our cheer captains, Angie and Corny, and of course our favorite Wildcat, Brittany!" The principal gestured to three chairs that had been arranged on the otherwise empty stage. The crowd murmured as Angie, Corny, and Brittany stood up and alighted upon the stage, looking at one another with smiles and shrugs, pretending to be surprised. *Who, us?*

Then the lights dimmed even further. There was a crackle as the sound system turned on. Then, way too loud:

"NOW I'VE . . . HAD . . . THE TIME OF MY LIIIIIIFE . . ."

Everyone was groaning and covering their ears, even Corny, Brittany, and Angie.

A black-clad figure leaped passionately onto the stage. He landed in front of the girls with a graceless thump.

"Oh my God," Virginia yelled over the song. "Is that Gerard?"

"Turn it down!" someone was screaming. "Turn it down!"

The song abruptly stopped. Gerard whirled around, looking confused. The girls looked at one another, obviously trying not to laugh.

"Now I've . . . had . . . the time of my liiiiiife . . ." The song began again, this time at a normal volume. Gerard raced backstage and then leaped out again, trying to re-create his entrance.

Virginia covered her face with her hands. She was laughing hysterically. Benny wished he could laugh, but all he could do was sit there grimacing as Gerard danced earnestly across the stage. His moves weren't even bad—they were obviously carefully choreographed and executed with an impressive degree of coordination. But the whole thing was just . . . painful.

Corny, Brittany, and Angie were avoiding one another's eyes, obviously afraid they'd burst out laughing if they looked at one another. There seemed to be an understanding among the cheerleaders, Benny had long observed, that Gerard was to be patiently humored and never made to feel bad about himself for being a dopey water boy and not a football star. But this was beyond dopey. This was beyond Gerard embarrassing himself; he was embarrassing the girls now too. Benny could see it in their strained, frozen smiles. Occasionally Gerard would dance *at* them, making intense eye contact and gesturing wildly.

Some people love watching other people make fools of themselves. Virginia was like that. She was having the time of her life watching Gerard leap about like an idiot in front of the whole school. But Benny couldn't bear it—he lacked the ability to separate himself from the embarrassment of others. He was embarrassed *for* Gerard, and he felt it as acutely as if it were happening to himself.

"I've . . . had . . . the time of my liiiiiife!" It felt like the song would never end.

Then there was a small commotion, and someone tumbled onto the stage. It was Trevor Cheek, half-dressed. His pants were falling off, and he was waving his tie over his head like a lasso. Before anyone knew what was happening, he had plunked himself down on Brittany's lap.

Gerard was so engrossed in his choreography, he didn't even notice. He continued snapping his fingers and doing spins, while behind him Trevor Cheek began giving Brittany a full-on lap dance. Trevor was wiggling his butt in her face and rubbing his rock-hard abs and smooth pectoral muscles. Angie and Corny looked at Brittany, as if for a cue. Was this funny, or appalling?

Finally Brittany burst out laughing, like she couldn't

contain it another second. Angie and Corny copied her, and the crowd copied them, and soon the whole assembly hall was laughing uproariously. A grin spread across Gerard's face. He began dancing with even more intensity, clearly thinking the laughs were for him and that his audience was captivated.

Behind him, Trevor got up and removed his pants. He was now wearing nothing but tighty-whities, and from his seat in the front row Benny could make out the entire shape of his genitalia. Trevor switched from Brittany to Corny, who covered her eyes in mock horror as Trevor gyrated his crotch in her face.

Then, midspin, Gerard realized what was happening. In about a millisecond his expression went from buoyant to confused to utterly furious. Benny had never seen someone's face contort so dramatically so quickly. His cheeks turned instantly red, and the veins of his throat bulged.

"Get off! GET OFF!" he screamed at Trevor over the music.

Trevor wagged his crotch even faster and shouted back, "I'm trying, dude! I'm trying!"

Angie and Brittany were laughing so hard tears were streaming down their cheeks. Corny was leaning her face away from Trevor's crotch, laughing and giving the audience a look like, *Is this guy crazy or what?*

"I've . . . had . . . the time of my liiiiiife!"

Finally the principal climbed onto the stage and shooed

Trevor away, throwing his pants after him. Everyone cheered, though whether it was for the principal or for Trevor was unclear.

"I've . . . had . . . the time of my li—" The music cut off abruptly, and then it was the principal, three hysterical cheerleaders, and a furious Gerard left onstage. Gerard threw Brittany the most woeful, bitter look Benny had ever seen. He almost expected to hear Gerard shout, *You betrayed me!* But instead Gerard just stomped from the stage.

"Aw, Gerard, we're sorry!" Corny called after him. But then she looked at Brittany and Angie, and all three dissolved into giggles again.

"All right, all right, let's get back to the program," the principal said. "I'll see you in my office, Trevor."

Everyone cheered loudly again. Even Virginia was cheering. Benny looked at her, feeling annoyed but also slightly envious. In a way, it must be nice to get swept up in things, to take a break from observing and assessing and actually participate in the moment. It was the difference between Being There and really just *being there.*

12:35 p.m.

It was about twenty minutes and three skits later before everyone fully calmed down. And occasionally someone would start giggling again, and you'd know they were thinking about Gerard's impotent rage and Trevor thrusting his tighty-whities in Corny's face, which would set off another round of snickering all around. Virginia had to take deep breaths continuously to keep from laughing every five seconds. Trevor was a disgusting idiot, of course, but it was still the funniest thing to ever happen in the history of high school.

"Our next act will also require some cheerleader volunteers," the principal was saying into the microphone. "About ten, you say?"

Zaire Bollo appeared onstage next to him.

"Let's get the whole squad up here," she said. "I promise I won't give you a lap dance! Unless it's a special request."

People barely laughed. Zaire could be clever, but she didn't have a reputation for being a jokester. She wasn't like Penelope Blailock, who could say the dumbest thing, and people would laugh hysterically because she was the established class clown since sixth grade. Reputations were carved in stone—Virginia knew this better than anyone. And Zaire's reputation wasn't for being funny; it was for being stuck-up and snotty and caring too much about grades. Zaire could say the funniest joke in the world, and people would just stare at her like she wasn't speaking English.

The cheerleaders filed onto the stage, smiling and giving one another little shrugs like, *Go with the flow, I guess.* Zaire wasn't one of "their" people. In fact, she was probably the last person you'd expect to find doing a skit for the spirit show, except for maybe Benny or that little goth ninth grader everyone made fun of.

Benny gave Virginia a look, like, *What's Zaire up to?* The look gave Virginia an unexpected feeling of pride. Benny was usually so closed-off and never said what he was thinking unless she specifically asked him. And here he was, giving her *looks*! *Communicating* with her, totally unbidden!

"Let's do a little experiment," Zaire was saying softly into the microphone. "Let's channel our Wildcat energy. Let's bring all our Wildcat energy together into a ball as big and bright as the sun. Bring your energy together. Relax and let your energy out. . . . Breath in, and out. In . . . and out . . ."

The cheerleaders looked at one another, as if consulting their hive mind to determine whether they were going to do this or not.

"Breathe with me," Zaire said firmly but gently. "Brittany, close your eyes and breathe. In . . . out . . ."

Everyone looked at Brittany to see if she would do it. Brittany narrowed her bright eyes at Zaire with a hint of suspicion, then she closed them. Her chest rose and fell as she breathed in and out. Within seconds all the other girls had followed. The audience was silent. There was a chill in the air, Virginia felt. And an itchiness on the part of the football players to go save their women from whatever creepy New Age thing Zaire was doing to them.

"Feel that energy seeping out of you, that Wildcat energy. Breathe in and out. . . . You're so relaxed. All that Wildcat energy is in a ball above our heads, and you're safe and relaxed and you want to go to sleep."

Virginia watched as some of the cheerleaders started swaying a bit, their heads lolling.

"When I count to five, go ahead and lie down. Lie down and take a nap. Don't worry if you touch someone. Just go to sleep like a heap of kittens. One . . . two . . . three . . . four . . . *five.*"

Instantly the entire squad dropped to the floor in a pile of blue-and-white skirts and flowing hair. In the audience, everyone started murmuring.

"Are they faking?" Virginia whispered to Benny. But Benny didn't answer. He was staring at Zaire, looking completely rapt.

"Sshhhhh . . . ," Zaire whispered into the microphone. "They're sleeping."

Something about Zaire's voice made Virginia shiver. She felt goose bumps go down her arms.

"Now, when you wake up, you won't be cheerleaders anymore. You'll be witches. You'll be evil witches from hell. When I count to five, you'll wake up and stand up, and you won't be cheerleaders anymore. One . . . two . . . three . . . four . . . *five.*"

Instantly all the girls opened their eyes and got to their feet. Virginia searched their faces. They looked strange. None of them were smiling.

"Can I talk to you, Angie?" Zaire asked, beckoning her with a finger. "I want to ask you a question."

Angie came forward. Her face was mean and blank.

"Angie, what's your favorite after-school activity?" Zaire asked.

"Eating rats," Angie said. It might have been funny, but her voice was so cold and rough. Nobody laughed.

"Interesting," Zaire said. "And if someone makes you mad, what do you do about it?"

"I put a curse on them until they die."

Someone behind Virginia whispered, "She's faking. She's so faking."

Zaire said into the microphone, "Thanks, Angie. Can I talk to Brittany now?"

Angie skulked back into the group of cheerleaders, swapping places with her twin. Their faces were identical masks of stony hate. The sight was deeply unsettling, but Virginia couldn't look away.

"Hi, Brittany," Zaire said. "Can I ask you a question?"

Brittany nodded lifelessly.

"Who do you love more, Jesus or Satan?"

"Satan."

The uproar was instantaneous. Everyone started talking and booing and yelling. Someone shouted "bitch" at Zaire, and someone else was yelling, "This isn't right! This isn't right!" And it *wasn't* right, Virginia knew. Brittany was the president of Winship's FCA chapter. She said "Oh my gosh" instead of taking the Lord's name in vain. She passed out WWJD bracelets every year on her and Angie's birthday. She would *never* say she loved Satan more than Jesus, not even as a joke.

The principal was on the stage in seconds. "That's enough," Virginia could hear him saying. "That's quite enough."

Zaire stared up at him defiantly.

"Unhypnotize them," the principal hissed. *"Now."* Virginia could barely hear him above the cacophony all around her. "She didn't mean it, Jesus!" someone shouted.

"When I snap my fingers, you'll be your mindless, vapid selves again," Zaire said flatly. Then she snapped her fingers. The microphone dropped from her hand with a deafening boom. She left the stage as the sound echoed off the walls. The cheerleaders were confused and glazed looking. They eyed one another like bewildered strangers.

"I've seen her do that before," Benny said.

"Hm?" It was so loud Virginia could barely hear.

"I've seen her do that before. I've seen her do it to people who didn't even know she was there." And then, without explaining himself, Benny got up and began squeezing his way out of the crowd.

Am I supposed to follow him? Virginia thought, annoyed. Not that she didn't know the answer. She was always supposed to follow him.

The library, 2:15 p.m.

Benny's head was pounding, the revelation pulsing like a heartbeat: *It was her, it was her, it was her.* It was her. It was Zaire Bollo, the girl you'd least expect to find at the center of anything related to their school. She was always at Winship's outermost edge, making everyone feel awkward with her pointedly foreign attitude. But it was her on the bridge in the video, and Brittany was the person she was trying to kill.

Benny wasn't surprised that someone like Zaire was capable of murder. She seemed to enjoy making people uncomfortable. She never relaxed the act; everyone, at all times, needed to understand that she didn't belong at Winship, that the entire school was beneath her. The spectacle with the mascot made sense. Zaire hated Winship and made no secret of her contempt for the distinctly American pageant of football and cheerleaders. What better way to exhibit her hatred than to literally kill the mascot? To drown the very embodiment of school spirit?

But it hadn't worked. Brittany wasn't in the suit that night; it was Choi. So rather than crushing Winship's spirit, Zaire's thwarted murder attempt had actually made Winship a better, safer place. The irony was incredible. *Zaire must be seething,* Benny thought. He felt agitated. Would she try to kill Brittany again? What exactly had been her plan? Was she hypnotizing people right and left? And how did that actually work? This was what the library was for: It was time to think. It was time to read. Virginia was going to freak out. Benny could just imagine her hyper reaction, and he didn't want to deal with it. He didn't want to face her barrage of questions until he had some actual answers. Probably his least favorite thing to say in the entire English language was "I don't know."

Across the heavy wood table Virginia couldn't even see Benny's face anymore. It was obscured by a huge stack of books with titles like *Mesmerism in History* and *Hypnotism in the Twentieth Century*. Benny was tearing through them one by one. This was the really boring part of Mystery Club, watching him speed-read like a robot in total silence. It was pointless to try to help him, Virginia knew. He'd let her do some research just to keep her busy, but then he'd reread everything himself to make sure she hadn't missed anything. He hadn't even bothered to explain what they were researching. Apparently Virginia was expected to read Benny's mind.

"You know, torture is a form of hypnotism," Benny announced with the authority of an expert and not someone who had just read it in a book five seconds ago. "Fundamentally, hypnosis is the act of manipulating the patterns of the mind to induce a state of highly suggestible consciousness. The same effect can be achieved with violence. You can torture someone into doing something they would never normally do."

He flipped through the pages. "It's amazing that hypnotism isn't illegal. It's amazing that its power is mostly used for, like, entertaining people at birthday parties."

Virginia wasn't paying attention. "Look at Margaret over there."

One of the cheerleaders, Margaret Inman, was leaning against the wall, holding an SAT practice book upside down, reading in a daze.

"These words sure look funny!" Virginia said in a ditzy voice.

Benny looked back at his books. "She does it to people who annoy her."

"Who, Margaret?"

"Zaire. She messes with people. I've seen her do it to Winn Davis twice. I just didn't realize it at the time. Winn didn't even know she was there."

"I didn't know you could hypnotize people from afar," Virginia said.

"Well, you can't. But what you can do is set up a signal in their minds that activates later. . . ." He flipped through one of the books called *True Mesmerism*. "There's a documented case of a guy who was hypnotized to jump into traffic if he ever heard the words 'the end is nigh.' Three years later he did it. Some homeless guy said the words randomly, and the man jumped into traffic and died."

Virginia wasn't listening. "Oh my God, look at Margaret."

Benny looked. Margaret had curled up in a ball on the floor and was using the thick SAT book as a pillow.

Benny snapped his fingers. "Virginia. Concentrate. This is the most important part of our work."

"Sitting in the library?"

"Expanding our intelligence."

"About hypnotism? What does that have to do with anything?"

"Hi, guys. Study date?"

Benny slammed his book shut, and Virginia looked up. It was Zaire. All around them, people were glaring at her, including the librarian. Zaire seemed to feel it, but held her nose in the air like she didn't give a shit. Virginia gave her a long look. Zaire had always been a little out of orbit, socially, but now she was just *gone*. There was no rebounding from that spirit show stunt. Making sweet, cherished Brittany say she loved Satan? Virginia couldn't think of a better way to get 99 percent of the school to hate you forever.

"Y'all are so cute together," Zaire said.

Virginia rolled her eyes. It was so annoying when Zaire said "y'all" in her snotty half-British accent.

"I've read that book," Zaire said to Benny.

Benny pretended to adjust his glasses. "Did you find it edifying?"

"I did! On an introductory level, at least."

For a second Zaire and Benny just stared at each other. Virginia didn't like it. It made her feel left out.

"So how long have you been into hypnotism, Zaire?" Virginia asked loudly.

"Oh, not long," Zaire said breezily. "About a year."

"Actually, at our age a year is quite long," Benny said. "Six point six percent of your life so far."

"Wow, I never thought of it that way!" Zaire exclaimed, fluttering her eyelids.

Is she flirting with him? Virginia thought. *Slut.*

"So, going to the big game tonight?" Zaire asked, with a mocking "hoorah" gesture.

"Maybe," Benny said. "Are you?"

"Oh, definitely."

"You are known for your school spirit," Virginia said, wanting to be in on the banter.

"And for my halftime show," Zaire added, giving Benny a wink—an actual wink.

Virginia glanced at him. He was half smiling, like he wanted to laugh but was too astounded.

Zaire glanced around and said, "Well I better get out of here. I'm feeling a few daggers in my back, if you know what I mean."

You should feel a few in your front, too, Virginia thought. Without meaning to, she eyed Zaire's chest, suddenly remembering how she looked naked. The image was so vivid in her mind, it was like she could see right through Zaire's clothes.

"You know, Benny, there's a much better book if you're interested in hypnotism. It's called *Field Hypnosis.* Virginia, will you go get it? It's on the same shelf."

"Um, *excusez-moi?*" Virginia balked at her. As if she would ever be Zaire's errand girl in a million years.

Benny gave her a harsh look. *Do it,* his face clearly said.

Virginia stared at him, daring him to make her.

"I'm very interested in reading that book, *Virginia*, if you would be so kind as to get it for me," Benny spelled out between gritted teeth.

"Fine," she said, and stood up so quickly her chair almost fell over.

"And put this one back while you're at it," Zaire said, picking up *True Mesmerism*. Virginia took it and headed to the nonfiction area, stepping over the still-napping Margaret. Margaret's cheerleading skirt was flopped up so anyone could see her pink underwear and half a butt cheek. Virginia considered covering her up, but then decided she didn't care enough to bother.

The nonfiction area had a disorganized "psychology" shelf containing a mishmash of college-level psychiatry texts, a slew of memoirs about anorexia, and a bunch of trashy true-crime books. But Benny had managed to find a few books about hypnotism hidden among the weird miscellany. Virginia scanned the titles for *Field Hypnosis* but couldn't find it. *Where is this damn book?* She couldn't go back empty-handed like a clueless helper who couldn't carry out the simplest chore. Zaire would love it too much.

Then there was a weird sound, like someone being punched in the stomach. Virginia peered around the shelf. At first she couldn't find Benny and thought he was gone. Then she saw that he was bent over in his chair, his hands on his knees. He was throwing up on the floor.

"What the hell?" Virginia said loudly.

Zaire whipped around and saw her. All the sly calm was gone from Zaire's face—she looked panicked and freaked out. Virginia turned from her to Benny, who was vomiting again, his barely digested lunch splattering onto the already vomit-colored carpet.

"What's happening to him?" Virginia demanded.

"I don't . . . I don't . . . ," Zaire said, looking slightly green. Then she started walking away.

"Hey!" Virginia shouted. But Zaire ignored her and pushed through the library doors.

The matronly librarian had scurried to Benny's side and was asking if he was all right, averting her eyes from the mess on the floor.

"I'm so sorry," Benny breathed. "I'm so sorry."

"Don't you worry. It happens! Will you take him to the nurse, sweetheart?"

"Sure," Virginia said, wrinkling her nose at the smell. "Can you walk?"

Benny nodded. He was clearly mortified, but he let Virginia take his arm. They walked slowly into the hall. Behind them, the librarian was calling the janitor.

"I don't know what happened," Benny said weakly.

"Don't worry about it," Virginia said. "Talking to Zaire makes me want to throw up sometimes too."

She'd meant it as a joke, but somehow it didn't seem very funny.

The parking garage, 3:00 p.m.

Fuck you, Trevor.

Winn stabbed the bayonet into the tire, then yanked it out with a grunt. Air hissed from the hole, and Winn felt a little calmer. He clutched the rifle in his arms, almost hugging it. Like all old guns, it was heavier than it looked. The brass was rusted in a few places, but otherwise was in good shape, thanks to generations of immaculate care by the Davis family. It even had a name, Bory, after General P. G. T. Beauregard, who defended the Confederate capital of Richmond from Union assault. The rifle was more than a prized possession—sometimes Winn felt like it was his best friend. Supposedly Trevor Cheek was his best friend, but best friends didn't wag their dicks in your girlfriend's face, did they? Best friends helped you castrate people who wagged their dicks in your girlfriend's face. Or at least castrate their cars.

Winn looked over his shoulder to make sure the garage was still empty. Then he moved around Trevor's ugly Hummer and stabbed Bory's faithful bayonet through the back tires. With each stab, he imagined stabbing the life out of Trevor's swinging, puffed testicles. No guy's balls but his own should ever have come that close to Corny's innocent pink lips. And the way Corny had just laughed, tolerating it, even seeming to enjoy it! And there'd been nothing Winn could do but sit there and watch while they made a fool of him, knowing he'd be an even bigger fool if he walked out or tried to stop it.

Now, as he stabbed and stabbed, Winn felt a tension growing in his crotch. For some reason, whenever Winn got really angry, he also got kind of horny. It was weird, but he tried not to think about it in a deep way. He just climbed into the driver's seat of his own tasteful blue BMW, unzipped his pants, and fished out his penis. Then he hurriedly jerked off, his dick in one hand and his gun in the other.

Fuck you, Trevor.

Fuck you, Trevor.

FUCK YOU, TREVOR!

In about five seconds he was shooting off all over himself. All his angry, righteous energy immediately went seeping out of him. He suddenly felt exhausted and as apathetic as a slug. He rested his head on the steering wheel. He waited for his breathing to get back to normal. Then he gave Bory a once-over to make sure he hadn't gotten any cum on the barrel.

Poor old Bory, Winn thought. The indignities this gun had endured in his hands! This noble weapon that had once been used to defend the South and cut down Yankee aggressors, now reduced to slashing tires and witnessing masturbation. And yet, Bory never judged.

There was the sound of a car pulling into the garage.

Shit. Winn quickly zipped up his pants and wiped his sticky hand on the seat. He slumped low to avoid being seen. He held his breath as the car drove slowly past, looking for a spot. It was a junky Fiesta, not a car he recognized. Winn heard its engine cut off and decided to just stay low until whoever it was had left.

TAP TAP!

Winn was so startled he jumped in his seat. He turned and saw an Asian guy rapping on his window. The guy was no one Winn had ever seen before. He had long hair and was dressed in a black T-shirt and jeans. Maybe thirty years old? It was hard to tell with Asian guys. Slightly panicked but trying to keep cool, Winn grabbed his letter jacket to cover the wet splotch on his pants. Then he rolled down the window.

"Yes?" he said, praying that this random guy hadn't seen him slashing Trevor's tires.

"Hey, man, you know where the Boarders is at?" the guy leaned down and said. "It's, like, a building?"

"Yeah, I know where it is . . . ," Winn answered.

"Can you give me directions?"

Winn looked at him suspiciously. Strangers were pretty rare at Winship. The campus was cloistered, the student body intimately small, and the teachers and staff were trained to question anyone they didn't recognize. Sometimes alumni would show up and walk around nostalgically, but this guy didn't have that look. Besides, if he were an alum he would know where the Boarders was.

"My girlfriend goes here," the guy said, sensing Winn's hesitation. "Virginia? Do you know her?"

"Yeah, I know her," Winn said. Virginia Leeds had a

boyfriend? He was surprised he hadn't heard. Virginia was the type to shove it in everyone's faces whether they gave a damn or not. Winn found it annoying when girls dated outside of the school. It was demoralizing for the guys, and for school spirit in general.

"She told me to meet her there, but this school is a fuckin' labyrinth."

Winn gave him a long look. "It's up the hill," he said finally. "Sort of away from the other buildings. You go down a gravel road."

"Oh, I saw that road!" the guy exclaimed. "I couldn't tell if it was part of the school or not."

"Yep," Winn said. Then, suddenly, he wished he hadn't said anything. Who was this random guy invading their school with his beat-up Ford and his long hair and his *jeans*? This always happened to Winn after he ejaculated—his senses became temporarily clouded, and he'd do something stupid, like telling Corny he'd go to her cousin's baby shower, or forgetting to close the porn tabs on his dad's laptop.

The guy was nodding gratefully, his long hair swishing like fringe. "Thanks, man. Hey, cool gun."

Winn looked at the gun in his lap. He'd forgotten it was there. It made him feel even stupider about betraying the location of the Boarders so easily. He was *Winn Davis*! He had a *gun*! This was *his* school!

"Thanks," Winn said dully. He didn't care anymore. Let Virginia Leeds have her creepy thirty-year-old boyfriend.

Let townie Asians flood the gates and take over the whole world for all he cared.

The stranger left, his footsteps creating an echo in the empty garage. Winn rolled up the window, closed his eyes, and arranged Bory in his arms. The rifle rested comfortably against his chest, and Winn's arms loosened and relaxed. Because when love is real, Winn understood but couldn't explain, you don't have to hold on so tight.

The nurse's office, 3:01 p.m.

"Drink up!" the nurse chirped, handing Benny a bottle of pink Gatorade.

"Don't drink it," Virginia said. "I think they're trying to lobotomize us." Virginia was always trying to use big words even when they didn't make sense. Benny wanted to roll his eyes, but his head hurt too much. He opened the Gatorade and downed half of it in a series of long gulps. Then he hopped off the cot.

"Now just a moment, you're not going anywhere," the nurse said firmly.

"It's after three o'clock," Benny said. "It's my right to leave school at this time." He needed to get out of there. He needed to get to the Boarders and see the video of the bridge again. Now that he was certain the shadowy figure was Zaire, it changed everything.

He smoothed his pants and walked out the door. Virginia followed him, and the nurse followed her, protesting with the exasperation of adults who assume, incorrectly, that being old somehow entitles them to respect. Eventually she gave up.

"I want to watch the video again," Benny said. "Can we go to the Boarders?"

"Sure," Virginia said. She knew better than to ask if he was okay. Benny hated being babied, and Virginia didn't believe in babying people anyway. If Benny was sick, he could deal with it himself. It's not like they were children. The thing Virginia really wanted to ask him was what he thought of Zaire. Had he noticed that she was totally flirting with him in the library? Did he like her? Old Virginia could have found out in a second, just by watching his reaction when she asked him. But New Virginia wasn't going to. Not just because it wasn't her style, but because . . . she didn't know. She just didn't want to do it. It was like, the new Virginia had self-respect, and only hung out with people who also had self-respect. She didn't want to watch Benny flounder and blush in front of her.

They turned down the road that led to the Boarders. They walked in silence, the only sound their feet crunching on the gravel. The air was muggy and a little too hot. It wasn't helping Benny's headache. He rubbed his temples, thinking. Then he finally said, "Zaire's not very good at this."

"Good at what?" Virginia asked.

"Pulling this off," he answered.

"Pulling what off? You never tell me anything."

"Whatever it is she's doing." Benny kicked a pinecone. "She's out to get the cheerleading squad or something. She tried to kill Brittany but ended up killing Choi."

Virginia squinted at him. "Huh?"

"Her plan went awry, and now she's making it worse," Benny went on. "She's a control freak. She thinks she's being some kind of puppet master, but really she's just screwing herself over. She was obviously threatened by the fact that I was reading that book. She should have just backed off and stayed cool. Instead she took the book away, and then tried to hypnotize me into not being interested anymore."

"Wait, you're saying Zaire Bollo is a murderer? You're saying I live across the hall from a *murderer*?"

Benny couldn't tell if Virginia was scared or thrilled. "Yeah," he said. "She tried to keep me off her track in the library. She started talking in this weird voice . . . I don't even remember completely. And she kept saying, 'It's so boring. Don't waste your intellect on this stuff. It's so boring, Benny. Hypnosis is so boring. It's so boring. It's so boring. It's so boring.' And the word 'boring' was actually, like, *boring* into my brain. . . . And then I felt like I was going to hurl."

"Zaire is definitely a control freak," Virginia said. *Not unlike you,* she added in her mind. "I remember when she was dating Gottfried, he'd be leaving with Corn Flakes or something, and she'd be like, 'What time are you coming back?' And he'd be like, 'I dunno, five?' And she'd be like, 'What time *exactly*?'"

"The key to getting away with something isn't planning it perfectly," Benny said. "It's *adapting* perfectly when the plan inevitably goes wrong. Control freaks can't adapt. They try to master their problems instead of adapting to them."

"Okay, but hang on. Are you sure about this? Why would Zaire want to kill Britt—"

"Shhh!" He hushed her quickly. They were at the Boarders now, and he didn't want anyone to overhear them.

Virginia opened the front door, and Benny followed her inside. The air was stuffy and thick. The Boarders didn't have air-conditioning, so they just kept the windows open until the temperature dipped below eighty degrees, which wouldn't happen until Halloween if it was going to be another Indian summer. Benny followed Virginia into the empty common room, and Virginia flicked off the lights. She hoisted herself up onto the refrigerator and reached behind it. After a moment of digging around, and the sound of tape ripping, she hopped down and held out the grimy flash drive to Benny.

Just then a girl appeared in the doorway and the lights flicked on. They both froze, the flash drive between their hands.

"Virginia, will you get your crap out of the hall?" Chrissie White said, folding her arms.

"What crap?" Virginia asked.

Chrissie gestured impatiently toward the hall, then turned and left.

Their hands were still touching. Their eyes met for half a second, then they both quickly drew back. Benny noticed Virginia wiping her palm on her skirt and was embarrassed. Was his hand sweaty?

Virginia walked past him into the hall. "What the hell?" he heard her say. He followed her. The door to Virginia's room was wide open, and some clothes were spilling out into the hall. He came up behind her and peered into the room. Every drawer was flung open, every book strewn on the floor. The sheets had been ripped from the bed and sat in a messy pile.

"Give me your phone," Virginia said.

Benny handed it to her, feeling the familiar reluctance. It's not that he had any secrets on there. It was mostly just apps for detective work (flashlight, encyclopedia, camera), and texts from Grandma, who didn't understand cell phones (*HELLO? HELLO?*). But it still felt weird and too personal as he handed it over.

Virginia had taken a business card out of her pocket and was dialing a number.

Benny stood awkwardly in the doorway.

Ring . . . ring . . .

"Hello? Detective Holling? This is Virginia Leeds from Winship. . . . Yeah, I just have a quick question. Are you going to trash my room every day until you find what you want? Because if so, I won't bother cleaning up."

She stopped talking and looked at the floor. Benny listened but couldn't hear what the other person was saying.

"My *room*," Virginia spat into the phone. "My room is ransacked. Again. And I haven't even gotten my stuff back that you took yesterday. And don't think I didn't notice that you totally stole my perfume, which I'd *just* bought, FYI. I should sue you for harass—"

Virginia listened again. She'd started pacing back and forth, kicking a path through the sea of stuff on the floor. Then she scowled suddenly and threw the phone on the bare mattress. Benny looked at her, afraid she might throw something at him next if he said anything.

"She said they haven't been here since yesterday," she told him. "She said it wasn't them."

The hall, 3:30 p.m.

No one had seen anyone going in or out.

"I just walked in and it was like that," said Chrissie White.

"And you came directly to the Boarders once classes let out," Benny confirmed.

"Yeah. I'm always the first one back. Everyone else goes to sports."

"Thank you," he said to Chrissie.

"Is this for your club?" she asked. "Like a training exercise?"

Benny peered into Virginia's room. She was making the bed, yanking the sheets around irritably.

"Training is over," he said.

Two minutes later he was in the common room with the door closed, waiting for the computer to buzz to life. He slumped in the chair and stared up at the ceiling, gently rubbing his temples.

Gottfried keeps cigarettes above the rafters.

Benny lowered his hands. Then he dragged the chair to the center of the room and stood on it. It wasn't high enough. He stepped onto the sofa and balanced on the back, careful not to tip it over. Now he could see just above the rafters, and he spotted a small dark lump. He grabbed it. It was a pack of Parliaments.

He jumped to the floor with a thump and pulled out his phone. He swiped through his photo gallery until he found the pictures he'd taken underneath the bleachers on Saturday. Dirty pieces of trash, a half-eaten hot dog . . . crumpled cigarette butts. Benny could just barely make out three dirty, blue letters: *ENT.* Parliam*ent.* So maybe Gottfried was at the football game after all, hiding under the bleachers. But what did that prove?

The computer screen flickered on. Benny dragged the chair back to the desk and plugged in the flash drive. The computer was so old and slow, it took a full twenty seconds before the icon popped up on the screen. *TOP SECRET,* it read.

"Christ, Virginia," Benny whispered. He heard his mother's voice in his head: *Don't take other people's Lord's name in vain.*

He clicked on the icon. It was empty.

He closed it and clicked it again. Still empty.

He pulled the flash drive out, blew on it, then plugged it back in. Nothing.

Two seconds later he was in Virginia's doorway. "Virginia."

She looked up from a pile of papers she was organizing on the floor. "What?" she said testily.

"There's nothing on this."

"What?"

"There's nothing on this," he repeated.

"It's just the computer," Virginia said. "It's a geezer."

"You showed it to Zaire," he half whispered, half hissed.

"What?"

Benny sighed impatiently and shut the door, a little more forcefully than necessary. "You showed the video to Zaire. Just tell me. I'm not mad; I just need to know all the facts."

"I seriously have no idea what you're talking about." She shoved a stack of papers into her desk drawer and slammed it shut.

"On Wednesday before the Sapphire Lounge. *I saw you.*"

"Oh my God, I didn't! I told you I didn't, and I wasn't lying."

"Then what were you doing? I saw you with her on the computer, and now the video is gone."

"I was fixing the Internet! I don't know! I barely remember! I just—I just—"

Is she about to cry? Benny was angry, but anyone could see she wasn't lying. He quickly changed his tone. "It's all right. She probably . . . she probably hypnotized you." As soon as he said it, he realized it made complete sense. "She hypnotized you," he said again.

"Wait, no way," Virginia said. "I mean, I think I would have known. She tried to hypnotize you and it didn't work."

"Well yeah, but your mind is . . ." *Malleable? Impressionable?* He was having trouble coming up with a way to say it that wasn't essentially *You're stupid.*

"Some people are better candidates for hypnosis than others," he said tactfully, sitting on the edge of Virginia's freshly made bed. "There really should be laws against it, but no one takes hypnotism seriously. That book I was reading, *True Mesmerism*, it said that a hundred years ago hypnotism was, like, a serious medical science. There are documented cases of hypnotism being more effective than anesthesia during surgery. You just alleviate the patient's anxiety about pain. Without anxiety, pain is rendered powerless. I mean, what *is* pain without the anxiety and discomfort of experiencing it? Nothing! It's nothing! Just . . . *signals* sent to the brain to indicate that there's a knife sticking out of you. Hypnotism disrupts those signals, you see?" Benny looked at Virginia's blank face and realized he was rambling.

"Well, my point is, at some point in the last century,

hypnosis got discredited, as we became a society less oriented toward holistic therapy and more toward prescription drugs. . . ." He could tell she still wasn't following. "Okay. Basically, hypnosis is powerful and potentially dangerous, but there is no regulation, because no one takes it seriously."

Virginia folded her arms. "My mind is what?"

Benny looked at the floor uncomfortably. Of course Virginia was only paying attention to the part about herself. "You're not very . . . focused," he said. "You're easy to manipulate."

Virginia glared at him. "I . . . I am not!"

"Yes you are. Think about it. You do whatever I say. I mean, it's good! I value that about you."

"I'm sure you do," Virginia said. Her cheeks were inflamed.

"Calm down; I'm not trying to insult you." He tried to explain. "You're easy to lead. It's a good quality. Some people can't be led, because they're too stubborn and full of ego. But that's not you."

Virginia wouldn't look at him. He went on. "The only problem is that Zaire took advantage of it. She used your mind against you to get the video. She must have heard about it from Gerard. . . . So it's your own fault, because if you hadn't told Gerard—" He stopped, realizing this probably wasn't helping. "We all have different strengths and weaknesses," he said conclusively.

"What's your weakness?" Virginia asked. She was still

sitting on the floor, looking at him challengingly, with a cocked chin and narrow eyes.

"Um . . . I dunno . . . maybe . . ."

"Maybe the fact that you think you have no weaknesses is a weakness."

"I know I have weaknesses," Benny said lowly. "Social weaknesses. I'm too polite. I give social constructs too much power."

Virginia frowned, obviously deciding whether or not it was worth it to keep arguing. "You were pretty rude to the nurse," she said finally. "That was cool."

"Thanks . . ." The truce felt flimsy and temporary, but Benny didn't know what else to say.

Virginia went back to folding her clothes. Benny sat awkwardly, wondering if he should offer to help. He didn't really know how to fold clothes. His mother always did the laundry and left everything in neat stacks on his bed.

"So what is the deal? Zaire was trying to kill Brittany?"

"Um, yes. Evidently. She's the figure in the video at the edge of the bridge. I think she tried to hypnotize Brittany to kill herself by jumping off the bridge. But it was Mr. Choi in the suit. . . . What's ironic is that if she hadn't done that crazy performance, I probably wouldn't have suspected her. And the way she meddled with you? She needs to learn not to interfere. There are moving parts in any plan. You have to just let them *move*."

"Why would she want to kill Brittany?"

Benny bristled a bit. Wasn't it obvious? "Because she hates cheerleaders. And school spirit. And Brittany is the mascot."

Virginia laughed, then quickly stopped. "Wait, are you serious?"

"Well, yeah."

Virginia looked at him. "Isn't that a little childish?"

Benny tensed. Who was she calling childish, Zaire or him? "It's immature, I guess. A lot of murderers are immature."

"Zaire's not."

"Well she . . . I dunno. I mean, it makes sense."

"No it doesn't."

Benny stared at her as she continued to fold her clothes. "Well what's your brilliant explanation?"

She shrugged. "I dunno. I'm just saying, I know Zaire. I've lived with her for a year. She doesn't give a shit about anyone but herself. Why would she bother killing Brittany just because cheerleaders are annoying?"

"Well . . . what about the spirit show?" Benny argued. "Why would she bother doing that?"

"To show off how great and amazing she is. But killing people? You can't brag about that. No one can ever find out how masterful you are. I'm telling you, she wouldn't bother."

Benny felt his mind straining to work around what she was saying. Somehow, without even trying that hard, Virginia just understood people. It was a skill Benny lacked, and one he was beginning to think was more important than he'd realized. He didn't want to believe her though. He liked his version of events. It made sense.

"But . . . I feel like I'm really on the right track here. The odd, out-of-control movements of the mascot? Zaire's obvious derision for cheerleaders? The fact that she tried to hypnotize a book out of my hands. She knows I'm onto her. I *know* it was her. I can feel it really clearly."

"I'm not saying it wasn't her," Virginia said defensively. "I believe you that it was her. I mean, the more I think about it, Zaire would totally probably kill someone. I'm just saying it wasn't because she hates cheerleaders. Zaire isn't that simple."

"Fine, okay," Benny said. "It's acceptable to know the *who* before the *why*. . . . Maybe Choi actually was her target. Maybe that was the plan, and the plan worked. Except how is she even connected to Choi? She's not a cheerleader, and she's not in band. . . . Maybe she realized he was a pervert, and just wanted to take care of it herself. . . ." Benny trailed off.

"That doesn't sound like Zaire either," Virginia said. "She's not gonna stick her neck out for a bunch of cheerleaders."

"Unless he was videotaping her, too."

"She's not his type though," Virginia argued, starting a new pile of folded clothes. "She's not cute or perky, she doesn't giggle and bounce around . . ."

Benny felt frustrated. Was he not seeing this clearly? "Zaire is smart," he said. "Why would she do that hypnotist act for the spirit show? Is she crazy? Drawing attention to herself like that . . ."

Virginia shut another drawer. "Zaire's not as smart as she thinks she is. She's not smart about boys."

Benny stood up. He needed some air and some time to think by himself. "If you see Zaire, don't talk to her. Don't even look at her, if you can help it."

"Are we gonna take her down?" Virginia asked, an excited grin taking over her face.

"We're not the Take Down Club," Benny said carefully, not wanting to start a fresh argument so soon after the last one. Virginia was unpredictable in how much antagonism she could take before snapping at him. "There's this philosophy in aikido that you stare death in the face not so you can fight it, but so you can understand it."

"Huh?"

Benny sighed. "Revenge and anger are petty reactions. I don't want to take Zaire down; I want to understand her and embrace her with compassion."

Virginia snorted loudly. "You want to hug her? For killing someone?"

"Well not literally. That's just a Zen saying. Whatever. What I'm saying is, you and me, we solve the mystery, and that's the reward. We use our power to understand, not to punish."

"Hm," Virginia said, and Benny felt his cheeks heat up with annoyance. *Hm.* It was way too similar to his mother's classic *Mm-hm*. He was so tired of being around people who *hm*'d at him like he was insane. How did the world get so messed up that having compassion made you a person to be *hm*'d at?

"And anyway," Benny added, "Zaire's sabotaging herself enough without our help. She'll bring herself down."

"You think so?" Virginia asked.

Benny paused for a moment, then said, "Yeah. She's out of control, even her own control. I got this vibe from her. . . . I don't know. I think she's going to do it again—another 'half-time show.' It could even be me or you, now that she knows we know."

Virginia shivered. "Omigod, you just gave me goose bumps! See? Look, do you see?"

"It's an issue of public safety at this point. Someone's going to get hurt."

Virginia wondered at what point a normal person would have called the police and handed over their information. Probably a while ago. But she knew Benny well enough to know he'd rather die than hand a mystery over to adults. It was kind of scary, his willingness to endanger his own life—and hers—to stay in control.

"Are you sure we shouldn't tell someone?" she asked.

"What would we say? That we think a straight-A student hypnotized a teacher to jump off a bridge? No way.

There's no proof. They wouldn't believe us, and even if they did, they'd just screw it up and make it that much harder for us to figure out anything. We can handle this ourselves. It'll be easy. Zaire's weakness is that she's a perfectionist. Her plans only work in a perfect world where everything goes perfectly. All we have to do is remove some element of the equation, and the whole thing will fall apart. . . ."

Benny's voice trailed off. The element was obvious.

The Wildcat.

The gym hallway, 4:00 p.m.

Virginia stepped between the enormous banners lying on the floor. Half-empty cans of paint sat nearby with abandoned brushes sticking out of them. The banners looked like they'd been painted by illiterates. *Wilscats killing you!! Go Wiltscat. Rildcats Roars! WILDdogd,* one even read.

"Does Winship have the stupidest cheerleaders on the planet or what?" Virginia said, shaking her head.

Benny looked down at the jumbled slogans. The mistakes were beyond spelling errors—whoever had made these signs was obviously on drugs or something.

He stopped at the door to the girls' locker room. "This is as far as I can go. You think you can do this?"

Virginia nodded. "As long as the hallway stays empty."

"I'll keep a look out. If someone's here, I'll knock. Knocking means don't come out."

"Okay."

"What does knocking mean?"

Virginia rolled her eyes. "It means come on out and sing a loud song."

Before Benny could say anything else, Virginia pushed the door open with a *swoosh* and disappeared inside.

It smelled like mildew and swimming pool, with an aggressive top note of body spray and vanilla air freshener. Virginia wondered if the boys even bothered trying to keep their locker room smelling nice. Probably not.

Pom-poms sat on the benches next to quilted Vera Bradley bags and pairs of Kate Spade clogs. It was a wonder any of the cheerleaders ever managed to go home with their own possessions—all their stuff was interchangeable. As Virginia passed the rows of gray lockers, she realized she was tiptoeing. *Act natural,* she willed herself. She had every right to be in there, after all—she was a girl, wasn't she? Which was the entire reason Benny needed her, apparently. Not because she was brilliant and talented, but because she was a girl and could go into the girls' locker room. But Virginia was trying not to feel too annoyed. At least Benny was letting her do something.

Someone was in the shower, and the hiss of the water echoed off the walls.

"Hello?" she said.

There was no answer.

She turned the corner to the pom-pom closet. She pulled

the door handle, half hoping it would be locked so she wouldn't have to do this. It opened.

The mascot head was sitting in the middle of the floor. Virginia hadn't seen it close-up since it washed up from the river. It had obviously been vigorously scrubbed—it was scratched and faded and smelled faintly of bleach. One of the teeth had chipped off. But mostly it looked the same, its creepy mouth still grinning, its bulging eyes staring relentlessly ahead.

"What?" she said, realizing how dumb it was trying to sound tough for a plastic head. She took a deep breath and bent to turn the head around so its lunatic eyes faced away. The fuzzy suit was stuffed inside the hollow plastic. Then she picked it up with both arms, leaning back to support its huge bulging girth. It felt gross to be touching it, to be holding it against her body. As she passed between the two walls of mirrors in the locker room, the Wildcat's lewd, psychotic smile reflected back at her seemingly into infinity. She stuck her tongue out at it. Which only made the Wildcat seem more nasty and gleeful in response.

Suddenly she noticed how quiet it was. The shower had turned off. She looked over her shoulder toward the showers to see if someone was coming. But it was too late. Someone was already there.

Virginia whirled around, the huge mascot head throwing her off balance. It was Corny Davenport. She was standing in a tiny towel in front of the sink, holding a pair of pink kiddie scissors.

Is she cutting her hair off?

"Corny?"

Corny's face looked deadened and blank. All the pink softness was gone from her cheeks. When their eyes met in the mirror, it was like Corny didn't even recognize her.

Snip. A little blond tuft floated to the floor.

"I'm just stressesed," Corny said, slurring a little. "It's normal. A lot of girls do it."

Virginia nodded slowly. Except obviously it wasn't *that* normal, or why was Corny bothering to explain herself when Virginia was the one absconding with a giant mascot head? If anyone should be explaining herself, it was *her*. A beat too late, Corny seemed to realize this.

"Who is that man?" She looked dully at the mascot head.

"What . . . man?"

Corny didn't answer. She turned back to the mirror and held the scissors up to her hair.

Snip.

As she raised her arms, the towel started to come undone. Her boobs threatened to spill out at any second. Her legs were brown and glistening wet, and her little feet had tan lines from flip-flops. It was sort of a competition among the Winship girls, who could keep their summer tans the longest. But despite her eternal bronze glow, Corny's face looked wan and sick.

"Are you okay?" Virginia asked.

"I have so much power," Corny was whispering. "I could cut all my hair off. Would anyone still love me? If I were bald?"

"Um, maybe?" Virginia said, trying not to laugh.

Then Corny threw off her towel and was completely naked. Virginia watched, sort of stunned, as Corny stumbled across the locker room, her round, tan butt jiggling as she hopped clumsily into a pair of blue cheerleader panties. It was one of the weirdest things about being a girl—other girls just got naked in front of you. *We're all girls here,* you heard all the time, as if that meant something.

"These aren't my clothes," Corny announced. "I'm just wearing them to blend in."

"Okay . . ." Virginia adjusted the mascot head in her hands. "Well, I have to go now. Bye."

"Good-bye. Forever."

At that Virginia burst out laughing, unable to help it any longer. Corny didn't seem to care. She was staring at herself in the mirror. Her stare was so intense, Virginia stopped laughing almost immediately.

"Have you ever seen yourself for the first time?" Corny asked. Virginia couldn't tell if she was talking to her or to herself. Her voice was raspy and hoarse, like she'd been screaming.

Virginia glanced from Corny's face to her own in the mirror. It was weird sometimes, looking into your own eyes—being inside and outside of yourself at the same time.

For a second she almost knew what Corny was talking about. *Have you ever seen yourself for the first time?* But then the gross, lecherous look of the Wildcat caught her eye, and the moment was gone.

The bridge, 4:30 p.m.

All around them, birds chirped and leaves rustled in the breeze. The clouds moved silently above their heads. The water surged below the bridge, hurtling over the rocks and frothing white, the same river it had been a hundred years ago. A thousand years ago. Benny felt intrusive, bringing their human drama into the serenity of nature like this. But there wasn't another option. He couldn't take the mascot with him without his mother asking a billion questions, and they couldn't leave it in the Boarders without Zaire inevitably finding it. And besides, there was a satisfying symmetry to dumping it back into the water.

"It was bizarre," Virginia said for the hundredth time. She'd been chattering excitedly the whole way to the bridge. Benny was only half listening at this point.

"She was cutting her hair off, but not, like, dramatically. Just creepy little snips. I guess she's having a nervous breakdown. Not that I blame her. It's probably hard to be that stupid."

Benny shrugged. He disagreed. Stupid people had it easy—they lacked the mental capacity to comprehend the true miserableness of the world.

"Ready?" He heaved the mascot head onto the low rail of the bridge. Its toothy smile was deranged, as if the prospect of being thrown over a bridge were one it met with utter excitement.

"Let me do it," Virginia demanded, jumping up and down like a kid about to ride a pony. The 150-year-old bridge groaned under her feet. It was a wonder it hadn't buckled and collapsed under the weight of all those cheerleaders and football players last week.

Virginia braced herself and gave the head a violent shove. It soared toward the water in an almost elegant arc, then hit the surface with a splash. Virginia clapped delightedly. Benny looked down. He almost expected the Wildcat's face to change, to suddenly look sad and anguished. *You killed me! You betrayed me!* But as it rushed away on the current, it looked as ecstatic as ever. *Wheee!* it seemed to say. *This is fun!*

He turned back to Virginia. "Hey, does your door lock?"

"No, they removed all the locks after . . . you know . . ."

Benny did know. In eighth grade one of the boarders had tried to kill herself by swallowing pain pills with liquid drain cleaner. They'd had to beat the door down with an ax because Mrs. Morehouse's master key snapped in half. What happened to the girl, Benny didn't really know. Her parents had picked her up the next day, and no one ever saw her again. Benny couldn't even remember her name.

"The front door has a lock," Virginia said. "We're pretty much fine."

Benny looked at her, and the sight of her stuff-strewn floor flashed in his mind. *We're pretty much fine?* Maybe the front door locked, but obviously that didn't make any difference; the windows were wide open half the time. It was creepy enough that her room had been opened up and trashed, but even creepier that Virginia didn't seem especially perturbed by it. It was like she'd lived in the Boarders so long, she'd forgotten she was entitled to normal things like privacy and nutritious food choices and basic safety. He felt a huge gulf between them suddenly. Of course, everyone was a little weirded out by the boarders, but Benny had never felt it as strongly as he did now. You couldn't feel sorry for them, because they were probably richer than anyone. But every year that they spent in that gloomy brick house, their potential to be normal diminished, while everyone else was forced to watch.

Benny cast a final look at the Wildcat head, which was just about to round the river bend and disappear. As it bobbed in the water, he could swear its bulging eye was winking.

See you soon!

Benny's house, 5:30 p.m.

"Light . . . cup . . . cloud . . . I think on Tuesday he said 'cloud.'"

Benny hunched over his calendar, filling in all the

blank boxes. His shoulders were tense, and his stomach was growling. He'd forgotten he'd thrown up his lunch. He ignored his hunger, determined to fill in the calendar, grab his flute, and get back to school as soon as possible. He'd ordered Virginia to avoid Zaire until the game tonight. But Virginia hardly ever seemed to listen to him, and imagining her wandering around and getting herself hypnotized off a bridge made him incredibly anxious.

The calendar was taking longer than usual, because he hadn't updated it in three days. He'd been so preoccupied with the case at school that he'd completely neglected his one duty at home. *Inexcusable,* he berated himself.

Rodrigo sat next to him on the sofa. Mrs. Flax and his grandma were at temple for a pancake supper, so it was just Benny and Rodrigo and his dad in the house. Mr. Flax sat in the La-Z-Boy fiddling with a Styrofoam model of a plane. Every once in a while he would try to fly it, his clumsy hands pelting it into the TV or the wall. Then Rodrigo would go pick it up and hand it back to him, saying, "Crash landing, Mr. Flax. Try again."

"Wait, he said 'cloud' twice?" Benny asked. He scanned the month of October looking for "cloud."

Rodrigo squinted, thinking. "I'm not sure. . . ." He set his bourbon down.

Benny took off his glasses and rubbed his eyes. The whole system was garbage if he missed a day. He had an urge to throw the entire calendar in the trash.

"Hey, it's okay! Relax," Rodrigo said. "Don't stress. You've got your life going on, and your dad knows that. Hey. Listen. It's good that you're doing this. It's good that you're paying attention. But you know what I've been wanting to tell you for a long time?"

"What?" Benny said, holding his head in his hands.

"What you're doing, you're sitting next to him, but you're not even looking at him. You're examining him. Maybe you could just hang with him."

"Hang with him," Benny repeated.

"Talk to him. Tell him how your day was. Give it a break with the calendar and the karate practice. Just hang. I'm telling you, he'll benefit a lot more from that."

Benny put his glasses back on. *Hold on,* he thought. This entire time, did Rodrigo think the calendar was dumb?

"I'm just—I'm tracking his language development," he said defensively.

"I know, and it's great!" Rodrigo said. "But you can do more. You're his only blood relation; did you ever think of that?"

Benny shook his head.

"Your mom, her mom . . . those aren't his blood bonds. Family bonds, yeah, but not blood bonds. His parents are dead, right? No siblings? So yeah, biologically speaking, you're the closest person to him on the planet. He recognizes you. He relaxes when it's just the three of us in a room. You ever notice that?"

Benny shook his head again. "No."

"There's a lot of stuff you'll notice if you just hang with him. Lose the highlighters and the bullshit. Talk to him."

"Talk to him about . . . what?"

"You know, just whatever. You obviously got a lot going on or you wouldn't have forgotten your calendar, right?"

Benny shrugged.

"Just relax. Have a bourbon. Well, don't have a bourbon— you're fifteen. Have a Coke."

An hour later Benny and his dad were alone. Benny found a Diet Coke Lime in the refrigerator, which didn't have the same vibe as plain Coke, but it was all they had. He sat on the sofa and cracked it open.

"Hi," he said, not looking at his dad but at the wall. He took a long sip.

Mr. Flax fiddled with the plane. He tossed it, and it hit a lampshade. Benny got up and grabbed it and placed it back in his father's hands. Then he slumped down in the sofa, wishing it were six thirty so he could turn on the news. It was awkward, sitting in silence.

What am I supposed to say? he thought. Suddenly the Coke felt stupid, like a sappy commercial. A son sits with his brain-damaged father while enjoying an ice-cold can of Coke. The father smiles, the first connection they've shared in over a year. *With Coke, miracles happen.*

Mr. Flax tossed the plane again. Benny waited for it to crash into a piece of furniture. But instead it sailed across the room, slicing the air with a soft *whoosh* and landing gently on the carpet.

"Whoa." Benny picked it up and handed it to his dad. "Nice landing."

He sat back down. Mr. Flax's eyes were doing that thing where they glazed over one second, and then became sharp and alert the next. Benny waited for him to throw the plane again, but he didn't.

Say something, Benny told himself. "I . . ." He stopped. "There's this girl at school. . . . She's really interesting. I wish I could know her better."

Benny sipped his Coke and snuck a look at his dad. He was glancing around vaguely.

"She's really closed off though. I don't think she'll let me near her. . . . I have a history test on Monday."

"Fine," Mr. Flax said.

Benny reached instinctively for a pen and a highlighter. "Fine" was one of Mr. Flax's main words. But then Benny took the calendar and turned it upside down on the table so he couldn't see it.

"It's on ancient Japan, so I already know everything. . . . This girl is so frustrating. She's smart, but the way she's using her intelligence isn't right. She tries to problem-solve her life instead of dealing with her life. . . . I don't know. Maybe I do that too, to a certain extent."

Benny took another sip of Coke. Once he'd started talking, it felt surprisingly easy. Why had he never tried this before?

"She has so many advantages," he went on. "A great mind. Incredible beauty. But she's messed up. I think some-one did something to her. I wish I could just ask her what's going on, but she'll never let me get close enough."

"Hrm," Mr. Flax said. His face twitched, drawing atten-tion to the deep craggy lines around his mouth. Mr. Flax's face was old for his age, prematurely wizened as the result of testing planes at supersonic speeds in the '90s. It made him seem more like a grandfather than a father sometimes. His current senility and lack of mobility made that feeling even stronger. It was getting confusing, who played what role in the family.

As Benny was thinking of what to say next, his father's face looked so normal for a moment that he could have sworn he was thinking too.

"Dad?"

Then the front door opened. Mrs. Flax appeared with an armload of grocery bags. "Benjamin, could you help your grandmother?" she said, not saying hello first.

Benny looked at his dad. His eyes had glazed over again, and he'd resumed clumsily fiddling with the plane.

You're the closest person to him on the planet. Benny heard Rodrigo's voice in his mind. He stood up and went over to the La-Z-Boy. He glanced toward the kitchen to make sure his mom's back was turned. Then he stooped and gave his dad an awkward half hug, patting him on the shoul-der. Benny couldn't remember the last time they'd hugged.

None of the Flaxes were huggers, except for his grandma, who wasn't actually a Flax.

"Thanks for the talk, Dad," he whispered. Then he pointed to the plane. "Keep practicing. I'm proud of you. You're doing great."

The football stadium, 8:00 p.m.

WILDCATS FOREVER AND EVER AND EVER AND EVER AND EVER AND EVER AND EVER AND EVER, the enormous sign read, the "ever"s getting tinier and tinier until they were barely readable. Virginia stared at it from the front row of the bleachers. The message was supposed to be affirming— Wildcats forever!!!—but instead it felt vaguely ominous. Wildcats *forever*? Virginia prayed not. Hopefully at some point her life would become interesting enough that the fact that she went to Winship would no longer be central to her identity.

The sign was at least twenty feet tall, supported with poles on either side by two football players. The pep band started hammering out "Hang On Sloopy." She could see Benny playing his flute, his head bobbing dorkily. Every time she started to think Benny was kind of a badass, she'd catch him doing something really nerdy, like using ten different colored pens to take notes, or playing his flute way too earnestly.

The entire stadium erupted into a cheer, even the half where the opposing team's fans were sitting. It was Catfight

Night, meaning the big game against the Lowell Lions. There'd been talk of canceling it after all the tumult of the week, but then it was decided that maybe a nice wholesome game of football was just what everyone needed. Not that tonight was really about football—it was about the cheerleaders. The huge, twenty-foot paper sign had been made with the idea that the girls would open the game by dramatically running through it onto the field. Everyone was there—even kids from Tate Prep and the Christian Academy had come, just to catch a glimpse of the magical twin from the "Cheerleader Survival" story. Even the little goth ninth grader was there, and Calvin Harker, who had a heart condition and never did anything. In fact, the only person who *wasn't* there, Virginia noticed, seemed to be Gerard. His usual spot on the bench by the water cooler was empty. Not that anyone really expected him to show his face after his total humiliation at the spirit show.

The cheerleaders appeared at the edge of the field. In the stands everyone stood and shouted and clapped joyously. For a too-long moment the clapping and exuberance went on, but nothing happened. Virginia squinted down the field. She could make out the two football players holding the posts on either side of the sign. They were gesturing toward the girls behind them, as if to say, *Come on!*

The clapping grew a little scattered. Virginia saw a bulge

at the center of the sign, like someone was leaning on it. Then it tore open, and a cheerleader fell through. She plopped onto the grass, and then didn't get up. Another cheerleader fell after her, and then another. Soon there was a little pile of cheerleaders lying half-inert on the grass as the sign tore wider and more cheerleaders came blundering through. She saw Corny Davenport fall forward on her face, as if toppled by the sheer weight of her boobs.

"What the hell?" Virginia said.

It was not the rousing display of spirit that was expected. It was a bunch of really-out-of-it-looking girls tripping over one another and seeming utterly unaware of the embarrassing spectacle they were making. It was one thing to screw up; it was another to do it in front of the Lowell Lions, their biggest rival. The Lowell side of the bleachers was roaring with laughter. Virginia wanted to laugh too, but she didn't. It was funny, watching the usually übercoordinated cheerleaders trip over one another, but also not funny. She tried to make eye contact with Benny in the pep band, but he was too far away.

Finally the cheerleading coach ran up and ripped the sign all the way open so the cheerleaders could come through without piling up like a bunch of zombies. The girls walked across the field in a daze to the track, where they ambled around looking lost. Some of them were trying to do choreography, their brows wrinkling in intense concentration as they swayed, seeming disconnected from

their limbs. Brittany and Angie looked particularly confused. Kirsten Fagerland started crying.

"*ZAIRE BOLLO, PLEASE REPORT TO THE SKY BOX
IMMEDIATELY,*" the principal's voice boomed from the
loudspeaker. Virginia's heartbeat quickened at the sound of
Zaire's name. She felt slightly queasy, a mix of excitement
and dread.

"Virginia."

She turned just as someone was squeezing into the spot
next to her. It was Min-Jun, the bass player from Asian Fusion.

"Um, hi!" she said. "If it isn't my biggest fan!"

"I thought *you* were *my* biggest fan," Min-Jun said.

Virginia looked down. "Well, I assumed it was mutual."
Then she forced herself to flash a smile.

"Oh, don't worry; it is. . . ."

He looked different in the bright stadium lights. At the
Sapphire Lounge he could have passed for late-twenties,
but here it was clear he was at least thirty-five. His teeth
were yellow, and she could see strands of gray hair among
the long, shiny black ones. But he was still good-looking,
in a sort of flawed way. And Virginia preferred flawed men,
really. They had more potential to be deep and fascinating
than the Winn Davises of the world.

"What are you doing here?" she asked him.

"I'm here to see you."

Virginia looked at him, expecting to see a big smirk on
his face. But he looked cool and serious.

The horn blew and then the game started. The boys on the field started smashing into one another.

"Football is so stupid," Virginia said. "You can't even see the ball half the time."

"That's why they have cheerleaders. To give people something to look at."

"Not much to look at right now."

Half the cheerleaders were sitting down with their legs splayed out like little kids. The other half were staring vacantly at the football field or one another. Min-Jun squinted at them.

"Yeah, what's the deal with those chicks?"

"They lost their innocence from being sexually traumatized," Virginia said. "They can't cheer anymore."

"I wonder what happens when football players lose their innocence," Min-Jun said.

"It probably makes them play even better."

The crowd cheered as the ball sailed across the end zone. Everyone stood up but Virginia and Min-Jun. It felt suddenly intimate, like they were in a cave together created by everyone's feet and legs. Min-Jun looked directly at her for the first time. His eyes were dark, almost black.

"I like you," he shouted over the noise.

Virginia was so startled she pretended not to have heard. "Wha—what did you say?"

"I like you."

Virginia narrowed her eyes. "No you don't. I know who you like."

"Huh?"

By now the crowd had quieted, and everyone was sitting back down.

"I saw your guitar case. I'm not your type." Virginia nodded toward Corny Davenport, who was on the track staring at her hands like she'd never noticed them before.

Min-Jun threw his head back and laughed. "You're a little snoop, huh?"

Virginia shrugged. How was *he* making *her* feel bad right now? He was the one with pinups of underage girls in his guitar case.

"Well, I like you better than her," he said.

Virginia scoffed. "'Cause I'm right here, and she's waaaaay over there?"

"No," Min-Jun said. "There's more to you than your proximity."

"Like what?"

"Like your legs."

Virginia's heart pounded suddenly. Her face was hot. She glanced down at her legs, wishing simultaneously that she could cover them up and show them more. She'd *just* been thinking this the other day—that her legs were totally nice but no one ever noticed. People only noticed your reputation at Winship, and Virginia's reputation wasn't for being a leggy sex kitten. Min-Jun wasn't from Winship, though. He wasn't even from the teenage universe. He had no idea what he was supposed to see.

"Thank you!" she breathed.

"And your business acumen," he added.

Virginia didn't know what "acumen" meant, so she just said "thank you" again. Her business acumen? Maybe that meant her body or her cool attitude.

"You know that guy?" Min-Jun asked, looking out at the field.

"What guy?" Virginia asked.

Min-Jun pointed. "That guy's been staring at you."

Virginia looked where he was pointing, expecting to see Benny. But it wasn't Benny; it was a football player—Winn Davis. He was standing on the sidelines, holding his helmet under his arm and gazing weirdly. At first it seemed like he was looking at the group of dazed cheerleaders. But he wasn't; he was looking *past* them. At *her*.

"Um, I don't really know him . . . ," Virginia said.

"Hey, no problem with me! I like a little competition. Makes me feel like what I'm getting's worth it." Min-Jun reached in his pocket and pulled out a small envelope. He handed it to her shadily, like it contained a big secret. Virginia took it and peeked inside. It was a bunch of twenty-dollar bills.

"I thought five hundred was a tad steep," he said. "But I'll give you four. You said you were Choi's 'little helper'?"

"Um . . ."

"That's half, in the envelope there. The rest is in my car if you want it."

Virginia didn't say anything. She just looked at the envelope, her mouth half open. Min-Jun glanced from her lips to the money.

"So do you want it?"

Pep band, 8:00 p.m.

The song was falling apart, and Benny was struggling to keep some semblance of order in the flute section, which was why he didn't notice what was happening on the field.

"ZAIRE BOLLO, PLEASE REPORT TO THE SKY BOX IMMEDIATELY."

At the sound of Zaire's name, he looked up. He'd been watching for Zaire ever since he got there, but so far she hadn't appeared. Was she there now?

He saw the cheerleaders ambling across the field. They were supposed to have exploded through the sign in a burst of cartwheels and dancing and backflips. But instead they looked like a bunch of freshly lobotomized mental patients.

"Keep playing!" the assistant conductor shouted over the confusion.

Benny played but kept an eye on the field. He looked for Virginia, but he couldn't see her. Usually she sat in the front row at games, but the stadium was so crowded today, she could have ended up anywhere. The horn blew and the game began, the cheerleaders still looking vacant and confused. Pom-poms hung from their arms like heavy pails of water.

On the ground next to Benny's flute case was a brown paper bag from Home Depot. Inside was a latch he'd bought for Virginia's door—or rather, his mother had bought it. Benny didn't have his own money, except for his bar mitzvah cash, which was all in a bank account. It had been awkward, trying to explain why Virginia needed a latch.

"The dorm isn't safe," he'd said, and even though it was true, his voice had cracked, which made it sound like a lie. Mrs. Flax had given him a cold stare.

"I don't see why anyone your age needs a lock on their door. There's nothing you should be doing that can't be done with the door open."

Amid the crowd, Benny noticed Zaire Bollo coming down the stadium steps with Principal Baron. As she passed, everyone turned and stared at her. From a distance it reminded Benny of a magnet pulling everything toward it.

Benny jumped off the bleachers, flute still in hand.

"Benny Flax!" the assistant conductor shouted. Benny ignored him. He walked across the track, trying not to be self-conscious of the fact that half the stadium was probably staring at him and wondering what he was doing. He could see Zaire and the principal standing in front of the cheerleaders. He caught up to them in time to hear Zaire saying, "Breath in. . . . Breathe out. . . . This is a safe space. A space where you can be yourself. . . . You can be a cheerleader. You can be yourself. Be yourself. Be yourself. When I clap my hands, this will all be over."

She clapped once.

Benny scanned the cheerleaders. Instantly their eyes looked brighter. Their cheeks even looked pinker. They started blinking at one another and giggling.

"There. That should do it," Zaire said flatly.

She turned to leave. The principal grabbed her arm roughly. Seeing it made Benny uneasy. There was hardly ever touching between the teachers and students, except for Mrs. Knox, who forced hugs on everyone and only got away with it because she was eighty years old.

"This isn't funny, Miss Bollo," the principal was saying in a low growl. Zaire's eyes flickered to Benny. Then the principal noticed Benny too, and immediately dropped Zaire's arm.

"If you can't unhypnotize them, we need to call a professional," he said, straightening.

"Look, they're fine," Zaire said. She gestured to the cheerleaders, who were staring around, looking bewildered but alive. Angie and Brittany were shrieking delightedly, "What are we doing here?" They started waving their pompoms, and the crowd erupted in cheers. Just then Zaire turned and looked Benny in the face. He was used to talking to Virginia, who was several inches shorter than him, so he was always looking slightly down. But Zaire was his exact height; their eyes met across an even, invisible plane.

"What," Zaire said, not a question.

"What—what?" Benny stammered. He felt suddenly intimidated by her physical beauty. Winship was full of beautiful girls, but Zaire was different. She wasn't like the other girls, who seemed to capitalize on being girlish and approachable. She was glamorous and imposing, like a statue. And she was a killer. She was pursing her lips and looking him up and down. She was probably thinking up ways to kill him right now. The thought made Benny's whole body tense. His hands felt tingly and numb.

"What are you doing?" she asked.

Benny shrugged dumbly. "What are *you* doing?"

She stared at him, not answering. Benny felt the need to look away from her eyes. He noticed Virginia in the bleachers. She was absorbed in conversation with a long-haired guy.

"Gosh, you better watch out," Zaire said, seeing them too. "As if Gottfried weren't enough competition."

"Gottfried?" Benny said.

"You didn't know? She likes him."

Benny narrowed his eyes at her. "I'm not sure that's correct. . . ." Then he looked back at Virginia. Who was that guy? He was sure he knew him from somewhere. . . . It took him a moment to recognize that he was the bass player from Asian Fusion.

Oh my God.

All at once, like a bat to the head, it was obvious who had ransacked Virginia's room, and why.

"Virginia!" he called out.

Zaire folded her arms. "Um, are we having a conversation here or not?"

"Virginia!" he shouted again. She didn't hear him. The bassist stood up with her, like they were getting ready to leave.

"Leave her alone," Zaire said. "You don't get girls by being a possessive Neanderthal."

"I'm not—I just—" There was no point trying to explain. He pushed past Zaire and wove through the cheerleaders, who had organized themselves into lines on the track.

"Virginia!" They were walking up the bleacher steps. Were they holding hands? Benny craned his neck to see. They weren't holding hands; the guy was leading her by the wrist.

He heard Angie's voice coming through the megaphone. "Y'all let's make the earth move! It's time for the Wildcat Stomp!"

Everyone in the stands stood up. The clapping started, and then the stomping. People spilled into the steps, blocking Benny's path.

Stomp! Stomp!

"Excuse me, excuse me," he said, trying to elbow his way through. The stomping filled his ears, and the ground trembled.

Stomp! Stomp!

"Excuse me!" he yelled. He could see Virginia disappearing and reappearing in the crowd. There was no way he would reach her at this rate. He knew he lacked the aggression to push his way through. It was his curse—his inescapable civility. Benny decided to double back around the stadium and catch them at the entrance. It would be about three times the distance, but at least he'd be moving. He turned and ran as fast as he could, the stomping reverberating in his chest. As he reached the edge of the stadium, it was suddenly pitch-black. Benny had to stop and wait for his eyes to adjust. To his right was the forest, to his left the dark underbelly of the metal stands. He ran toward the entrance and turned in circles, looking for Virginia.

There.

She was getting into the passenger side of a badly parked Ford Fiesta on the side of the road, where only teachers were supposed to park.

What does she think she's doing? he thought frantically. *Don't get in a car with him!*

"Virginia, stop!" he shouted. "Virginia!"

He started running again. But Benny was an endurance runner, not a sprinter. He was still about fifty yards away when the car lights turned on and it pulled out of the parking spot.

"Virginia! Get out of the car!"

In seconds the car was gone. Benny was panting from

running so hard. He felt his hand stinging and looked down. He was still gripping his flute, his knuckles white, the keys pressing into the skin of his palm.

He pulled out his cell phone and stared at it, as if waiting for it to tell him what to do. There was no one to call. Even if his mom could come pick him up, he had no idea where Virginia and the Asian Fusion guy were going. He should have made Virginia get a cell phone. That was obvious now. But he hadn't wanted to embarrass her by pointing out that she was the only girl in school who didn't have one. And now she was driving off with a pervert and a room ransacker and who knew what else, all because Benny couldn't shove his way through a crowd, or endure the social awkwardness of telling Virginia she needed a phone.

He stood there on the street, not knowing what to do. *Virginia can take care of herself,* he thought. But he wasn't sure if he really believed it.

The track, 8:30 p.m.

Stomp! Stomp!

Zaire sat on the bench next to the water cooler, waiting for the god-awful Wildcat Stomp to be over so she could leave. The principal was watching the whole thing, making sure the de-hypnotism worked this time. Because God forbid the world should be without a bunch of imbecilic girls screaming into megaphones about how great it is to be a Wildcat.

The mascot suit didn't appear. Someone had gotten

rid of it or something—that was the rumor anyway. Zaire didn't know. She didn't care, either. Kirsten Fagerland was jumping around in what looked like pretty much a burlap sack with a pair of plastic eyes and ears glued to it. Kirsten had obviously been instructed to be as energetic as possible to make up for how awful and cheap it looked. The bulging eyes looked manic and imploring. *Love me! Love me!* But it wasn't possible. Never again would anyone at Winship look at a mascot and be anything but creeped out. The thought should have made Zaire very pleased with herself, but it didn't.

It was getting harder and harder to feel satisfied. She used to get a rush of power from her little pranks, but lately nothing seemed to penetrate her numbness. So what if she could make Brittany say she loved Satan? So what if she could make Winn Davis spill his orange juice? It didn't feel powerful anymore; it felt pathetic and masturbatory. Zaire knew what she really needed to do, but she couldn't seem to do it. Her first plan had gone completely haywire, and now apparently Benny Flax was watching her, which was annoying because she couldn't hypnotize him. He had too many mental walls or something. Zaire didn't know. She wasn't an expert on this stuff. She'd only started doing it to get close to Gottfried.

Gottfried was famous in the Boarders for his insomnia. Back in Germany he'd seen an experimental sleep therapist who'd used hypnotism as a sleep-inducing device. Learning this, Zaire had immediately set about teaching herself to do it, as an excuse to be alone with him in his bedroom. She was good at it, which shouldn't have surprised her. Zaire was good at everything she set her mind to. All it took to be a hypnotist was confidence and tranquility, and for one's subject to have the right kind of mind—loose, willing, pliable. Soon Zaire was hypnotizing Gottfried to sleep at least five times a week. Gottfried relied on her, *needed* her. And Zaire had seized on that need like a parasite. But it wasn't enough. Gottfried needed her, but he didn't love her. He loved "American girls."

She spotted him in the front row of the bleachers. A fat blond woman with cheap highlights was practically sitting in his lap. She was feeding him a hot dog and occasionally licking ketchup off his lip. Gottfried had the stupidest grin on his face. Zaire wished she could hate him, but she loved those idiotic expressions of his. She envied his goofy charm and effortless happiness. He was the only person Zaire had ever met who seemed to actually live in the moment, instead of just pretending to.

Zaire watched as the woman whispered something in Gottfried's ear. Gottfried laughed delightedly. Zaire had never been able to make Gottfried laugh. *She's ugly!* Zaire thought, wanting to shout it in Gottfried's face. Why did he like ugly old trailer park hags better than her? What was wrong with him?

What's wrong with me? Zaire thought, which was the

real question. She was smart and sophisticated and mature. Why didn't he want her? She pretended to examine her nails in case Gottfried caught her staring at him. Not that he would. He was too wrapped up in his big-boobed, puffy-lipped, cheetah-print-wearing white-trash cougar to notice anything else.

I have to finish this, Zaire thought, suddenly determined. *I have to get this done. No more dicking around. Benny Flax can fuck off and go to hell. I'm finishing this tomorrow.*

Chatahoochee Mall parking lot, 9:15 p.m.

A security cruiser circled past slowly. Min-Jun didn't seem anxious about it. He just checked the rearview mirror to make sure it was gone, then started rolling a joint on his knee.

"You smoke?"

Virginia shook her head. Maybe she should have said yes, to stay in character. But Min-Jun didn't seem to care either way. He lit the joint and inhaled deeply. Virginia looked at his hands. They were smooth and long-fingered. Musician hands. When he blew the smoke out, he said, "Mind hotboxing?"

Virginia shrugged, not knowing what he meant. She looked out the window for the reassuring presence of the cop car. She knew it was stupid to wish it would come back with the Fiesta full of pot smoke—they'd probably be arrested—but she had the anxious feeling she'd be safer in jail than alone with Min-Jun in the parking lot of this vast, empty strip mall. Half the stores had closed down in the recession, so it was mostly dark, desolate storefronts abutting a shoddy discount warehouse with its rows of forty-cent soda machines and grizzled old cashiers who must have screwed up pretty badly in life to be ringing up condoms and quarts of milk at the age of eighty-five.

What am I doing? Virginia had asked herself at least five hundred times since deciding to get into Min-Jun's car. But then she'd hear Benny's voice in her mind: *Do you want to contribute or not?*

"So," Min-Jun said. "Here's the deal. I've got an international distribution network, but no inside guy anymore. The money's not fantastic—I mean it's just tits and ass—but at least I can sleep at night. I'm voyeur-only, that's where I draw the line. With underage girls it's way dicey. I need to sleep at night, you know?"

Virginia looked at him. "Uh-huh . . ."

Min-Jun took another hit of the joint. Then he unbuckled his seat belt. For a second Virginia was alarmed, like maybe he was about to pull down his pants or something. But he just twisted in his seat to reach into the back. He rustled around for a while. His face was so close to Virginia's that she could smell his unwashed hair. Finally he produced a small stack of videotapes. He thrust them into Virginia's lap. *Locker Room Wildcats Vol 4, Locker Room Wildcats Vol 8.* The covers were splashed with cheap clip art of pom-poms and still-shots of boobs.

"We use old-school tech because it's harder to rip off. I bet you've never even seen a VHS, have you, you little baby. . . ." Min-Jun leaned back in the driver's seat and looked at her with a cool, admiring grin on his lips.

Virginia was having trouble breathing normally. It was scary, the way he was looking at her, but also undeniably flattering. No one had ever looked at her like that before— like they wanted to eat her. Like she was a scrumptious, very-bad-for-you dessert.

He kept staring at her. "I'll be the only one on the scene with an inside *girl*. I bet you can get me some real slumber party shit, can't you?"

Virginia shrugged. Then she asked, in what she hoped was a matter-of-fact tone, "How was Choi getting all this footage? Was he always in the mascot suit?"

"Nah, nah," Min-Jun said. "Volumes one through ten were made with crappy little hidden cameras. We thought we could ratchet up the price if we got more *intimate* footage. Up close and personal with your fave Wildcats, you know?"

"Totally," Virginia said, starting to feel a little ill. *Breathe,* she told herself. Then she realized maybe it was the pot smoke making her feel strange. *Don't breathe.*

"So is it true the football players realized he was in the suit and chased him off the bridge?" Min-Jun asked.

"No, that's just a rumor."

"So what the hell happened?"

Virginia shrugged. "Maybe he had an attack of conscience."

Min-Jun scoffed. "I doubt it. Like I said, I sleep at night. It's just a little skin. They're just girls. What they don't know can't hurt 'em."

"Deep," Virginia said.

Min-Jun laughed. "I like you, Vir-gin-iaaa," he said, stretching out her name as he stretched himself out too, leaning back even farther in the driver's seat. "You're a cool girl. So let's take a look at Choi's final chef d'oeuvre, shall we?"

"Well, I don't have it on me," Virginia said.

"Oh, where is it?"

"Um . . ."

"Listen, if this is about the price, we can negotiate. I can go as high as three hundred. Three-fifty. Four hundred."

"Can we open a window?" Virginia asked.

Min-Jun shook his head. "Not a good idea. The smell. So where's the video?"

Virginia took a deep breath. "I really need some air." She reached for the door handle and pulled it. It was locked. She yanked on it. Still locked.

"Girl, chill." Min-Jun laughed.

"Just let me open the door a crack."

"Chiiiiill . . ."

Virginia looked at him. He was staring at her, that weird grin still on his face. He licked his lip, his tongue flicking out like a lizard. Suddenly he didn't seem very attractive anymore. His thin lips and his expressionless eyes made Virginia want to throw up. She looked down. But what she saw at her feet made it even worse. It was a pair of girl's underwear, blue spandex with a white *W* sewn into the side. It was the kind all the cheerleaders wore under their little skirts, flashing when they did flips and cartwheels.

"Oops," Min-Jun said.

Virginia looked up, terrified that Min-Jun had noticed her noticing. But he didn't seem to care. His indifference disturbed Virginia more than anything. It was almost as if he'd put the panties there on purpose, so he could enjoy watching her reaction. He took another hit of the joint, his eyes never leaving her face.

"Wanna try 'em on?" he asked, nodding toward the panties, sounding half serious.

"I'm not a cheerleader," Virginia said.

"I know. That's what I like about you," he said back.

Virginia glanced at the door. In the darkness it was hard to see where the lock was, and she didn't want to reach for it again until she knew exactly what she was doing.

"I thought you said you were voyeur-only," she said. Then it hit her. "Oh my God. Did you go through my room? Was that you?" She shouldn't have said it. Now he knew that she knew. Min-Jun just laughed, seeming really stoned.

Get out of here, she told herself, eyeing the door again. Where was the lock? And where was the cop car? If only it would just cruise past again, she could bang on the window and scream for help.

"Just try 'em on," Min-Jun said. "They'll look good on you."

In the midst of her panic, it occurred to Virginia how hypocritical he was being. If he liked that she wasn't a cheerleader, why was he pushing her to put cheerleader underwear on? *Make up your mind!* she wanted to scream at him. *Make up your mind and let me out of this car!*

She felt a hand on her thigh. She screamed.

"Whoa, whoa!" Min-Jun said.

"GET OFF ME! GET THE HELL OFF ME!" Virginia barely recognized the sound of her own voice, it was so shrill and hysterical. Her hand flew to the door and she hit it over and over, looking for the lock.

"Jesus, I thought you were cool!" Min-Jun said, snapping out of his daze.

Finally her fingers found the lock, and she yanked the door open. Smoke spilled out. She tried to lunge, but realized she was still wearing her seat belt. Frantically she fumbled with the buckle and flung it off. Min-Jun's hand had found her thigh again and was squeezing it hard.

"Girl, be cool! It's cool! Get back here!"

Virginia screamed in his face and wriggled out of his grip. Then she hurled herself from the car, tripping over herself and tumbling onto the concrete. She felt her knees and palms scraping as she skidded. Half stumbling, she got back to her feet and started running. She didn't know where she was going. She didn't know if he was following her. She didn't look back. She just ran from the darkness into further darkness, her feet pounding on the concrete as her heart pounded in her ears.

Then she had to stop. She wasn't in good shape like Benny. She slipped into a shadow next to the closed dollar store to catch her breath. She scanned the parking lot for Min-Jun. The dingy Ford Fiesta was sitting by itself at the far end. And Min-Jun was still inside—she could just barely make out his round, white face though the windshield. She thanked God he hadn't chased her, but her relief was short-lived; it was scarier, somehow, that he was just *sitting* there. He must have known she was there. He must have seen her ducking into the shadow. And maybe the second she tried to run, he'd start the car and mow her down.

Can he see me? Virginia looked down at her hands. She was pretty sure she was completely shrouded in blackness. It was safe in the darkness, but she was trapped in it. There was another patch of shadow next to the deserted bank, but how could she get there without exposing herself to the parking lot's floodlights? It was like that game everyone played as kids—lava—where you die if you touch the floor. Except in this version, you die if you touch the light.

Virginia had only meant to stay there long enough to catch her breath. But the longer she stood still, the more impossible it became to make herself run again. She was frozen. She just stared at the car, and felt it staring back.

The Boarders, 11:00 p.m.

"Hello?"

Benny stood on the front porch, deciding whether to go in. The door to the Boarders was wide open. Moths were fluttering toward the light. Benny had been walking back and forth in front of the school entrance for an hour, hoping that every car he saw magically contained Virginia. Then he'd remembered there was a back entrance that wound around the campus. Maybe he'd missed her. He'd run to the Boarders and found the front door hanging open like the saloon of a ghost town.

He called again. "Virginia? Hello?" Nothing. He took a tentative step through the doorway. In one hand was his flute, and in the other the paper bag from Home Depot. It was a little pathetic, coming over to put a lock on her door when she was already off somewhere with a dangerous pervert. What good was a lock going to do now?

Stop freaking out, Benny told himself. Installing the lock was less about Virginia and more about keeping himself calm. He'd decided that if he didn't hear from Virginia by midnight, he would call Detective Disco and ask him to put an APB on the guy's blue Ford Fiesta. So it was just a matter of keeping himself together until then.

The house was empty. Everyone was probably at the OK

Café, which was where Winship kids went after games to drink milkshakes and hang out. Benny was walking down the girls' hall toward Virginia's room when he saw that her door was wide open, just like the front door. And there were sounds coming from inside.

"Virginia?" Benny called hopefully. He ran the last couple of steps to her room. The first thing he saw was a pile of clothes flying through the air. Then he saw who was throwing them, and it wasn't Virginia.

"*You?*"

For a second Gerard froze.

"Get out of here!" Benny shouted at him. "What do you think you're doing?"

Then Gerard immediately started yelling, "Where is that video? Tell me! Where is that video? I'm giving it to the police! You won't humiliate me again!"

"Get out!" Benny repeated. "This is a private room, for Christ's sake. What do you think you're doing?"

Gerard's face was red. He opened a drawer, threw its contents on the floor, then slammed it shut. "Where is it? Tell me!"

"She doesn't even have it anymore. It's gone. Now get out of here, you creep!"

Gerard's mouth gaped open. "Me, a creep? ME, A CREEP? I'm the only guy at this school who ISN'T a creep! If I were a disgusting rapist like Trevor, I'd have all the girls I wanted. But what do I get for being a nice guy?"

He swiped his arm across Virginia's desk, sending all her stuff crashing to the floor.

"Get out of her room," Benny said firmly. "Now."

"Get out of my face!" Gerard said back, tossing more of Virginia's stuff on the floor.

"GET OUT OF HER ROOM, YOU FUCKING CREEP!" Benny screamed. "GET OUT OF HER ROOM OR I'LL KILL YOU!"

Gerard stopped. All the redness in his face suddenly went white.

Benny realized how hard he was breathing. He'd never screamed at anyone like that in his entire life. He stared at Gerard, not backing down.

"*Kike,*" Gerard hissed under his breath, which Benny pretended not to hear. Gerard stormed past him into the hall. Benny watched to make sure he left. Then he sat down on the bare mattress of Virginia's bed, the sheets tangled in a pile at his feet. He dropped his flute and his Home Depot bag and put his head in his hands. He was so tired all of a sudden. He wished he could go to sleep and not wake up for twenty hours. He checked his watch. Forty-five minutes until midnight.

Benny was having a hard time getting his breathing to normalize. He felt a huge lump in his throat. Was he about to cry? He couldn't remember the last time he'd felt this upset. Virginia was probably dead. Or raped. And even if she wasn't one of those things, she probably would be sooner or later, because the Boarders had no security, and she was so stupid she'd get in a car with anyone. He should have done a better job looking after her. It was his club, after all!

He checked his watch again, but he could barely read it because his hand was shaking. Forty minutes until midnight.

"You okay, man?"

Benny looked up. Gottfried was standing in the doorway.

"I hear da shouting . . . ," Gottfried said, his eyes flickering around Virginia's trashed room.

"It's okay," Benny said, more to himself than to Gottfried. "It's okay."

"You are very stressed?" Gottfried asked. "Sometimes I feel dis way. I feel so . . . I don't know. I feel so disconnected. Like I'm running away. Like my mind isn't real. Like my mind is a small dog dat lives inside me, you know?"

Benny looked at him. "Not really."

Gottfried leaned into the doorway. He chewed his thumbnail. "When I feel dis way, Zaire helps me. Shall I find her for you? She does her hypnotism, and I calm right down and go to sleep."

"You let Zaire hypnotize you?" Benny asked.

"Oh *ja*," Gottfried said. "Many nights a week. She will do da same for you if you wish. You will go right to sleep."

Benny searched Gottfried's blank smile for a sign that he was trying to trick him or something.

"Thank you, but I'm fine," he said finally. "Actually, I need to call the police." Benny pulled out his cell phone. The midnight deadline was stupid. If Virginia was in trouble, he needed to call Detective Disco now. He started dialing.

"Da police? Dat is my cue to leave!" Gottfried exclaimed. "I am underage drinking!"

"Bye," Benny said. Then he heard the sound of crunching gravel coming from outside. He looked up from his phone. It was a police car coming slowly down the road.

Oh my God, he thought. The phone dropped from his hand. *She's gone. She's gone.*

11:25 p.m.

"I hope you've learned your lesson," the officer said as they turned down the road to Winship. He was a big man with a mustache. Big in a husky way—only slightly fat. He was nice, or at least had nothing better to do than take Virginia back to school. She must have stood in the shadow of the dollar store for an hour, just staring at Min-Jun's car and praying that he would give up and leave. But the car just sat there and sat there, as if daring her to try to get past it. Then finally, mercifully, the police cruiser had circled back on its patrol route. Virginia had flung herself from the shadows and frantically waved it down. Within seconds, Min-Jun's car had screeched away.

"No more gettin' in cars with strangers," the officer was

saying. "You kids got no idea how dangerous it is out there. Take it from me."

Virginia rolled her eyes. She hated it when adults acted like they were so great. You know what pretty much every bad guy in the world was? An adult. *They* were the reason the world was so dangerous.

"How come cops always eat donuts?" she asked.

The officer gave an irritated shrug. "You shouldn't stereotype people. I don't eat that crap." He gestured toward a protein shake that was sitting in the cup holder.

Virginia picked it up and examined the nutrition facts. "You may as well. There's forty-five grams of sugar in this."

"The hell there is!" He grabbed the protein shake and squinted at the label. "Daaamn!"

The car pulled up to the Boarders. It looked quiet and empty, but the front door was hanging wide open.

"This is where you live?" the officer asked dubiously. "Looks like a haunted house."

"It is," Virginia said. She opened the door. "Thanks for the ride."

He leaned over and called, "No more getting in cars with strangers! Unless they're me. And I'm not a stranger anymore—I'm Officer Good Guy! You call me any time."

He waved. Virginia loitered for a minute, waiting for him to give her a personal number or something. But he didn't. How was she supposed to call him if she didn't have his number? Dial 911 and ask for Officer Good Guy?

Whatever, Virginia thought. Adults were such liars. They said they wanted to help, but really they just wanted to dump you at the curb of your haunted house and get back to their business.

She slammed the car door and started trudging away. Her bloody shins and knees stung from skidding on the cement. She hoped there were some Band-Aids or Neosporin in the house.

"Virginia?"

She looked up. Someone was standing in the doorway, the light creating an unmistakable Benny silhouette.

"Hey," she said.

"Virginia, oh my God." He flew down the steps. His eyes ran up and down her bloody arms and legs. "Oh my God, no no no, what happened." It didn't sound like a question, and he sounded like he dreaded the answer. Virginia blinked at him. Was he crying? Were there tears in his eyes?

"I'm fine. I fell down. Aw, damn it. . . ."

"What? What?" Benny said.

Virginia rubbed her eyes. Then she reached into her jacket pocket and pulled out an envelope. "I accidentally took his money."

Benny's mouth fell open. "What did you . . . what did you *do?*"

"Oh my God, *nothing,*" Virginia said. "He wanted to buy the video. But obviously I didn't have it. Come on, I need to clean up."

Five minutes later they were in the small first-floor bathroom, sitting on the wide sink and dabbing cotton balls with disinfectant on Virginia's scrapes.

It could have felt weird, Benny invading an environment clearly designated for girls (tampon machine, no urinal, a fruity Febreze air freshener plugged into the wall), but it was actually very calming. The collection of hairbrushes crowding the countertop—who knew there were so many kinds? The bouquet of pastel-colored razors in a cup, their blades identical to men's razors, only disguised with curving pink plastic and lavender-scented moisture strips. The pink and purple toothbrushes with stripes of glitter. The row of deodorants, all lilac colored and green and baby blue, promising "freshness" and "lasting, romantic fragrance," never actually saying the word "sweat." The Band-Aids Virginia had found in a drawer, which Benny couldn't even tell were Band-Aids; they just looked like stickers of clouds and kittens and glittering stars. *There's a girl version of everything, isn't there?* he realized. Even their toothpaste contained glitter. Normally such obvious marketing would have bothered Benny, but at the moment it was strangely comforting. Why shouldn't girls have special things? They deserved them.

"So I don't know," Virginia was saying, unwrapping another brightly-decorated Band-Aid. "He has this gross little porn ring, but I don't see the point of getting involved. . . ."

"Wait, that one's still bleeding. Here, let me." Benny took a paper towel and pressed it against Virginia's knee, watching the blood seep through in small dots.

"I mean, I think *Locker Room Wildcats* is over. He needs an inside guy to replace Choi, but I can't imagine him finding anyone, especially not with all the attention on the school right now. . . . Maybe I could have done some undercover thing, but I think I blew that. I kind of freaked out on him. He probably thinks I'm a narc now."

"It's okay," Benny said, lifting the paper towel to inspect the scrape. "I wouldn't have wanted you to do anything like that."

"But I could have," Virginia said. "I really could have. I was doing fine until he grabbed me."

"I know you were," Benny said, placing a sparkling-puppy Band-Aid across her knee. "I know you could do it."

Virginia looked at him. Did he mean it? His face was so hard to read. He pressed another wet paper towel against her knee. His touch was very gentle and deft. It surprised her. For some reason she always expected him to be awkward.

"But please don't do anything like that again," Benny said. "Not without asking me first. These things need to be planned."

Virginia didn't say anything. She peeled another Band-Aid. She was starting to look like a human sticker book.

Benny went on. "I know you have abilities. I take those

abilities into consideration when I make plans. You need to trust me."

"I do trust you," Virginia said. "It's you who doesn't trust me."

"Well it's hard to trust you when . . ." His voice trailed off. It didn't seem the greatest time to mention the restraining order he'd found in her file on Principal Baron's computer. But was there ever a good time to tell your friend you'd willfully invaded her privacy and investigated her behind her back?

". . . when you repeatedly show poor judgment. Yes, there are things I trust about you. For instance, I trust you to always do your best. I trust you to never be lazy or defeatist. But no, I do not trust you to make good decisions. You should never have been in a situation where you were alone with a suspect in an unknown location. That was incredibly stupid and dangerous. Which is why you will let *me* make decisions from now on. That's nondebatable if you want to stay in the club."

Benny bent to place a final Band-Aid on Virginia's shin. But at the last second she moved her leg away.

"Actually, you know what's nondebatable?" she said suddenly. "If you want to use my abilities, you have to treat me better. I didn't join Mystery Club to be your slave."

Benny scoffed. "I think 'slave' is a tad hyperbolic."

Virginia scoffed back. "Barely! You never let me do

anything. If it were up to you, we'd do nothing but sit around all day thinking."

"*Thinking* is the most important part!" Benny snapped. "Why can't you understand that?"

"Well *think* about this," Virginia said. "Without me you'd be nowhere. *I* flirted with those Asian Fusion creeps. *I* stole the mascot head. *I* found out about *Locker Room Wildcats*. *I* hid the video and got my room trashed while you stood around like a marble statue of a nerd."

"Hang on. *I* was the one who told you to flirt with the Asian Fusion guys, if you recall. You didn't even want to do it."

"Well *you* couldn't have done it at all," Virginia argued.

"What do you want, credit or something? Are you building a résumé to join some other Mystery Club that I'm not aware of? In *this* club, the goal isn't glory seeking. It's to improve our minds, and, by extension, the world, through mystery solving."

"Oh my God!" Virginia shouted. "Why do I have to be in Mystery Club for the exact same reasons as you? Why can't I have my own reasons?"

"Because it's *my* club!"

"And what does that even mean, improving your mind and the world or whatever? Why do you actually do this? What is your weird deal?"

Benny gawked at her. His *weird deal*? He liked solving mysteries and was good at it. Why did it have to be a *deal*?

"What—I— It means what I said it means!" he sputtered. "What do *you* mean?"

"You sound like a kindergartener. You can't control everyone, Benny! God! You and Zaire should totally be boyfriend-girlfriend, because you are exactly alike."

"We are not!" Benny yelled. His voice echoed off the tile walls, and the sound of it startled him. He glanced at his reflection in the mirror. His cheeks were red. *Calm down,* he told himself. Benny never could have imagined himself fighting like this with someone, especially not a girl. Usually he kept his feelings under the surface where they just kind of simmered uselessly. Yet here he was, in the girls' bathroom where he had no business even being, screaming at his fellow club member who was *bleeding*. He felt embarrassed and ashamed.

"Sorry . . . ," he said, struggling to think of something to say that could bring the conversation back from the brink. "Um . . . okay. Do you want to be vice president?"

Virginia lit up instantly. "Yes. Wait, really?"

"Sure."

"Yes!"

Benny frowned at one of the pink Band-Aids on Virginia's shin, which was turning brown from blood. "Except if we're both officers, it means we're a club with no members."

"It means we're a duo!"

"Well, I'll have to make a chart outlining the division of

power," Benny said before she could get too excited about the promotion.

"Um, sure, if you seriously don't think two people can work together without a *chart*."

"I'm just saying, for efficiency's sake—"

"I'm just saying, having a relationship is probably more efficient than having a chart."

Benny immediately looked down.

"Not, like, a *relationship*, obviously," Virginia quickly said. "Just like, when two humans have a relationship in which discussions occur. Oh my God! You know what I mean."

"Fine, fine, no chart."

"I mean, I don't even care. Chart, no chart, whatever. *I* don't need a chart. If *you* need a chart—"

"I don't need a chart!"

They both stared down at the floor. The bathroom felt painfully quiet.

Abruptly Virginia hopped off the sink. She gathered up the bloody paper towels and Band-Aid wrappers and threw them in the trash. "I'm going to bed. Can you get home?"

Benny nodded and pulled out his phone. "I'll text my mom. Um, just one thing, though. I got you a lock for your door. Let me just install it real quick. Is there a toolbox anywhere?"

Virginia shrugged. "I think there's a hammer in the closet."

"I need a power drill. I just assumed y'all would have one."

"We don't have anything."

Benny thought for a moment. "Okay, I'll come back first thing in the morning to put this lock on. Tonight, I guess . . . just stack some books in front of your door. Make sure you're the last one up, and that the front door is locked and the windows are closed before you go to sleep. Okay? You'll do those things?"

"Got it," Virginia said, yawning. She went into the hall, and Benny followed her. She opened the door to her room. "Oh my God. *Again?*"

Benny had forgotten the mess. "Oh yeah. Gerard's the one who's been trashing your room. I caught him doing it. He was looking for the video."

"Gerard was in my room? Ew!"

"I don't think he'll come back though. I yelled at him pretty bad."

"You yelled at him? Cool."

Benny shrugged. "Don't go to sleep without making sure the front door is locked," he repeated.

"I won't, I promise."

"Okay, well . . . good night."

"Night!" Virginia waved and went into her ransacked room. Benny stood in the hall for a second, hesitating to leave her alone with just Gottfried upstairs. What if Min-Jun came back? For a second he thought about asking Virginia to come stay with him. She'd be safer at his house. But then he thought of the circus of awkwardness that would entail—his mother's glares, his grandma's fascination (a girl in the house! With hair as yellow as a Crayola crayon!), and everyone assuming they were up to some hormone-fueled shenanigans. Worse—the idea of his dad and Virginia in the same room made Benny almost physically uncomfortable. What if his dad did something embarrassing? Would Virginia laugh? He just couldn't deal with it.

"I'll be back in the morning," he said. "Stay safe. In fact, just stay in your room."

"Okay, Dad."

Benny paused. Virginia was picking stuff off the floor and dumping it on the bed. He couldn't tell if she was joking, or if the "Dad" had been a genuine mistake, like that time at the Sapphire Lounge.

"Well . . . see ya."

"See ya," Virginia said back distractedly. Benny watched her shove an armful of clothes into a drawer, not bothering to fold them this time. Why didn't she ever seem scared? Did she just not show it? Or did she lack the common sense to be scared? If that was the case, in a way, Benny envied her.

He went outside, and soon the headlights of his mom's Subaru appeared at the end of the dark road. As he opened the car door, he gave a backward glance at the Boarders. The bulb in the streetlamp flickered like a camera flash on the old brick house. He could see Virginia's light on the first floor, and her shadow moving across the gauze curtain. Why did they have the girls on the first floor and the boys on the second floor? It made no sense. It would be safer to have the boys on the first floor—no one wanted to spy on boys or watch them undress. Why did no one think these things through?

"Benjamin?"

"I'm coming."

He got into the car. There was a granola bar waiting for him in the passenger-side cup holder. He was hungry, but the sight of it displeased him. How was he expected to become a man in a life filled with granola bars planted here and there to satisfy his slightest hunger? He folded his arms, resolved not to eat it. He'd cook something when he got home. Benny didn't have the slightest idea how to cook, but he'd just have to figure it out. It's what adults did.

"Did you see I brought you a granola bar?" his mother asked.

Benny sighed and unwrapped it, his resolve having lasted about five seconds. He didn't want his mom to feel unappreciated. And besides, he really was hungry.

The woods, 12:30 a.m.

Forgive me, Jesus. I love you!

Corny said a quick prayer before slurping up the gelatinous pink goo. The first time Corny ever got drunk, she'd felt so awful the next morning at church that she'd promised Jesus she'd never do it again. And she'd only done it three times since then, so that wasn't so bad. There were girls at Winship who got trashed every weekend, like Chrissie White, who had the worst drunk eyes of anyone. And besides, this was a special occasion. It was a beautiful, festive night, the boys had won the game, there was a keg, and Brittany and Angie's stepmom had made pink Jell-O shots for the girls. Jell-O shots were Corny's absolute weakness. They were the most magical substance in the world—pink and sweet and you couldn't tell there was vodka in them at all! Corny's philosophy was that it was healthy to sin once in a while, because afterward when you repented, you felt closer to Jesus than ever before. And the buzz of holy forgiveness lasted for days, unlike being drunk, which only lasted a few hours.

The party was on the other side of the bridge, which was technically off campus, so as long as things didn't get too rowdy, no one would get in trouble. There was a fire in the fire pit, and everyone had brought camping lanterns and flashlights and marshmallows, and "Sweet Child o' Mine" was playing on the boom box, and the whole thing was like a Girl Scout camping trip, except even better because *boys* were there.

The darkness made everyone a little bolder. Usually Winship parties started with all the girls on one side and the boys on the other, like an elementary school square dance or something. But tonight everyone was so excited, and the night air felt so heavenly, and boys already had girls sitting in their laps, and girls were downing Jell-O shots and giggling and twirling their hair. Corny couldn't wait for Winn to get there so she could sit on his lap and twirl her hair too.

She texted him again: *Almost here? <3<3 <3<3 xoxoxx*

Winn had disappeared after the OK Café and apparently gone home. She'd practically had to beg him to come back out for the after-party. Winn was like that sometimes—he was sensitive and moody and needed to be alone. Corny found it very manly and tried to humor his moods as much as possible. But this was kind of unacceptable. The woods at night were romantic, but they were also spooky. What if that scary voodoo freak Zaire Bollo came out and put a spell on everyone again? Winn needed to be there to protect her. Corny barely remembered anything from that day since the spirit show, but apparently someone screwed with her hair, because all the layers were choppy and funny looking. But whatever! She'd put some cute barrettes in for now and had an appointment at Flair tomorrow to get it fixed. Nothing was going to spoil this magical evening of victory and s'mores and cloudless night sky.

Margaret Inman passed by with another plate of Jell-O shots, and Corny grabbed one.

"Where's Winn?" Margaret asked.

"Oh, he's coming," Corny assured her. She downed the Jell-O shot and licked the sticky sugar residue from her lips.

"Careful, girl!"

"Now I've . . . had . . . the time of my liiiiiife . . ."

There were squeals of laughter as Jamie Bannish turned

up the volume on the boom box to max. A bunch of girls collapsed into giggles. Jamie was pretending to be Gerard, and Steve Sommer was pretending to be Trevor, which would have been funny, except it was the third time they'd done it since the party started, and the drunker they got, the gayer their reenactment got, with Steve practically humping Jamie's leg at this point. It was starting to feel uncomfortable and ruining the romance of the evening. Corny looked around to make sure Gerard wasn't there before she dutifully laughed along with the other cheerleaders.

"Y'all!" she chided good-naturedly, wishing they would stop.

"Now I've . . . had . . . the time of my—"

A scream pierced through the song. Corny whirled around. It didn't sound like a scream of excitement—it was like someone having a nightmare. And it was immediately followed by another scream. Someone ran past her, slamming into her shoulder.

"Ow!"

A plate of Jell-O shots flew threw the air, the pink blobs splattering across the ground like pieces of exploded brain.

"RUN! RUN!" someone was screaming.

"What's happening?" Corny shrieked.

And then she saw it.

A shadowy mass of fake fur and plastic teeth was crouching in the shadows, like it was hiding. As soon as Corny saw it, it leaped out at her. Its arms were wide open, as if to say, *Hug me! Love me!* But its grin was malicious and insane. Corny stumbled backward, almost falling. Then she turned and ran. The mascot followed on thumping feet, its paws outstretched to catch and crush her.

The woods, 12:30 a.m.

It wasn't Virginia's first campfire party. She'd gone to all ten of them last year—campfires were always the best for gossipmongering. The darkness brought out everyone's wild side. Virginia remembered night skies dotted with twinkling stars, and people dancing around a blazing fire like in a music video for a country song. But as she looked around now, it didn't seem that way. There were no stars; the sky was ugly and bruise colored from the city's light pollution. The fire was puny and smoking. No one was dancing except Jamie and Steve, who were only making fun of Gerard's spirit show performance. And people's laughter didn't sound magical and delightful, it sounded drunk and coarse. Had Winship parties always been this stupid? What gossip was there to be had? *BREAKING NEWS: Football Player Acts Like Idiot. Ginger Rollins Wears Hideous Shirt. Corny Sits on Wrong Lap Thinking It's Her Boyfriend's.* Who cared?

Virginia wished Benny were there. Not because he'd be such a great date—in fact, the idea of socially navigating him through the evening was exhausting—but because genuinely interesting things seemed to happen when Benny was around.

"Now I've . . . had . . . the time of my liiiiiife . . ."

The song seemed to be mocking her. The only reason she was even at this party was because Chrissie had begged her to come. Chrissie hated going to parties by herself, which Virginia didn't understand at all. Going to parties by yourself was pretty much the coolest thing a person could do. Just stride in alone like the most mysterious and unfathomable creature on the planet. But Chrissie was so insecure she could barely tiptoe to the bathroom without checking her face for zits first. It was the same routine as last year: Chrissie changing her clothes a million times (as if a pink V-neck and jeans were any more or less exciting than a blue V-neck and jeans) and then clinging to Virginia for an hour or however long it took to down five Jell-O shots and be drunk enough for Virginia to ditch.

"Want one?" Chrissie asked, holding up a pink jiggling square.

"No thanks," Virginia said. She'd seen how stupid people got on that stuff. As if anyone at Winship needed assistance to act like an idiot.

Chrissie heard the screaming first.

"Did you hear that?" She looked around.

"Hear what?"

Then there was another scream, one that came from right behind them.

Virginia spun around. People were running, dropping their drinks and marshmallows onto the dirt.

Oh my God.

The mascot emerged from between two trees, looking ghastly in the dim firelight. The suit was dirty and muddy and matted. The plastic head was off center. As Virginia stared at it, the mascot raised its furry hands and adjusted its face slowly until its huge white eyes stared back at her. Then it lunged forward.

Virginia shrieked. She looked around for Chrissie, but she was gone. She could hear people screaming in the woods all around her. The mascot took another giant step. Virginia didn't know whether to stand her ground or run.

She ran. Everyone else seemed to be running toward the road. Virginia ran toward the bridge. Her feet pounded onto the 150-year-old wooden slats. She made it to the center and then stopped and looked back. Was the mascot following her? Who was inside? And how had it resurrected itself from the river? She couldn't see anything but a spot of yellow campfire amid the blackness of the trees. Below her, the river rushed past, its sound dulling the screams. Virginia stood, frozen.

"Virginia."

She jumped and whirled around. There was a man on the other side of the bridge. He stepped toward her, a silhouette of blackness. She recognized his outline immediately. No boys at Winship had hair like that.

"Are you . . . are you following me?"

"Yes."

Virginia's heart slammed in her chest. She started to back away.

"It's cool," Min-Jun said. "Be cool."

Virginia stopped.

"I had to find you again."

"Well . . . here I am."

He closed the distance between them slowly. Then he leaned on the low railing and looked out at the river. Virginia found herself relaxing a little. Not much, but a little. Min-Jun's body language was casual; at least he wasn't blocking her path. Virginia inched away the tiniest bit, but tried to seem casual too. She glanced across the bridge, preparing to bolt.

"Did you tell on me? To that cop?"

Tell on me? It was something a ten-year-old would say. You don't "tell on" a child pornographer; you "report them to the authorities." Virginia gave Min-Jun a sideways look.

"No," she said. "I didn't tell on you."

Min-Jun sighed, relieved. "Whew. Wow. I knew you were cool. I just freaked you a li'l, didn't I? You're a cutie. No one's touched you before."

He looked at her, and Virginia immediately looked away.

"I don't—that's not—"

Shut up, she ordered herself. If she couldn't be cool, she needed to be quiet. She looked around. Where was the mascot? Where was anybody? Everything was quiet all of a sudden.

Min-Jun laughed. "So . . . you gonna keep my money? Or give it back?"

"Give it back," Virginia said.

"Okay then, hand it over. No hard feelings. You're just not up for this."

"Yes I am!" Virginia said. *Why am I getting insulted?* she thought. It's not like she wanted to be in a porn ring. But even though Min-Jun was weird and gross, she didn't want him thinking she was a priss. She still wanted to be cool. Was that pathetic?

Min-Jun smiled. "Maybe next year, cutie. So where's my cash?"

"It's in my room," Virginia answered. It was the truth.

"Let's go get it! I'd love to see your room. What color is your bedspread? Pink?"

"It's toile," Virginia said.

"What's *twall*?"

"It's like, pictures of flowers and goats."

Min-Jun chuckled. "Okay, let's go see these goats and get my money."

"Um, I don't know. We're not supposed to have guests. . . ."

"I'll sneak in your window."

Virginia shook her head. "I'll just . . . I'll give it to you tomorrow."

"Give it to me tonight."

Now he was facing her. In the darkness his long silky hair was blacker than black. The river seemed louder all of a sudden. It was the blood rushing to Virginia's head. She felt dizzy. Min-Jun was touching her hand. His fingers were cold and clammy.

"Don't freak out," he said. "We'll go reeeal slow."

Then there was a loud rumble of thunder. Virginia reflexively looked up. But the sky was still cloudless and mauve. In a split second she realized it wasn't thunder. It was thundering footsteps pounding across the bridge.

THWACK!

A hulking shadow slammed Min-Jun's head against the rail. Virginia jumped back.

"Awww!" Min-Jun moaned, crumpling in a ball.

"STAY AWAY FROM HER!" the shadow growled. "THAT'S MY GIRLFRIEND!"

A wave of golden hair and blue letter jacket became apparent in the darkness.

"Oh my God, Winn?" Virginia said.

He'd knelt down and was punching Min-Jun's face. Each punch landed with a grotesque *smack*. "THAT'S. MY. GIRLFRIEND."

Virginia heard a terrified squeal behind her.

"*Winn!*" It was Corny. Her phone was open in her hand. "What is he doing?" she shouted at Virginia.

"I don't—I don't know!"

"We're on the bridge," Corny said into the phone. "Please hurry. Winn! Stop! Stop him, Virginia!" she yelled. "Why is he beating up your boyfriend?"

"He's not my boyfriend," Virginia said. She turned back to Winn, who was continuing to pummel Min-Jun, probably breaking his skull with his fists. The sound of each punch made Virginia feel more sick.

"Winn!" she shouted. "Stop it! What are you doing?""

Winn whipped around. His face looked crazed. He grabbed Virginia's head. "STAY AWAY FROM HIM," he snarled at her. "HE'LL FUCK YOU."

He yanked her by the hair, so hard she felt her scalp burn with pain. He dragged her across the bridge, away from the bloody heap of Min-Jun.

"Ow! Let go!" Virginia shouted. "Let go of me!"

"WINN!" Corny shrieked. At the sound of her voice, Winn let go of Virginia's head. A small tuft of blond curls came away with his hand. He looked at Corny. Then he looked at Virginia.

"Winn?" Corny said in a tiny, confused voice.

Winn swayed unsteadily. Then he tipped forward and threw up. Vomit splattered across the wooden bridge.

"Ew!" Corny yelled, jumping back.

Virginia peered past him to Min-Jun, who was lying motionless. Had Winn killed him?

"Freeze! Everybody freeze!"

Virginia turned. Flashlights were shining in her face. She squinted, blinded. Then she heard a woman's voice—

"There. I told you that was her."

The road, 1:00 a.m.

There were three cop cars, with officers piling a different guy into each one. The first was Min-Jun, bloody and barely able to stand. The second was Winn, a brown stain of vomit running down his shirt. Corny was crying and pleading with the officer handling him. "Be gentle! He's a sweetie; he just doesn't know his own strength! I love you, Winn!"

Winn looked dazed as he disappeared into the back of the car.

The third was the mascot. Except he wasn't the mascot anymore, he was just a dumbass in a letter jacket.

"GRRROOOWL!" Trevor Cheek yelled, grinning as he ducked into the car. "I'm gonna get you! I'm gonna GET YOU!"

"Shut up," a cop snapped at him.

The mascot head and soggy suit sat in a heap next to a tree. The story was that Trevor had found them washed up on the riverbank next to the football field and thought it would be hilarious to scare everyone. That was so Trevor. Other people's fear seems hysterical when you're a linebacker and no one can touch you.

The cop cars lit up the scene with their red and blue lights. Virginia watched from a little ways away. Everyone was trying to leave, but one of the cruisers had blocked the exit to the road. Virginia gingerly touched the spot on her head where Winn had ripped out a small patch of her hair. Her fingers came away with a little blood on them.

"Some night, huh?"

Virginia turned around. Detective Disco and Detective Holling were standing together with their arms crossed. Their flashlights pointed toward the ground, creating a spotlight at their feet. They looked like they were posing for a TV show about cops busting kids. *Bad Teens*, it would be called.

"You can't arrest me," Virginia said immediately. "I haven't even been drinking."

Detective Disco narrowed his eyes. "Why would we want to arrest you?"

"I don't know. I'm just saying . . ."

"Do you need to be arrested?" Detective Holling asked. Car doors slammed behind them.

"No," Virginia said.

"Can you tell us what that fight was about? On the bridge?"

"I have no idea . . . ," Virginia said, bolstered slightly by the fact that she wasn't even lying. She really had no idea. Did Winn know about *Locker Room Wildcats* somehow? Was he defending Corny's honor? "I guess Winn thought that guy was hitting on his girlfriend."

Detective Holling nodded toward the first cop car, the one with Min-Jun in it. "Do you know him? He doesn't look like a Winship student to me."

Virginia shook her head slowly. "I don't know him. I was just standing there."

Detective Disco stared her down. He looked even taller than she remembered.

"Where's your friend?" he asked.

"What friend?"

"Your pal with the glasses. The one in charge."

Virginia scoffed. "He's not in charge! We're both in charge."

Detective Disco gave a phony smile. "Sure you are. You wanna give him a call? Ask him what to say?"

"I can say what I want."

"Which is . . . ?" Detective Holling prompted.

"Which is *nothing*," Virginia snapped. In her mind she frantically tried to remember what the official story was. Mr. Choi snuck into the mascot suit to watch cheerleaders undress, and then flung himself off the bridge? For no reason? She wished Benny were there. He could remember who knew which details better than she could. He could see the big picture. *Just keep your mouth shut,* she told herself.

"What is going on at this school?" Detective Disco asked flatly.

Virginia shook her head. She started backing away, half expecting them to stop her and cuff her and throw her in the car with Trevor. They didn't. They just stared at her.

"Can I take that?" she asked, pointing to the mascot suit on the ground.

The detectives glanced at each other.

Oops. That was a mistake. Now they looked really suspicious.

"The coaches were looking for it," she said. "It cost, like, three thousand dollars. . . . I know where it goes."

Detective Disco let the moment hang. Virginia raised an eyebrow like, *What?*

"Sure," he said finally. "Take it."

Quickly Virginia picked up the suit and plastic head. She turned and started walking toward the Boarders, not looking back in case he'd changed his mind. There was a chill in the air as she crossed the bridge.

What am I doing?

She hadn't intended to pick it up. She didn't know what she planned to do with it. She just felt this weird connection, like she couldn't leave it there. But she hated it. She adjusted it in her arms so its eyes faced away, gaping out into the darkness.

The Boarders, 3:30 a.m.

Someone was crying.

It wasn't the most unfamiliar sound in the world. People cried in the Boarders all the time. But this was different. It wasn't the crying of someone who was lonely or stressed or having a bad dream. It was the crying of a ghost—hopeless, drained of life, not knowing or caring whether anyone overheard.

Virginia got out of bed. She opened her door a crack and listened. It was coming from Zaire's room. She crossed the dark hall on bare feet. Then she knocked lightly.

Oh wait, damn it, she thought as soon as her knuckles hit the wood. It wasn't something Benny would have done. She should have called and asked him first. But it was too late. The door was opening.

She'd never seen Zaire without makeup on. It was kind of a hideous sight. She had puffy circles under her eyes, her nose was shiny, and her chin was dotted with purplish zits. Her lips were pale and cracked and gummy. She stared down at Virginia through watery eyes, looking confused and angry.

"You?"

Virginia shrugged. "Um, who were you expecting?"

"Nobody. Gottfried. I was hoping you were Gottfried." Her voice was hoarse.

"Jesus, why?" Why would Zaire want any boy to see her like this?

Zaire turned and threw herself on the bed, not seeming to care whether Virginia stayed or left. Virginia noticed a tall, half-empty bottle of gin on the desk, along with a cocktail shaker and a jar of olives.

"Want one?" Zaire asked, her face half smushed into a pillow.

"Sure. Is it a martini?"

"What does it look like?"

Virginia folded her arms. "How should I know? Am I a teen alcoholic or something?"

"I don't know what the fuck you are." Zaire sat up and

302

dragged herself to the desk. She poured a drink sloppily into a martini glass. Only Zaire would have actual martini glasses in her dorm room. She handed it to Virginia, poured herself one, and sat down on the edge of the bed. Virginia sat down next to her. Zaire had stopped crying, and it was quiet.

"Are you just drinking by yourself?" Virginia asked after a long silence.

"Not anymore. Now I'm drinking with you." Zaire smiled, but it was a grim, lifeless smile. "Cheers." She clinked her glass against Virginia's, spilling most of her drink. She flopped back on the bed, resting the glass on her stomach. Virginia did the same. The easiest way to get people to be comfortable around you, Virginia knew, was to imitate them.

"You still going to Boca Raton tomorrow?" Zaire asked, her eyes closed.

"Nah. Staying here."

"That's too bad. . . . Sure you won't come to Spain?"

Virginia shrugged. She lifted her neck to take a sip of her martini. She wrinkled her nose. "I think I like sidecars better."

"Everyone should have a signature drink. Mine is gin with a splash of tears."

Virginia stared at the ceiling. She could feel a feather from Zaire's plush down comforter poking into her arm. "What is this about?" she asked suddenly.

"What is what about?"

"You drinking and crying and stuff. I know you don't give a shit about Brittany. I know you don't give a shit about Choi."

Neither of them said anything. Their martinis bobbed gently up and down on their stomachs as they breathed. *It's so much easier to talk to people when you don't have to look at their faces,* Virginia realized. Maybe it was because they were both lying down. Or because Zaire looked like garbage instead of her usual perfect, overdone self. But something made it feel like the most natural conversation in the world.

"I don't give a shit either. I swear I'm not going to turn you in. Choi was vile. He deserved to die." Virginia didn't know if she really believed what she was saying. Obviously Choi was vile, but did he deserve to *die*? That seemed a little dramatic. It's not like he'd even touched anyone, as far as Virginia knew. But it seemed like what Zaire would want to hear.

Zaire sighed. "Choi, Choi, Choi. If I never hear the name Choi again, I'll die happy. You know what 'choi' means in Korean? Pinnacle."

Virginia turned her head slightly to glance at Zaire. *Pinnacle?* Was that supposed to be deep? Zaire could translate Korean words all she wanted; it wasn't going to fool Virginia. *You're a killer.*

Zaire sat up a little and took a sip of her martini before

lying back down again. Virginia did the same. The gin burned her throat going down. "So what's it about, then?" she asked, coughing a little.

Zaire started crying again. Then she stopped. "I have no one to talk to."

"You can talk to me."

"No I can't. You'll put it on your stupid gossip site."

God damn it, Virginia thought. Was Winship Confidential going to follow her around the rest of her life?

"I'm not like that anymore," she said. "I shut that site down, like, five weeks ago."

"Then you'll tell Benny Flax."

"Benny doesn't care about other people's business."

"He does when it's *mysterious*," Zaire said in a mocking voice.

"I won't tell him. This is just between me and you. Because we're friends."

Zaire turned her face to look at her. Virginia did the same. This close, Virginia could see some of the beauty in Zaire's face that was there naturally, despite the tears and acne and lack of makeup—the strong line of her nose, the intensity of her eyebrows, the shade of brown that was unique to her skin.

"Well . . ."

Virginia stiffened, sensing that Zaire was about to open up. But just then Wildcat hopped on the bed. He started rubbing against Zaire's face and purring.

"Wildcaaaat," Zaire cooed, petting him fondly.

Virginia reached out to pet him too.

"Better not," Zaire warned as Wildcat shrank from Virginia's outstretched fingers. "He only likes me. Actually he doesn't. Not even Wildcat isss my real friend." She was beginning to slur. "I hypnotize him to be nice to me."

"Wait, you can hypnotize animals?" Virginia said.

"Sure. I can hypnotize anything. Except I can't get Gottfried to love me." Her voice squeaked, and then she was crying again.

"You know, Gottfried's not that great," Virginia said, looking up at the ceiling again. "I'm sure you could get someone else. Have you tried college guys? Like Emory guys, maybe? They have Yankees at Emory. New Yorkers."

"I don't want a Yankee," she whispered, half sobbing. "I want Gottfried. I love him. I love him. I love every inch of him. I love his body. I love his heart. I wish I could *be* him. All my love is for him. I hate everything that isn't him. I hate the world. I hate you. I hate me. I love *him*." Zaire continued to ramble, repeating "I love him, I love him" over and over, until the words barely seemed to have any meaning.

This is getting weird, Virginia thought. It was like Zaire wasn't even talking to her, she was talking to herself. Like she was hypnotizing herself. Tears streamed down her cheeks. Her martini jiggled on her stomach as she cried. Virginia was afraid to look at her. It was shocking to see

Zaire so emotional. Virginia had no idea this much passion had existed under that stiff, haughty exterior. Why didn't Zaire show her feelings more? It actually made her more likable, in a weird, unexpected way. Maybe Zaire was a little demented, but demented was better than just plain bitch.

"Zaire, you need to stop hooking up with him."

Zaire sat up so abruptly her drink fell over. She glared at Virginia. "What did you say?"

"You need to give yourself space to get over him. He dumped you, what, six months ago? Right before prom?"

"Oh my God! What is with you and other people's business?" Zaire snapped. She got up and started making herself another martini. "You need to get a life."

"I have a life. I have two lives! Look at my palm . . . there are *two* life lines. A psychic told me."

Zaire rolled her eyes and stumbled back to the bed. She ignored Virginia's outstretched palm and downed her drink.

Virginia went on. "You can't be friends with benefits with someone you're in love with."

"Like you're an expert. You've never even had a boyfriend."

That one stung. Virginia sat up. "You don't have to be a relationship expert to see that you're hurting yourself."

"Seriously, get a life, Virginia, and stay out of mine," Zaire said.

"You're the one who needs a life. All you do is study and obsess over Gottfried. At least I have Mystery Club."

"Mystery Club?" Zaire spat. "You and Benny are the biggest five-year-olds in the whole school. You realize that everyone makes fun of you behind your back."

"Well at least I'm not letting a guy totally use me," Virginia spat back.

"At least I'm not going to *Boca* for holiday."

"I said I'm *not* going to Boca."

"Yeah, even worse, you're staying here, because no one wants you."

Virginia stood up. Her drink splashed to the floor. "Shut up," she said.

Zaire grinned. "Gosh, hit a nerve, did I?"

"Shut up," Virginia repeated. Then she walked out of the room.

"Aw, come on," Zaire called.

Virginia ignored her. She stood in the hall for a second, deciding whether to call Benny or go to bed. Then she chose a third option. Without planning to, she went upstairs to the boys' hall. She knew she was lapsing into Old Virginia—inserting herself into other people's drama—but Zaire was obviously incapable of managing her own business, and it was hard to just sit there and watch her self-destruct. Zaire probably wasn't that bad underneath—she was just messed up from being yanked around by Gottfried for so long.

The boys' hall was dark, except for a single light coming from under Gottfried's door. Virginia knocked.

"Come in."

She opened the door.

"Ah," Gottfried said, surprised. "I am sinking you are Zaire."

"She thought I was you," Virginia said back. "You're meant for each other."

Gottfried's room was a mess. It was pretty much the opposite of Zaire's room, which was neat and organized and full of expensive things. Gottfried's floor was scattered with junk-food wrappers, notebooks, and posters of German metal bands that had fallen from the wall. It was like looking into both of their minds: Zaire's resembled a well-curated museum; Gottfried's resembled a knocked-over garbage can lived in by a raccoon.

"You need to stop hooking up with Zaire," Virginia said bluntly. "She can't get over you, and it's turning her into a bitch."

Gottfried looked confused. "What?"

"Hooking up? It means, like, having sex?" Virginia explained awkwardly.

Gottfried nodded. "*Ja*, I know. But me and Zaire, we are just friends."

"I saw you."

"What?"

Virginia lowered her voice, remembering that Zaire was

in the room right below. "I know it's hard, because she throws herself at you. But you have to say no. You have to be really firm. No. *Nein*."

"Ehh, we broke up long ago," Gottfried said, looking embarrassed. "We do not have da sex."

"But she—I saw—" Virginia stopped talking. Without another word to Gottfried, she turned and went back downstairs. She glanced at Zaire's door. It was closed. Then she went into her own room and picked up her phone. She dialed the number of Benny's cell.

"Heelllo? Are you okay?" Benny's voice was raspy and sleep-steeped.

"I'm fine. Do you want to hear something weird? Zaire's been hypnotizing Gottfried."

"Yeah I know," Benny said, still sounding groggy. "He has insomnia. Hypnotism is actually a very effective technique—"

"No," Virginia interrupted. "She's hypnotizing him to hook up with her. To have sex with her."

She could barely bring herself to say the actual words: "She's raping him."

Saturday
The Boarders, 7:00 a.m.

The sky was a sheet of thin gray clouds, soon to be dispersed by the rising sun. A dim gold line ran across the horizon. It was colder than Benny expected. He shivered and rubbed his arms, watching his mom's Subaru disappear around the corner. He hadn't been able to go back to sleep after Virginia's call. "She's raping him." The words had hit him like a tidal wave. The words were staggering. Who *was* this girl? What did she want—dominion over every person in school? And what was Benny supposed to do about it? Put a lock on Virginia's door and let Zaire continue on her path of destruction?

He was halfway up the steps to the Boarders when he noticed a weird shadow next to the magnolia tree. He stared at it, and an outline slowly emerged before his eyes. It looked like the silhouette of an old-timey soldier. For a second Benny thought it was a cardboard cutout.

But then it moved.

"Hello?" Benny called out.

A figure stepped forward. It took Benny a moment to recognize Winn Davis. He was clutching his old Civil War rifle, like he'd come to protect the Boarders from Yankee assault. Yellow light from the rising sun created a golden halo around his already golden head. What was he doing here? According to Virginia, he'd been picked up by the police last night for pummeling Min-Jun. Had they just let him go? Benny supposed they would have had to if Min-Jun had chosen not to press charges, which was smart under the circumstances. But why hadn't Winn just gone home? Why was he loitering around the Boarders at seven a.m.? Was he waiting for *him*?

"Hi . . . ," Benny said hesitantly.

Winn said nothing.

"What's up? What are you doing here?"

Winn continued to stare at him. Benny started to panic. Was this about the tire slashing? Did Winn somehow know that he knew? Benny quickly rehearsed a small speech in his mind: *I won't tell anyone, I promise. It's not a big deal. What do I care if a bunch of spoiled rich kids get their cars damaged? Just leave me alone.*

"I think my girlfriend's cheating on me," Winn said suddenly, stepping closer. Benny eyed the rifle in his arms. The thing was more than one hundred and fifty years old; it couldn't actually shoot, could it? Not that it mattered if it could shoot. The point of the bayonet could easily pierce him through. He wanted to run, but felt oddly frozen.

"Oh . . . ," he said. "I'm sorry to hear that."

"With that German guy. And a Chinese guy."

"That's very . . . international," Benny managed.

"She's a whore."

Whoa, Benny thought. He glanced at Winn's rifle again. Winn was stroking it like it was a docile pet. And there was something scarier about that than if Winn had been pointing it straight at his head. Benny looked toward the road, praying that, for some random reason, his mom would come back. But the road was empty.

"You want my girlfriend too," Winn said. His voice was flat and expressionless. "I've seen you with her."

"Noooo, no no no," Benny said quickly. "I do not want her, I swear."

"Then you're a fag." Winn adjusted the rifle in his arms. It was almost like he was hugging it. His knuckles were bruised and bloodied. And Benny could see tiny dots of splattered blood all over Winn's face and clothes. Benny's heart slammed in his chest, imagining the kind of punches that would produce such a spray of red. It wasn't fair— Winn had the fists of a street fighter *and* a gun. Benny had nothing. Benny was going to die.

"So . . . what brings you to the Boarders?" he asked, trying to sound casual but failing.

"My girlfriend's in there," Winn answered, taking another step toward him. Benny felt the stone wall against his legs and realized he couldn't back up any farther. He glanced over his shoulder at the Boarders. It was gloomy in the early morning light. He willed the sun to rise faster, as if the morning light would save him.

"Huh. Okay. Well. Are you sure she's not at home? It's kind of early."

"Are you trying to mess with me?" Winn asked flatly.

"No. Huh? No no no."

"How stupid are you to mess with me?" He raised the gun, pointing it vaguely at Benny's head.

"Please put that down," Benny said. "It's dangerous."

Winn didn't put it down.

I should scream, Benny thought. *I should scream right now and run.* But he knew he wouldn't; he knew himself. He would stand right there and get shot by a football player and die. It was who he was. *Shut up,* he told himself. *Stop freaking out.*

He looked from the gun to Winn's face. It was hard to tell in the dim light, but his eyes looked glazed and deadened. He was either really stoned, or . . .

"Winn, who's your girlfriend?"

"Corny." He answered without hesitation.

"And what does Corny look like?"

"She's pretty. She has blond hair."

Benny frowned. Blond hair didn't really narrow it down. "What's her most . . . *remarkable* feature?" he asked delicately.

Winn shrugged. He lowered the gun a little. "She's pretty."

"I know, but . . ." Benny felt his cheeks getting hot. "What I mean is, is she quite . . . well endowed?"

Winn blinked at him. "Huh?"

"Does she have really big . . . *boobs*?" Benny said bluntly, holding his hands out to indicate large handfuls of breast.

Winn looked confused. "I don't . . . I dunno, bro. . . . She's pretty. She's in there." He pointed with his gun toward the Boarders. "Guys just won't quit. Don't they know she has a boyfriend?"

She has a boyfriend.

Suddenly a lot of things made sense, things Benny hadn't even been thinking about. The pom-poms at Virginia's door. The yellow rose, the notes on their lockers. Corny wearing Virginia's perfume. And now the fact that Winn couldn't seem to remember whether his girlfriend had huge boobs or not. *For god's sake, Zaire,* he thought. *Is there no end to the reach of your arm?*

"Listen, Winn," Benny said calmly. "Put the gun down. I think I know what's going on. I know you're worried about Corny. But I was just talking to her, and she loves you. You're the only one she loves. She doesn't care about Gottfried or that Chinese guy."

"But they'll still try to fuck her!" Winn cried. His glazed mask of a face suddenly contorted with emotion. "I have to keep them away from her! I have to watch her!"

"You look exhausted," Benny persisted, trying to imitate the soothing tone Zaire used onstage with the cheerleaders.

"You need to go home and go to sleep. Go home. Go home."

Winn appeared to consider it dimly. He started nodding his head, but then it sort of morphed into a shake. "No. I gotta stay here." He stared at the ground. For a second Benny wondered if he might have fallen asleep standing up.

"Winn?" Benny snapped his fingers. "Winn? Are you listening?"

Winn said, "Yeah."

"I think you need a break," Benny said. "Let me take care of Corny. I'll guard her."

Winn looked him up and down, and Benny could read the foggy conflict in his mind. Benny knew he presented as wimpy. He had the classic signifiers: glasses, curly hair, dorky clothes. He'd never felt the need to broadcast masculinity before; it seemed like something only insecure guys did. Except now he needed Winn to trust that he was man enough to take care of his woman.

"I have a brown belt," he said, which wasn't a lie, but of course a brown belt in aikido didn't mean the same thing as a brown belt in karate or tegumi. Aikido was mostly about mental training and achieving spiritual harmony, and the moves were all defensive. Benny didn't know how to beat someone's brains out. He really didn't want to know.

"Listen, Winn, I've got this." Benny did a quick ax kick that had nothing to do with aikido, but at least it looked impressive. This was definitely the weirdest moment of his life: doing bad karate at seven in the morning to convince a half-stupefied football player holding a gun that he could protect Corny Davenport, who wasn't even there, from a harmless German exchange student.

Winn was drooling slightly, apparently overwhelmed by the amount of thinking Benny was demanding of him. Benny wished he knew his trigger so he could snap him out of this trance and get him out of there.

"I'm your bro, Winn. Bros stick together." Benny grimaced slightly, feeling like ten thousand of his brain cells died every time he said the word "bro." But it seemed to be working. Winn was nodding again.

"Bros," Winn affirmed vaguely.

"Best bros!" Benny exclaimed.

"What's your name again?" Winn was squinting at him.

"I'm Benny Flax. Is that your car?" He nodded toward a blue BMW parked behind a magnolia tree.

Winn nodded.

"Okay, well you just drive on home and get some sleep, okay? I'll make sure no guys—foreign or otherwise—lay a hand on Corny. Okay? She loves you. Don't forget it."

"Okay. Thanks, bro," Winn said, reaching out and enveloping Benny in a tight hug. Benny stiffened reflexively. The rifle was squeezed between their chests, jabbing Benny's ribs. The hug lasted what felt like an abnormally long time.

Then Winn pulled away and shuffled off toward the car, the rifle's barrel bobbing on his shoulder. Benny watched him turn on the ignition, and kept watching until the tail-lights had disappeared around the corner.

Benny took out his phone and dialed Virginia's room number. She picked up after one ring.

"Benny?" she said immediately.

"Yeah," Benny answered. "Come outside right now."

"Where are you?"

"I'm out front. I think Winn Davis has been stalking you." Benny heard a snort of laughter. "I'm serious. Come outside and I'll explain."

The Boarders front porch, 7:45 a.m.

The sun was coming out, its glow obliterating the gray veneer of clouds. It felt the same in Benny's mind—the truth radiating and dispersing everything in its path.

A black town car had pulled up to the Boarders and was parked a ways away, apparently waiting for someone. The driver leaned against the front door looking at his phone. Benny watched him suspiciously, but the man didn't seem to have any interest in him.

Virginia came outside, wearing pajamas. He'd never seen a real-life girl in her pajamas before. They were light blue with little cowboy hats stitched on them. The shorts were too small, he couldn't help noticing. Almost her entire leg was showing as she plunked down next to him on the front steps, still bruised and scabbed and covered in Band-Aids from her fall last night. It was something he'd noticed before about Virginia's clothes—they were always a little too small. He'd assumed she was just following the style; all the girls at Winship wore their skirts as short as they could get away with. But now he suspected it was because her clothes were all old, that she'd outgrown them, that no one had bought her any new ones.

"What's going on?" she asked. She sounded alert, but her eyes were puffy and tired.

"Whisper," Benny whispered. He nodded toward the house. "Zaire."

"Oh, she's not here," Virginia said. "I just passed her room. It was empty, and her door was wide open."

"Whisper anyway. Listen, this is all Zaire. Everything weird, everything crazy, it's all her. I think she hypnotized Winn into thinking you're his girlfriend so he'd keep you away from Gottfried. Zaire thinks you like him. She's jealous."

"Wait. Oh my God," Virginia groaned.

"What? What?"

"He was in my room. I thought I was dreaming. It was last Saturday after Gottfried kissed me."

"Wait, Gottfried kissed you? Winn was in your room?" His voice raised. Christ, who *hadn't* been in Virginia's room? It was like a freaking train station in there, with every creep in town coming and going as they pleased.

"Just on the cheek," she whispered quickly. "Anyway, that night there was someone in my room. Only I thought I was dreaming. Then on Wednesday, after Gottfried and

319

I came home together, and I guess I was really drunk? There was a guy standing outside my window, which I had totally forgotten about until just now. And then last night someone threw a football at Gottfried's head. It was Winn! What a freak!"

"Well, in his defense he barely knows what he's doing. Zaire did a really crappy job on him, and he's totally confused."

"And last night at the party, he clobbered Min-Jun. I mean, he nearly killed him with his fists. He was like a caveman! And he ripped my hair out, see?" She lifted a lock of curls to reveal a small patch of exposed, bloody scalp. "He was actually, like, ten times scarier than Min-Jun."

Benny felt his jaw clench. She'd told him about the party on the phone, and alluded to some insane thing with the police, but she hadn't told him she'd been physically *hurt*.

"I told you to stay in your room," Benny said, knowing he sounded like a dweeby babysitter.

"Well it's a good thing I didn't, or I would have missed everything."

"You could have gotten in real trouble," Benny said. Except if he were honest with himself, that wasn't what was really upsetting him. It was that he'd missed all the action because it happened at some party that no one had bothered to invite him to. Not even Virginia.

"I would have called you," Virginia said quickly, seeming to read his mind. "I thought it was just going to be a dumb party. I wasn't, like, trying to Be There without you."

"I believe you. . . ."

"God, Zaire is out of control," Virginia said. "She's crazy about Gottfried. *Crazy* about him. She'd, like, hypnotize the world to turn backward on its axis if it meant he would like her again."

Neither of them said anything for a moment. They sat side by side with Benny's bag from Home Depot between them. Benny reached inside and held up the power drill. "Is it too early to use this? Will I wake everyone up?"

"Everyone's up already packing for break. . . . You going anywhere?"

"Nah. It's Yom Kippur, so . . . I'll just be reflecting on my sins."

"That doesn't seem fair. You're like the one guy in school who actually deserves a vacation."

Benny looked down, feeling a small jab of shame. Maybe Virginia wouldn't think that if she knew he'd snooped in her file behind her back. He wasn't going to say anything, though.

"It's kind of sad. . . . Actually, it's really sad," Virginia said tiredly, not making a move to get up.

"What is?"

"Zaire . . . Why can't she get over him? Why does she love him so much? He's not that great. But it's like he's the only guy in the world to her. It's like every other person is just a windup toy, and he's the only one who's real."

Benny looked at her, uncertain how to respond. She seemed more interested in the fact that Zaire was still in love with Gottfried than the fact that she'd tried to murder someone. But he didn't want to be insensitive, so he waited a beat before saying, "What I can't understand is what the mascot has to do with anything."

"Hm?" Virginia was resting her chin on her hand, apparently deep in thought.

"The mascot. I mean, that's where everything started. Did she know Choi was inside it? How would killing Choi help her get Gottfried back?"

"Oh. I don't know. . . ."

Another minute passed, the colors around them growing brighter as the sun rose. Everything was still. Then, at the edge of the woods, a flash of yellow and blue and brown caught Benny's eye.

"Wait," he said suddenly. "Where did you say you put the mascot?"

"In my room. I could barely sleep with it staring at me. I threw a blanket over its head, but it didn't really help."

Benny pointed to the trees.

"What the hell?" Virginia said. "Jesus Christ. You know what? I think that mascot is possessed."

"Quiet," Benny said. He dropped the Home Depot bag and the power drill on the porch. He started walking. Virginia followed.

The temperature had dropped even more since yesterday. It was like the weather had realized it was fall break already, and that it better get with the program. It even smelled like fall all of a sudden. The wind was sweeping thick clouds across the sun, making everything look sunny one second, and somber the next.

The mascot was shuffling through the trees, kicking up patches of leaves. It seemed to be leading by its heavy, plastic head. Occasionally it looked like it might fall over. Benny and Virginia followed at a distance.

"Who's inside it?" Virginia whispered. "Is it Trevor?" But she already knew it wasn't. Trevor's moves were campy and over the top—he was trying to scare people. Whoever was in there now was just bumbling along, almost toppling over with each step.

The mascot lurched to the left, and Benny grabbed Virginia and ducked behind a tree. But the mascot didn't see them, or at least didn't care. Benny kept walking. He held her wrist and kept her half a step behind him. An enormous gust of wind blew in their faces, as if trying to push them back.

It was obvious where the mascot was going.

The bridge.

They followed slowly as the huge furry beast stumbled between the trees. Its yellow shirt popped brightly in the light one moment, then turned dull as the sun disappeared behind a cloud. The wind blew so hard it actually whistled.

Virginia whispered, "It sounds like Zaire with her Coke bottle."

The sound of the rushing river grew louder as they approached the bridge. The mascot stopped at the edge. Benny and Virginia crept closer. They were about ten feet away. Then, slowly, the mascot turned. Its bulging eyes stared at them. Its white plastic teeth were frozen in a smile.

Virginia's arm was going numb, Benny was holding it so tight. But she didn't want him to let go. The mascot looked at them. They looked back. Virginia wanted to look at Benny, but couldn't tear herself away from the mascot's huge, unblinking eyes.

Then she heard a voice calling.

"Jump."

The mascot turned again. As soon as it moved, Virginia could see Zaire across the bridge. Even from a distance, she could tell it wasn't the same Zaire who had been drowning herself in martinis last night. This Zaire was perfect—perfect hair, perfect poise, her face stony and clear. Then her expression changed when she noticed Benny and Virginia.

"Hey! Get out of here!" she shouted over the sound of the river gushing below.

Benny let go of Virginia's arm. She looked down; her skin was bright white from his grip. Before she knew it, Benny was walking toward the mascot and lifting the enormous head from its shoulders.

"Don't!" Zaire shouted. "Benny, don't. I'll stop. I'll stop! Just don't take the head off. Please. Please!"

Benny looked at Virginia. Virginia shrugged. Benny dropped his hands and backed away.

Zaire started stomping across the bridge. Her four-inch-high heels hammered on the old wood. "Lie down," she ordered the mascot. "Relax and lie down." The mascot immediately plopped down on the ground and stretched itself out.

"Nod if you feel relaxed," Zaire said, looking at Benny.

"Um . . . ," Benny said.

"Not you, *him*." Zaire nodded to the mascot. Its enormous grinning head lolled to the side, apparently nodding.

Benny looked down at it. "I know who's in there. You can't hide him."

The wind whistled and blew Zaire's shiny black hair across her face. She brushed it away.

"I know you know," she said. "I'm not trying to hide him. I just don't want to see him." Her voice wavered slightly, barely noticeably.

She loves him, Virginia thought. She wondered what that must feel like, loving someone so much that you want to kill them and can't stand to see their face. Was it even love anymore at that point?

The three of them stood there on the steep bank, the river rushing past, the breeze swishing the leaves, the mascot lying at their feet. Their eyes flickered between one another: Benny to Virginia, Virginia to Zaire, Zaire to Benny. It was like they were all trying to decide which of them was in charge. *Obviously not me,* Virginia thought. She looked at Zaire's face. Up close, she could tell she hadn't slept. Even with her mask of makeup on, she looked ragged and hungover.

"Aha!" Benny exclaimed suddenly. The girls both looked at him.

Zaire snorted. "Did you actually just say 'aha'?"

"I just figured it out! Gottfried is *German.*" He smiled widely, like this was incredible news.

"Uh-huh," Zaire said, and gave Virginia a look, like, *Since when is Benny stupid?* Virginia was thinking the same thing, but it felt disloyal to gang up on Benny, especially with Zaire.

"He has a *German* mind," Benny went on excitedly. "In Germany they use the twenty-four-hour clock. Even if he's adapted to our twelve-hour system, deep in his subconscious mind, he's still hardwired to German time."

"Oh my God," Zaire said, slapping her forehead.

"Wait, what?" Virginia asked. "I don't get it."

Benny ignored her. "You hypnotized Gottfried to jump off the bridge at nine o'clock p.m. But to Gottfried, nine o'clock p.m. is *twenty-one hundred.*"

Zaire's mouth fell open. "Oh my God, you are so right."

"You must have hypnotized Gottfried earlier, right? Maybe Friday morning?"

Zaire nodded.

"Because it worked. We saw Gottfried the next day on the football field around nine o'clock. *A.M.*"

"Shit, really?" Zaire said. "Bloody hell . . ."

"You never meant to kill Choi at all. He had nothing to do with this. He was just in the mascot suit at the wrong time, spying on the girls. You never wanted to kill Brittany either. It was Gottfried the whole time. He's the only person you wanted dead."

He's the only person she loves, Virginia thought, and it gave her chills. She couldn't wrap her mind around love like that. She looked at Zaire's face. It seemed like she was about to cry. Her eyes were glassy, and her lip was trembling. But then she took a deep breath through her nose and wiped her eyes aggressively.

"I don't care what you think you know or don't know," she said.

Benny raised a finger. "Here's what I'm wondering though. How did Choi end up hypnotized at all? You must have hypnotized Gottfried long before the game. Why did you go back to the locker room? Why did you mess with him again? Or the person you thought was him?"

Zaire didn't answer.

"She just wanted to see him one more time," Virginia said. "To say good-bye."

Benny waited for Zaire to confirm. She didn't. "Okay . . ." he said. "I'm also wondering, did Choi lock Brittany in the pom-pom closet, or did you?"

"You think I'll just tell you?" Zaire snapped. "Because I'm overwhelmed by your detective genius?"

"I think it was you. I think you hypnotized her so she'd forget that she'd seen you, which is why she didn't scream or bang on the door for the other cheerleaders to get her out. It's also why she was so spacey on Monday when Corny finally rescued her. The hypnosis hadn't worn off. She was wandering in a half daze all over school, people thinking she was a grief-stricken Angie. . . ."

Zaire didn't confirm or deny. She stared glumly at the mascot, watching its soft stomach rise and fall as it breathed.

"Or maybe you locked her in the closet, then Choi locked her in the closet again?"

"I put her in a shower stall," Zaire declared, suddenly exasperated by Benny's guesses. "Choi must have found her and moved her to the closet."

"The shower!" Benny exclaimed. "I knew the shower was significant!"

"Well there you go."

Benny was making his thinking face. "You must have thought you'd accidentally killed Brittany at some point. Didn't that bother you?"

Zaire shrugged. She didn't look particularly bothered. She just looked numb.

"You don't care that your plan was so sloppy you could have killed an innocent girl?" Again, Zaire said nothing.

Benny exhaled. "Well what do you propose that I do with you? Obviously I can't let you kill Gottfried. Or do anything else to him. You need to leave him alone."

Zaire rubbed her temples. "I can't leave him alone if he won't *leave*. Every semester I pray to God that he won't come back, that I won't have to see his face again. . . ."

"Aha!" Virginia exclaimed. It didn't sound as natural as when Benny did it. Benny and Zaire looked at her like they'd forgotten she was there.

"I mean . . . that's why you wanted him in the mascot suit. You couldn't do it if you had to look at him. That makes sense to me. It would be hard to murder someone you love. So you disguised him as something you hate. Which is this school."

On the ground, the mascot lay motionless. A leaf had fallen between its plastic teeth.

"Huh, wow. Is that correct?" Benny asked Zaire.

"Yes."

"Nicely deduced, Virginia!"

The level of surprise in his voice annoyed her.

"This is so stupid," Zaire sighed. "I'm so tired."

"Do you think you deserve to be punished for what you've done?" Benny asked her. "I'm genuinely curious what you think of yourself right now."

"Every second of this hellhole is a punishment," Zaire answered. Virginia couldn't tell if by "hellhole" she meant Winship, or just life in general.

"You know what?" Virginia said suddenly. "You're not the only one who thinks Winship is stupid. We're all stuck here. We all wish we could be somewhere else. We just have to make the best of it, you know? It doesn't have to be *that* bad."

Zaire glared at her. "Easy for you. I'm sure Winship is heaven compared to *Florida*."

"Um, excuse me?"

Benny kicked some leaves around. "Okay, let's focus please. Zaire, you've killed someone, and now you've tried to kill again. I don't know what I'm supposed to do with you. I'm a mystery solver, not the hammer of justice."

"Just leave me alone, then," Zaire said.

Benny shook his head. "I don't think I can. What do you think, Virginia?"

She looked at him. Was he really asking her opinion? Or were they just screwing with Zaire's mind?

"I don't know. I guess she should go to jail like a regular killer and rapist."

Zaire scowled. "Rapist? What the hell do you mean, rapist?"

"You need to examine your actions," Benny said. "You'll find they meet the criteria for sexual assault."

"Myopic fixation," Virginia remarked. "She thinks it doesn't count because she loves him."

Zaire's hand flew out and whacked Virginia across the face. It was so fast, Virginia didn't even realize what had happened until she felt the stinging on her cheek. Then she felt a whack on her other cheek, this one so hard she stumbled backward and tripped over the mascot's huge furry feet. She fell to the ground, landing hard on her back.

"Christ, ow!" she groaned, rolling over.

"Hey!" Benny yelled at Zaire. Then he bent down to Virginia. "Are you okay?"

"Ow, yeah . . ."

Benny pulled her to her feet. They looked around. For a second it was like Zaire had disappeared into thin air. Then they saw her sprinting down the path. She'd flung off her high heels and was barefoot. Benny immediately set off after her. Virginia paused to look at the inert lump of mascot by the bank.

"Should I stay with him?" she yelled.

"Um, uh—" Benny shouted back. "Just do what you think!"

Just do what you think. For a second it was like being overwhelmed with power. She could do whatever she wanted? But the only thing she could think of was to run.

She darted through the trees, keeping her eyes fixed on Benny's back. He was way ahead of her though, and he ran too fast, and by the time she reached the edge of the forest, she lost him for a second. Then she heard the sound of crunching gravel and saw him sprinting toward the Boarders. In the driveway, Zaire had thrown herself into the black town car in a flash of luxurious hair and cashmere and slammed the door.

"She's in there," Benny said breathlessly as Virginia caught up to him.

Virginia banged on the dark tinted window. "Hey! Get out!"

The driver started the engine.

"Zaire! Get out here!" Virginia shouted again. She was so angry all of a sudden. Zaire thought she could just jump in her Town Car as if Virginia were totally invisible. All her snotty comments. The way she acted like she was thirty years old and the rest of them were children to be ignored. Virginia slammed her hands down on the hood.

"I can see you! Don't run away, you stuck-up coward!" She realized the driver thought she was talking to him. He looked confused, but also incredibly pissed that some kid was banging on his car. She could hear Zaire yelling in the backseat. The car lurched forward a foot, making Virginia jump. She backed away a second, then threw herself on the hood of the car.

"Careful!" she heard Benny yell. "Oh my God, get down!"

The car jolted forward, just enough to make Virginia almost fall off the hood. Then she felt a pair of hands around her waist. Benny was yanking her down. They tumbled to the ground, and Virginia felt the gravel scrape her already scraped-up arms and knees. The car sped forward before Virginia could get back up. In seconds it disappeared around the corner, leaving them in the dust.

Then it was quiet. After a moment Benny picked himself up and brushed the dirt off his pants.

"He wouldn't have run me over," Virginia said. A pink

Band-Aid was peeling from her arm. She ripped it off, revealing a scab that had opened up and was bleeding again.

"Zaire was yelling at him to call the police."

"Well you should have just let her!"

Benny shook his head. "No, it wouldn't have been good. Zaire's not even on Detective Disco's radar, whereas we . . . It would have looked bad."

"Whatever." Virginia plunked down on the front porch steps. While they were gone, suitcases had appeared up against the wall. Virginia could hear people bustling around inside. It was the only time the Boarders ever seemed to come to life—when everyone was getting the hell out of there.

"What was that yelling?" Chrissie White poked her head out the door, looking bedraggled and hungover.

"Just saying farewell to Zaire," Virginia said glumly.

"Oh my God, did she leave? She was supposed to give me a ride! Now I have to call Mrs. Morehouse? Oh my God!" Chrissie stood there for a minute, apparently waiting for Benny and Virginia to chime in with outrage, as if anyone besides her cared whether she made it to the airport or not. Finally she slammed the screen door and went back inside.

"So . . . what now?" Virginia asked. "There's time before her plane takes off. We could still call the police."

"I don't know . . . ," Benny said.

"She should be arrested," Virginia insisted.

"It would never get that far. There's no evidence, and the

case is absurd. Her family has ungodly amounts of money to throw at lawyers. There wouldn't even be an indictment. She's obviously deeply in denial about her actions. She needs therapy, not jail."

"So we seriously just do nothing," Virginia said.

Benny struggled with the answer. His existential philosophy—seek the truth, but don't be a hero about it—was trickier when applied to real life. Maybe the truth was pointless if you didn't use it to prosecute rapists and voyeurs and people who got away with murder. Maybe the world needed heroes more than simple truth-seekers. But Benny couldn't see himself that way. He wasn't a hero. He was just a person who wanted life to make sense.

Virginia pressed, "Should we at least tell Gottfried?"

Benny paused then shook his head. "It doesn't feel like our business."

"We kind of made it our business," Virginia said.

Benny knew she was right. But the idea of giving Gottfried life-changing information when he hadn't asked for it was too overwhelming.

"I'm not ready for that responsibility," he admitted. "Let's just see what happens when Zaire gets back from fall break. We'll watch her closely. Maybe we can help her."

"Okay," Virginia said, dropping it. It felt very rebellious against society to keep the secrets of criminals. In a small way, Virginia knew it was wrong. But in a bigger way, it made her like Benny more. He was . . . unconventional.

She stood up. "I'm gonna get a Coke; you want one?"

Benny shook his head. "I don't think I can drink that stuff anymore. All that sugar. Yuck."

"Yeah, it's pretty bad once you realize. Maybe I shouldn't have told you."

"Nah," Benny said. "It's better to know. Some things, anyway."

One Week Later, Saturday
Gainesville, GA, 4:15 a.m.

This was the best part—the blond twins lovingly rubbing mayonnaise on each other's faces as a moisturizing mask. He watched it through his tears, clutching a pair of pristine blue panties to his chest.

It's over.

Normally Min-Jun wasn't this pathetic. He made money off pathetic guys; he wasn't supposed to be one of them. Yet here he was, pigging out on honey chili Korean Doritos and weeping into a pair of girls underwear. He'd even grabbed a jar of mayonnaise from the refrigerator and begun dabbing it on his cheeks so he could feel what the girls on the screen were feeling. But his face was too tender from getting bashed in by that crazy asshole jock last weekend. So he just held the mayo to his nose and smelled it.

You wouldn't believe the kind of stuff girls put on their faces. Min-Jun had seen it all in that locker room. Mayo, bananas, toothpaste, fat-free yogurt—all the condiments imaginable—it was fascinating. Girls didn't *eat* food; they applied it to the surface of themselves. And clearly its magic worked. They were all exquisite, like the one hundred forbidden daughters of a god.

Christ, get a grip, Min-Jun told himself. He shoved a handful of Doritos into his mouth and hit fast-forward on the remote. What was he going to do now? He had eight thousand dollars in advances for *Wildcats Up Close and Personal,* and the idea of returning the checks made him want to cry, as if he weren't already crying.

Most of the money was from a backer in Boca Raton who wanted more cameras and more variety of girls, not just cheerleaders. Min-Jun had planned to coast on that perv all the way to the bank, but without Choi, the whole system fell apart. There was an assistant soccer coach at Lowell who said he could get cameras in the locker rooms there— *Locker Room Lions* had a nice ring to it. But the backer said it had to be Winship or he was pulling his money. Min-Jun had been annoyed at first—girls in their underwear were pretty much all the same, weren't they? Who cared if their pom-poms were yellow or purple, if they were Wildcats or Lions or Baboons for God's sake. But now he suddenly got it. These girls were special. They were the brand.

What was he supposed to do now? That Virginia girl had seemed game, but Min-Jun couldn't figure her out. Maybe she was a narc. Or maybe she was just a virgin. He certainly didn't have a problem with *that.* The problem was she had four hundred dollars that belonged to him. He imagined it hidden in her room—in her underwear drawer—the dirty bills pressed against fresh pairs of lacy pink thongs and B-cup bras. It was cute, but not cute enough to sit back and let some child rob him.

On the screen, the girls whizzed around in fast motion. Min-Jun hit play again as two of them reached out tenderly to hug each other. There was something about watching girls hug each other, feeling excluded from their girlish bond . . . it gave Min-Jun a weird, jealous boner. He hit fast-forward again, skipping to the part where the girls came out of the shower, dripping in their skimpy towels. He knew the video by heart, and every girl in it. It wasn't just the money he'd miss, it was *them*.

Saturday
Hartsfield-Jackson Atlanta International Airport,
7:05 a.m.

Benny gazed at the enormous *Yangchuanosaurus* skeleton. Sunlight poured down from the atrium's glass ceiling, making the curves of the fossils shine. He adjusted his glasses and read the little plaque:

> THE ASIAN GIANT. At 33 feet (10 meters) long, *Yangchuanosaurus* is one of the largest carnivorous dinosaurs ever discovered. Its main prey was likely the plant-eating dinosaur *Tuojiangosaurus*, a Chinese relative of the widely-known spiked *Stegosaurus* from North America.

"I never thought about a Chinese dinosaur," he said.

Virginia burst out laughing. "That's the funniest sentence I've ever heard. 'I never thought about a Chinese dinosaur.'"

"Seriously though," Benny said. "Isn't it fascinating how

we attribute nationality to life-forms that existed more than a hundred million years ago? Not only is 'China' a set of artificial boundaries that exist only in our minds, 'China' didn't even exist as a physical reality during the Jurassic period. The continent had only just begun to break up at that point. The world was basically still Pangaea."

"You're obsessed with Pangaea," Virginia said.

Benny looked at her. "Am I?"

"You talk about it all the time."

"Do I?"

"You're also the only person in the history of this airport who has ever looked at the dinosaur exhibit."

This seemed to be true. Hartsfield-Jackson was famously the busiest airport in the world. More than 260,000 people passed through the airport each day, and not a single one, it seemed, was interested in pausing to examine a *Yangchuanosaurus* on their way to Chicago or Toronto or Rome.

Benny looked at his watch: 7:08. People had begun trickling through the international arrivals gate. He used to come here all the time with his mom, waiting for his dad to come home from conferences. Now he was here with Virginia, waiting for a murderer to come home from vacation. It was amazing how much your life could change, and yet you always felt like the same person somehow.

"Ask those ladies if they were on the red-eye from Barcelona," he told Virginia.

Without hesitating, she went up to them.

"Excuse me. Are you coming from Barcelona?"

They had loud print jackets on and alligator purses. Their hair was fluffy and dyed rust colored. They reminded Virginia of the women at the Sapphire Lounge, except their clothes fit better and were obviously expensive.

"Yeah," one of them said, not even looking at her. Virginia scurried back to Benny and the *Yangchuanosaurus*.

"Yeah, this is it," she said.

"Okay, eyes open. Don't even blink."

"She's kind of hard to miss," Virginia said.

The trickle of people became a stream. Caffeine-powered men in wrinkled suits trying to get ahead of the line, parents dragging sleepy-headed kids and snapping at each other in Spanish, tourists still wearing their half-deflated neck pillows and bumbling with their customs forms. Old ladies stopping in the middle of the path to fish through their purses. A man with a plastic briefcase, who made Virginia feel depressed. Wasn't there enough money in the world for every man to have a decent briefcase? It must be horrible to be a man and to have so little to show for your life that your briefcase is made of plastic.

People kept streaming by, with no sign of Zaire.

Virginia approached an academic-looking man in a tweed jacket. "Excuse me, are you coming in from Barcelona? Flight 881?"

"Uh, *non*," the man said. His voice had an accent. "Parees."

Virginia shook her head at Benny. They kept waiting. Zaire didn't appear.

"Let's go to the baggage claim," Benny finally said after twenty minutes of standing there watching foreigners stream into the atrium.

They found the carousel for the Barcelona flight. Only a handful of bags still circled around, watched by an old couple who seemed lost. A duffel bag, a chrome hard shell, a few generic black suitcases.

"None of these are Zaire's," Virginia said, surveying the unclaimed baggage. "She has a burgundy Tumi set."

Benny looked at his watch again: 7:45. The carousel hummed loudly, making him feel slightly brain-dead as he watched it go around and around. *She's not coming back,* he realized. There was nothing he could do about it. But strangely, he didn't feel thwarted or defeated—he felt relieved. It seemed like confirmation, somehow, that his role in the universe was to solve mysteries, not to dispense justice. His calling was to make the unknown known, and he'd done that.

"So what next?" Virginia asked.

"I have no idea," he said. "I think . . . I think we're done."

"Okay, cool."

Benny looked at her. The casualness of her reply confirmed it—Virginia didn't really care about this, did she? She was just along for the ride. She'd proved she could be useful to him—she was dauntless and resilient and relentlessly observant—but what use was he to her? What was she getting out of this?

"Oh hey, I wanted to show you this," Virginia said. She reached in her jacket pocket and handed Benny something. It was a woven bracelet with some white letters sewn into it.

"Uh, what does this mean?" he asked. "WWBD?"

"What Would Benny Do!" Virginia shrieked, clearly thrilled with herself. "I had it specially made so I won't screw up as much."

"Wow . . ." Benny handed it back to her.

"I think everyone should wear one," Virginia said, hooking it onto her wrist. "The world would probably be a lot better."

Benny thought about it. It was tempting, the idea of a world where everyone shared his values. It would certainly be an orderly world, a peaceful world even. But would it be right?

"No," he said. "There'd be no mysteries if it were a world of Benny Flaxes. And so none of the Bennies would have anything to do. And as a result they'd all go insane from lack of stimulation. And ultimately chaos would reign."

"Oh," Virginia said.

"I mean, you can still wear it. If you'll find it helpful."

"Okay! I will!" She tightened it and held out her arm to look at it.

Benny sat on the edge of the baggage carousel, feeling

like an unclaimed suitcase himself—dumped at the end of a trip, apparently going nowhere. Virginia looked at him and felt her mood slumping; why couldn't Benny just be happy for five seconds?

Above them, a row of bright screens listed all the departing flight information against an electric-blue background. They glowed like a patch of unnatural sky amid the dull grays and whites of the terminal.

"You know, we could just get out of here," Virginia said. "I have four hundred dollars. There's a flight to Havana in an hour."

Benny rubbed his temples, suddenly wishing he were alone. Obviously Virginia was jealous of Zaire and wanted to prove that she could run away too. He sighed, feeling obligated to humor her.

"Oh yeah? What would we do in Havana?"

"We'd stay with my stepdad. He's awesome. He has a hacienda."

Benny looked at her. *A hacienda? Christ.* She sounded like one of those pathological liars you met in grade school who convinced everyone that their mom knew Princess Diana.

"Sounds great, but we can't just leave. We have to go to the homecoming dance next month. I mean, not to *go*," he qualified quickly. "To Be There. Something always happens at dances."

"Oh, okay!" Virginia said, abandoning her Havana dream swiftly enough.

"I'm on the invitations committee. You should be too."

Virginia looked at him, appalled. *Invitations? Christ.* Why did Benny have to constantly sabotage himself? It was like two roads diverged in a yellow wood and Benny chose the dweebiest one every time.

"God, do you have to?" Virginia groaned. "Can't we go in, like, a non-nerd capacity?"

Benny's mouth twitched. "Invitations are the best way to have an exact count of everyone who will be in attendance. You can do what you want. Scan for action on the dance floor, maybe. That would be helpful."

Suddenly it hit Virginia that this was life with Benny: being in the same place at the same time, but never actually together. In a way it was annoying, but it was also strangely ideal. Virginia liked being alone at dances; it filled the night with more possibility. People held each other back; that was everyone's main problem. There was mystery in life—Virginia knew this now. And Benny might have been clueless about a lot of things, but about one thing he was absolutely right: Your only hope was to Be There.

acknowledgments

All my gratitude to the generous brains of Nico Carver, Liesa Abrams, and Sarah McCabe. And to my creator, Stephen Barr.

The mysteries heat up in Book Two.
Turn the page for a peek!

Only at Winship Academy would an evening science expo turn into a criminal fiasco. First, there's the anonymous boy in the girls' bathroom handing out drugs to anyone with the secret password. Then the student body president is maimed in a horrifying and tragic accident—but was it an accident or an attack?

Benny Flax and Virginia Leeds are right at the center of it all. And so is the headmaster's son, Calvin Harker, an oddball poet whose interest in Virginia sets off alarm bells for Benny. As the case bleeds from Winship Academy to the surrounding city, the deep fault lines of racial tension in Atlanta's history reveal explosive hatred still simmering under the city's surface.

Outside the gym, 6:30 p.m.

Benny felt like an imposter. He always did on these occasions.

It was the clothes—khaki pants, blue blazer, tie. The outfit wasn't mandatory, technically, but it's what every single guy would be wearing. It wasn't what he'd planned to wear. He'd planned to wear his dad's gray wool suit, which had been hanging in the closet since the accident, immaculate and untouched. It was still in the plastic bag from the dry cleaners. The crease in the trousers was as perfect as if it had been ironed yesterday, not eighteen months ago. Seeing it, Benny had stopped. He wasn't really going to wear this, was he? This was a man's suit, and he was just a kid. What if it didn't fit? What if he messed it up or spilled punch on it? What if his dad needed it? That last question was ridiculous, Benny knew. Benny's dad had severe brain damage from a plane crash and wouldn't be needing a suit tonight or possibly ever again. But still, what if he suddenly felt better, and wanted to go out for a nice dinner in his suit, and when he went to the closet it was gone, and the shock sent his brain back into its foggy maze? The idea was ludicrous, but as soon as it had germinated in Benny's mind, he knew he wouldn't be touching that suit.

He sat on the curb outside the gym, waiting for Virginia Leeds to appear. They were going to the science expo together. It was not a date, as if that needed to be established.

He'd never heard of anyone going to a science expo as a date. He wasn't exactly sure why they were going together at all. Ostensibly it was for Mystery Club, but really it was just a habit they'd developed of meeting each other places—in the hall after assemblies, by the apple stand during break, in the cafeteria if they had the same lunch period. They'd report any unusual observations—usually there weren't many—then they'd go their separate ways.

Benny had founded Mystery Club on the basic philosophy that mysteries were everywhere, and that the greatest advantage in solving one was to Be There. Be watching, be a witness. Don't wait for mysteries to come to you, because they won't. Benny had learned this quickly enough. When he'd first created the club, he'd expected to be barraged with inquiries: Who started that rumor that I tongue-kissed a dog? Who put a bag of peanuts on the peanut allergy table in the cafeteria? Weird things were always happening at Winship, but people seemed too self-absorbed to care. Except for Virginia. Virginia cared—cared too much maybe. She was obsessed with other people's business and always had been. Sometimes Benny wondered if she'd only joined Mystery Club as an excuse to spy on people.

"Hey."

Benny twisted around and saw her approaching. She was wearing a soft black sweater and a gold skirt that Benny recognized as having belonged to Zaire Bollo. It looked expensive, and was short enough to glue anyone's eyes to her legs. It was definitely inappropriate for an academic event that was mostly a spectacle for parents. Benny's own mother was already inside, examining every tenth grader's project to assess the competition.

Benny was about to stand up, knowing there was no way Virginia could sit on a street curb in that skirt without flashing the entire world. But Virginia either didn't know or didn't care. She plunked down next to him, immediately scooching away a bit, apparently having misjudged how close to him she'd landed. Benny stared ahead. Just because her underwear was probably showing didn't mean he had to look. In fact, it was his duty not to.

"You look like a calculator salesman," Virginia said.

"I look the same as everyone," Benny said, nodding toward a very athletic, sandy-haired boy climbing out of a blue Mazda who was wearing the same combination of khakis and blue blazer as him.

"Oh yeah, you're clearly twins separated at birth."

Benny gritted his teeth. Virginia always managed to blithely zero in on whatever anyone was insecure about and broadcast it to the world. Did she do it on purpose? Benny didn't know. Perhaps she'd enjoy it if Benny pointed out that she was wearing Zaire Bollo's designer cast-offs and her underwear was showing. *At least I didn't steal my outfit from a murderer,* he imagined saying back. But he knew he wouldn't. It might feel good for a second, but then Virginia would get that crinkled, hurt look on her face, and Benny would be consumed by guilt for days.

Clothes, clothes, clothes, he thought dismally. These events always revolved around clothes. Winship was a uniform school, which meant that on the occasions when people had free reign to wear what they wanted, it became a matter of intense public display and scrutiny. The irony was that everyone ended up dressing the same as one another anyway, but as a collective decision rather than a mandate from above, which seemed to be an important distinction.

Virginia was picking at a large scab on her knee. She'd been picking at it all week. It was never going to heal at this rate, and the skin around the scab was red and infected. Benny was about to say as much when she sat up abruptly and began digging through a small brown bag that didn't match her outfit at all.

"So, um, I got you something." Virginia handed him a small velvet box. Benny examined it warily.

"What is it?" he asked. The last time she'd gotten him a present, it was a bracelet with the letters W.W.B.D.? (What Would Benny Do?) sewn onto it, with a matching one for herself. It had been touching but embarrassing.

"Just open it," Virginia insisted.

He snapped open the box. Inside was a silver ring. He turned the ring over in his palm, and saw that it was composed of a pair of dials, one engraved with letters and the other engraved with numbers. It looked expensive.

"It's a decoder ring," he said. "Wow, thank you."

"I got us both one!" She held up a second ring. "For writing messages. You're always complaining about the notes I leave on your locker, so . . ." Her voice trailed off, and Benny saw that her cheeks were bright red.

Benny had always found Virginia somewhat irritating-looking: her heart-shaped face prone to flushing, her blank staring eyes, her Afro of blond curls. But in the warm evening light, her features seemed to morph slightly, her face at some middle point between an awkward, chunky cherub and a Renaissance angel. It was an undeniable flash of . . . *cuteness*. Benny didn't like the word—it evoked ponies and puppies and cupcakes—but there it was.

"You need to learn to control that," he said, a little louder than he'd meant to.

"Control what?" Virginia said, turning her face away.

"Your cheeks. You're blushing. If you want to be a great detective, no one should ever be able to tell what you're thinking."

"Oh yeah?" Virginia snapped, looking at him suddenly. "What am I thinking?"

Now Benny was the one blushing. "I . . . I don't know. I'm just saying . . ." He stared down at the decoder ring, pretending to be fascinated by the dials. He could sense that Virginia was glaring at him. Seconds passed.

"So what's your project?" Virginia asked, back to picking her scab.

"A study of anomalous recoveries from neurological damage. What's yours?"

"Trees of Georgia. I dunno. I suck at science."

Virginia's wouldn't even be the worst project, Benny knew. The science expo was mandatory for all students. Winship's science program had recently been called "lacking" in the *Guide to Southern Prep and Boarding Schools,* a slander the administration was obsessed with correcting. But by making the expo mandatory, the result was that people who had no business contributing clogged up the works for the people who were serious. But Benny tried not to be bothered. He believed in inclusivity and that everyone deserved a chance. But at the same time, he couldn't help noticing that the chance seemed to be wasted on 99 percent of humanity.

He stood up. "I better go set up my booth. See you later."

"See ya."

"Um, thanks for the ring." Benny made a small show of sliding it onto his finger.

"You're welcome," Virginia said back, not looking up from her scab.

Benny lingered a second, then gave up. He'd screwed up the moment somehow, and now it was over.

Booth 29, 7:30 p.m.

Why is everyone so willing to be boring?

It was a question Virginia asked herself almost every single day. Why did anyone do homework? Or wear navy? Or date the same person for three years? The other day in Ethics class, they'd gone around the room saying what everyone wanted to be when they grew up, and Corny Davenport said, "A real estate agent, just like my mom!" It was pretty much the most depressing thing Virginia had ever heard.

She'd been looking forward to the science expo all day. In her mind she'd conflated it with a dance somehow, imagining dim lighting and the promise of romance, except with science projects everywhere. Only now was she realizing how non-conducive to romance the science expo environment was. The gym's fluorescent lights assaulted every corner. It was loud, and the roving panel of judges were making everyone uptight. This was going to be as boring as school, wasn't it? Except worse, because at least at school you didn't normally have to be around a hundred million parents.

On the "Trees of Georgia" poster she'd made, several of the dried, crumbling leaves had fallen down, and another was lopsided. She'd known it wasn't a great project, but now it seemed actually pathetic. As she looked around, some of the other projects seemed barely even related to science. A group of juniors were doing a project on *The Fast and the Furious* that was just pictures of exploding cars and Vin Diesel quotes. And Trevor Cheek had a project called, simply, "Hunting," which was showing off all the heads of deer he'd killed. If Virginia had known you could just do whatever you wanted, she would have done a project on classic cocktails, or Body Language of the Rich and Powerful.

In the booth next to her, Yasmin Astarabadi was erecting an immense pair of metal wires, one of which kept drooping perilously toward her. Virginia leaned away, not wanting her outfit to get stabbed. It felt different, wearing expensive clothes. It made her more conscious of her posture and of potentially ruinous stabbing wires. She'd never cared about perfect clothes before, but she loved this outfit and would probably literally cry if anything happened to it. You couldn't find clothes like this in Atlanta. All of Zaire Bollo's clothes had come from Paris and London and Milan. And back to Paris and London and Milan they'd gone after Zaire failed to return from fall break—except this one particular outfit, which Virginia had swiped from her closet and intended to wear as often as possible until she grew up into a person who bought clothes like this all the time.

"What is that?" she asked Yasmin, who was bending the wire back into place.

"A high-voltage traveling arc," Yasmin said, not looking up from her weird equipment.

"What does that mean?"

Yasmin sighed impatiently and gave a long answer involving the words "cathode voltage drop" and "heated ionized air." Virginia wished she hadn't asked.

On the other side of her, Lindsay Bean had a project called "Pudding Inventions," which seemed to involve making pudding out of the grossest flavors imaginable, like seaweed and diet popcorn and lobster. Sophat Tiang and Skylar Jones, the biggest stoners in school, had wandered over to sample them. Virginia tried to look busy putting the falling leaves back on her pathetic poster. Skylar acted like she wasn't even there.

Hello? Virginia thought, getting annoyed. Skylar always ignored her as if they hadn't totally had a thing last year. Not a huge thing, but enough of a thing that she deserved some respect from him. She'd only liked him because he seemed different from everyone else at Winship. He wore *sandals*, and a hemp necklace, and had once said, "I'd rather have a bottle in front of me than a frontal lobotomy," which Virginia had found unbelievably clever until someone told her it was a famous quote.

"Is it going to explode?" Skylar was asking Lindsay. He was grinning and pointing at a cylinder full of white frothy substance.

Lindsay giggled. "Maybe!"

"It looks like jiz. I think it wants to be released." Skylar and Sophat laughed. Skylar reached across the table and rubbed the cylinder up and down obscenely.

"Skylar, stop. Skylar! Don't!" Lindsay squealed. Virginia considered giving Skylar a shove to make him quit, but then decided it was better to remain aloof from his gross immaturity. Lindsay could fend for herself. But then, as she was turning back to her leaf poster, she heard a squishing noise and felt a hot thick liquid all over her neck.

"Ew!" She touched her shoulder and her fingers came away sticky with a white, fishy-smelling goo. Skylar and Sophat were slapping each other's backs and laughing hysterically.

"Skylar, you moron!" Virginia hissed at him.

"Was it good for you, too?" he said, grinning hugely.

Virginia turned to Lindsay and pointed to the nasty white smear covering half her sweater. "What the hell is this?"

"It's lobster paste."

Skylar laughed even harder. "What can I say?"

Virginia grabbed a paper towel from Lindsay's table and started dabbing at the ugly splotch. She felt angry tears sting her eyes. *Does lobster paste stain?* She felt like kicking Skylar in the balls, but what if she didn't kick hard enough and accidentally gave him a boner or something? It was just impossible, trying to get the upper hand with boys.

Skylar and Sophat had moved on to poking Brook's gigantic metal wires. Yasmin was ignoring them and messing with a transformer box. Nerds like Yasmin were used to this kind of thing, Virginia figured. They just conducted their lives as best they could amid constant disruptions from people who couldn't build anything of their own, so they tore everyone else down. She couldn't decide which side of the dynamic was more pathetic. Virginia grabbed more paper towels and started toward the bathroom, dabbing at herself.

"Wait!" Skylar shouted at her, suddenly not laughing anymore. "Are you going to the bathroom?"

Virginia paused. Why did Skylar care if she went to the bathroom or not? Was he going to invite himself along? She glanced at Yasmin, who was giving her a blank, weirdly hostile look, as if to her, she and Skylar and Sophat were all the same. *I'm not with them*, Virginia wanted to tell her.

"You don't wanna go in there," Skylar was saying, his face serious. Sophat and Yasmin looked from him to her, like something was about to happen.

Virginia narrowed her eyes. "Why, did you do something gross?"

"*No*," Skylar said. "Just trust me, dude. Don't go in there."

Virginia tossed her hair and kept walking. You couldn't take anything that loser said seriously. But then, the second she crossed into the hall, she sensed a shift in the air. It was quieter, and brighter. The hum of four hundred voices was instantly muted. Without daylight streaming through the windows, the fluorescent lights gave the white walls an eerie glow. A group of girls was huddled by the water fountain, talking in urgent whispers. They looked like paint swatches, each with a different vibrantly colored cardigan set. Virginia walked past them and was almost at the bathroom door when she heard her name.

"Virginia," one of them was whispering. "Virginia, don't go in there."

about the author

Maggie Thrash grew up in the South. She is the author of *Strange Truth* and the graphic memoir *Honor Girl* and is a contributor to the online teen magazine *Rookie*. She attended Hampshire College and the Sewanee School of Letters. She now lives in Delaware.